To.

Options

Written By
James Douglas Mann

LONDON BOOK PUBLISHER

16 East Croft House, 86 Northolt Road,
Harrow, England, HA2 0ER,
United Kingdom

ISBN (Paperback)
ISBN (Hardback)

Cover Design by London Book Publisher

For more information, visit www.londonbookpublisher.co.uk

Dedication

For Michelle, the love of my life.

ACKNOWLEDGMENT

My thanks to John, Lilly, Frank, Anna, and all those behind the scenes at London Book Publisher for their patience and astonishing hard work, and to my wife, Michelle, for her painstaking editing and encouragement.

And my thanks to all the rogues I knew back in the day, some of whom have been recreated in the novel.

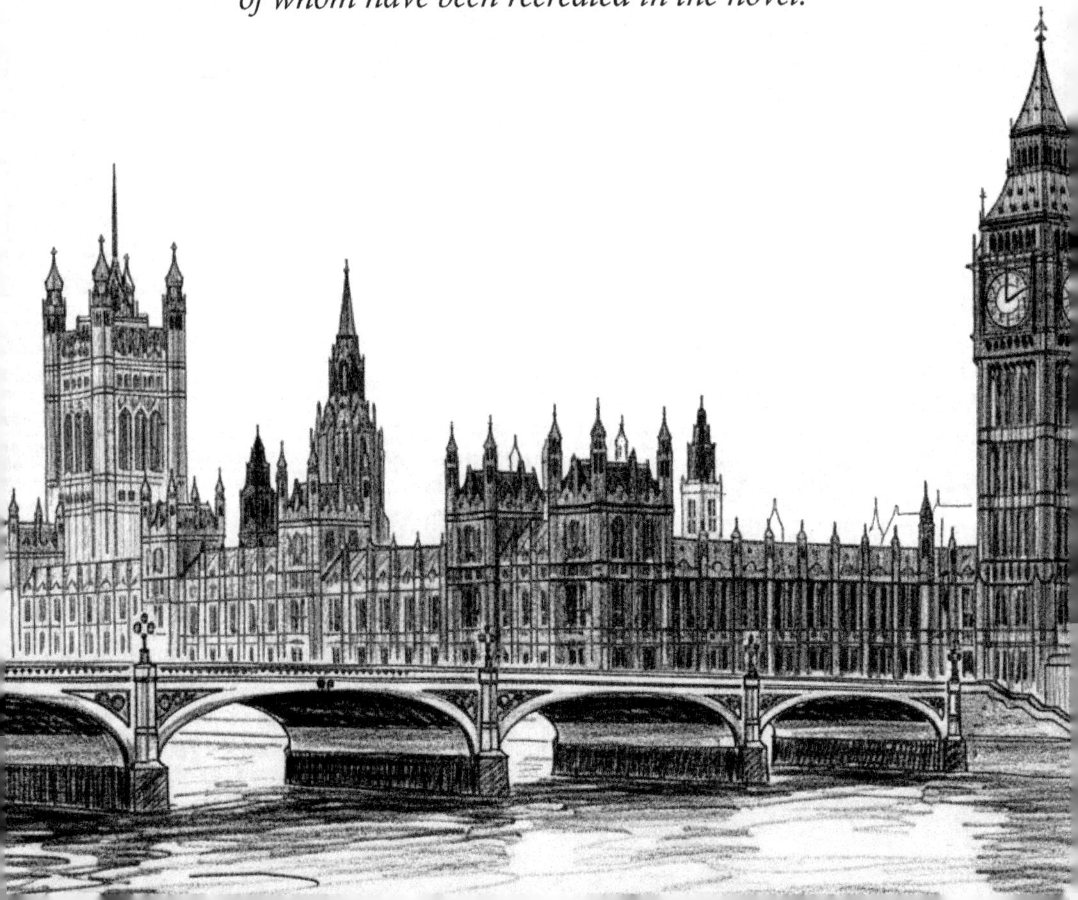

TABLE OF CONTENTS

CHAPTER 1

— June 1983

Walthamstow High Street was quiet now, a stark contrast to its usual bustling self. The deserted street seemed to echo with ghosts of the day, the laughter and bartering now replaced by the dull slap of damp against cobbles. A stray newspaper page tumbled along, catching on a lamp post and rustling like dry leaves.

The market stalls, vibrant and overflowing with produce during the day, were now shrouded in darkness, their boisterous cries of "Two for a fiver!" and "Get your fresh fruit 'ere!" replaced by an eerie silence. Even the distant hum of traffic felt muffled, as if the world itself was holding its breath. In the early hours of Sunday morning, a chill hung in the air, a dampness that spoke of the coming dawn.

Inside the Archer Brothers' betting shop, the only illumination came from a single bare bulb hanging precariously from the ceiling, casting long, distorted shadows across the room. The walls felt close, lined with grime and age, as though they too had witnessed the night's horror. The air stank of stale smoke and whisky, mingled with the cold bite of fear. Joss poured his brother another generous measure of Scotch whisky, the amber liquid sloshing against the sides of the glass, and then emptied the remaining contents of the bottle into his own, not bothering with niceties.

As he raised the glass to his lips, his hand slightly trembling, and swirled the oaky liquid around his mouth, he reflected, not for the first time that night, that this was much-needed 'medicinal' treatment following the utterly traumatic events of the previous night. The taste of the whisky, usually a source of pleasure, was now tinged with a bitter edge of disbelief and anger. He shifted in his chair, feeling the weight of responsibility settle on his shoulders like a lead coat.

"It's at times like this," said his brother Wayne gloomily, his voice a low rumble that barely disturbed the silence, "that you wish Ronnie and Reggie were still around."

He spoke of the Kray twins, the notorious gangsters who, thirty years earlier, had held a vice-like grip on the East End, representing an unofficial, and brutally efficient, version of the area's police force. Their methods were legendary, their reputation a cocktail of fear and grudging respect.

In Wayne's mind, they represented a twisted kind of order, a stark contrast to the chaos and vulnerability they now faced. Wayne let the Scotch burn his throat, not caring about the taste, only the numbness it promised. His fingers drummed against the glass, betraying an anxious energy at odds with his drawled cynicism.

Joss sighed deeply, a sound that seemed to emanate from the very depths of his being, put down his glass with a dull thud on the cluttered desk, and peered around the room. His gaze lingered on the empty safe, its heavy steel door yawning open like a broken jaw.

The safe sat like an accusation in the corner. Its gaping mouth seemed to mock them, daring them to fill it again, to try to reclaim what was lost. It should have been concealing a hundred thousand pounds in used banknotes – the hard-won spoils of their most successful night – except for the unfortunate, and violently unexpected, set of events that had transpired a mere two hours earlier.

The room felt violated, the air thick with the residue of shock and disbelief. Around them, betting tickets and newspapers lay strewn across the floor like confetti from a party that had ended in violence.

Joss and Wayne Archer were turf accountants, more commonly known as bookmakers, and the previous evening, a Saturday night, had been the most lucrative in their careers. The venue for this triumph, and subsequent disaster, was the White City Stadium, the iconic home of greyhound racing in London.

Each year, this stadium played host to the final of the Greyhound Derby, the pinnacle of the sport, and on this particular June evening, as it was every year, the Shepherd's Bush stadium, a sprawling concrete edifice, had been packed to the rafters with a diverse and boisterous crowd. Joss could almost hear the dogs barking in their kennels, the roar of the crowd rising like a tide.

Punters and fans from every walk of life across the social spectrum had converged on the stadium, their hopes and dreams, their fortunes and losses, all tied to the swift legs of the greyhounds. He remembered the way money changed hands so quickly it felt unreal, so much wealth, so many dreams riding on a single race. These included the working men, for whom a night at the dogs was a weekly ritual, a brief escape from the drudgery of their daily lives; couples, dressed in their Saturday best, seeking a bit of excitement and a shared thrill; boisterous stag parties, fuelled by lager and bravado, celebrating impending nuptials; sophisticated office parties, the women in elegant dresses and the men in ill-fitting suits, letting their hair down after a long week; celebrities, drawn by the glamour and the chance to be seen; and, as Wayne liked to call them, with a hint of disdain and a touch of envy, "hoorays."

This referred to the new breed of enthusiasts from the affluent enclaves of nearby Chelsea and Fulham, most of whom worked in the City's high-powered financial sector and who seemed to have only recently discovered that an alternative form of gambling existed beyond either the hallowed turf of Royal Ascot, with its champagne and socialites, or the green baize of London's exclusive casinos, with their high stakes and air of hushed intensity.

Wayne's voice, when it came again, was hoarse. "We should've hired more muscle. We knew it was a big take tonight."

The bitterness in his tone was directed at himself as much as at his brother. Neither replied. The silence stretched, thick as the smoke curling from the ashtray between them. The sport was enjoying a resurgence, its popularity, even on an average Saturday night, almost back to the heady levels not seen since the golden age of dog racing between the two world wars, a time when the working classes flocked to the tracks in their thousands, seeking a bit of excitement and a chance to win big.

Outside, a siren wailed far off, a lonely, accusatory note that reminded them the city never truly slept. The night felt like it might never end.

Joss and Wayne owned the number one pitch at White City. It was more than real estate; it was an unspoken declaration of dominance in a world where reputation mattered as much as odds. It was a position of considerable prestige and advantage. It was so called because its prime location gave the brothers access to the largest number of punters, being situated not only in the first row of the four lines of bookmakers' pitches, but also, crucially, in the very middle of the front line, directly facing the main stand.

This afforded them maximum visibility and ensured a constant flow of potential customers. Even from a distance, punters could see their bright signage and hear their booming banter, impossible to ignore.

The reality, however, was that the location of the brothers' pitch might just as well have been irrelevant, such was the formidable reputation of the Turf Accountants Archer. Their pitch stood out amongst their rival bookmakers like a shining beacon, a lighthouse in a sea of more mundane offerings. It drew people in with a promise of action and bravado, of stakes so high they set the heart racing. Whereas their rivals were largely a motley collection of surly old men, weathered veterans who had been in the trade for most of their lives and worked to safe, slender margins, content with small but consistent profits, the Archers had only been in business for five years and operated with a very different philosophy. They would accept bets and liabilities of a size that their competitors only shuddered at, amounts that spoke of confidence, audacity, and a healthy disregard for conventional wisdom.

To many in the trade, it was reckless.

To the punters, it was thrilling. Not that they needed to, but Joss and Wayne wanted the public, and their competitors, to know without any doubt that they were the men, the ones to be reckoned with.

So vociferous were they, so flamboyant and theatrical in their approach, that during a night's racing, either brother could easily have been mistaken for a stand-up comedian playing to a large and appreciative audience. They knew it was part of the sell, that people weren't just betting; they were buying into a show. Their patter was legendary, their voices booming across the betting ring, drawing in punters like moths to a flame.

"Come on now, who wants a wager? Six to four the field!" Joss would boom, his voice echoing across the stands, his presence amplified by his loud white suit, a sartorial statement that screamed confidence, and the voluminous gold jewellery that adorned his wrists and neck, catching the light with every gesture.

He loved the way eyes followed him, the attention that turned a simple transaction into theatre. Wayne, not to be outdone, would drag on an enormous Cuban cigar, the smoke curling around his head like a halo, and add his own characteristic flourish.

"Alright, hoorays allowed as well! Where are you yuppies tonight... still quaffing bubbly at Royal Ascot?" His grin was wicked, knowing exactly how to get a laugh or a groan from the crowd.

The crowd, a diverse mix of hardened gamblers and casual punters, would often erupt in laughter, appreciating the showmanship as much as the odds on offer. They relished the energy, the insults traded with good humour, the sense that they were part of something bigger than themselves. They would exchange banter with the two brothers, the air thick with the smell of beer, cigarettes, and anticipation, before the serious business of wagering began. It was a carnival atmosphere under the cold floodlights, a world of noise and smoke where fortunes changed hands with the flick of a pen.

Punters would scour the betting ring, their eyes darting from bookmaker to bookmaker, seeking the best value, the most favourable odds. They would compare prices, weigh their options, and, more often than not, settle on Joss and

Wayne, whose prices on the better-fancied dogs were generally bigger, and certainly more enticing, than those offered by their rather staid and predictable opposition. It was a calculated gamble by the Archers, knowing the risk but also the lure of being the boldest bookmaker in the ring. The punters loved them because they added an element of excitement, a sense of theatre, to the overall experience, transforming a simple act of gambling into something more akin to a sporting event. Some came just to watch the banter, even if they didn't place a bet.

And on a good night from a bookmaker's perspective, those glorious evenings when the majority of favourites were unexpectedly beaten, when long shots came in and the form book was turned on its head, Joss and Wayne would regularly take home profits in the region of twenty to thirty thousand pounds. Their faces would be wreathed in smiles, their good humour infectious, even on the relatively few nights when the much-fancied 'jollies' kept winning, when the favourites lived up to their billing and the punters went home happy. Win or lose, they performed the same ritual: a shared drink back at the shop, recounting every bet, every quip, relishing the memory of the crowd's roars.

Part of the appeal of the intrepid brothers, the source of much speculation and rumour, was the curious question of how they had come to be bookmakers in the first place. Both men were in their late forties, a time of life when most men had settled into comfortable routines, and their flamboyant lifestyle and unorthodox career choice intrigued many. They seemed larger than life, almost fictional to those who only heard about them in whispers at pubs or read about them in the papers. One of the tabloids, always eager for a human-interest story, had recently run a feature on Wayne, its headline a witty, if somewhat predictable, pun:

HOW MY CAREER WENT TO THE DOGS

The article detailed his past life as a chartered accountant, a world of audits and endless meetings, of spreadsheets and balance sheets, that he had willingly, and perhaps somewhat inexplicably, traded for the unpredictable, often chaotic, world of odds, a smoke-filled betting shop in the gritty heart of East London, and evenings spent juggling numbers and calculating liabilities at a handful of London's greyhound stadiums. It was a transformation that seemed to amuse him as much as it baffled others.

When asked about his interests in the article, his typically laconic reply had been, delivered with a wry smile and a twinkle in his eye, "My greyhounds, my jewellery, and Charlton Athletic."

Nobody seemed to know much about Joss, a fact that only added to his mystique. He was the more enigmatic of the two, a man of few words outside the betting ring, and this air of mystery fuelled a rich tapestry of speculation and rumour. Some said he'd been in trouble years ago, others whispered about debts paid off in blood. But if Joss knew the stories, he never confirmed or denied them. He let the silence do the talking.

"I 'eard 'e spent 'alf 'is life in the nick," was one commonly whispered comment, the East End vernacular adding a certain dubious credibility to the rumour. There was always someone ready with a new theory about Joss, especially after a few pints at the local.

"He was a failed comedian," was another popular theory, perhaps fuelled by his theatrical pronouncements on the betting pitch and his natural flair for the dramatic. That one always got a laugh, especially since Joss, intentionally or not, often delivered lines with the timing of a seasoned comic.

The previous evening, the fifty-third running of the *Daily Mirror* Greyhound Derby, a race steeped in history and tradition, had proved to be the high point of Joss and Wayne's bookmaking careers to date. It was the kind of night that could either make a man legendary or ruin him entirely. That morning, they had diligently 'scratched a few buttons' – a bookmaker's term for making a small profit – from the earlier meeting at Hackney Wick, another of London's iconic greyhound tracks, before returning to their shop in Walthamstow in the afternoon.

There, amidst the familiar surroundings of their own establishment, they had gratefully watched winning outsiders run riot on the final day of the prestigious Royal Ascot horse racing meet, their profits steadily mounting. The combination of luck and skill had left them almost giddy, their eyes flicking between screens and slips, already dreaming of what the evening might bring.

"Like pilgrims on the way to Mecca," Joss had declared with characteristic grandiosity as they set off for White City in the late afternoon, driven by their loyal and long-suffering clerk, Colin.

Colin had long since given up trying to temper Joss's dramatics, though his eyes often rolled behind the wheel. He and Wayne shared the onerous responsibility of meticulously recording literally thousands of bets over the course of a major evening such as this, their hands cramping from the sheer volume of transactions.

But while Colin's duties were primarily driving and handling the necessary clerical tasks, ensuring that every bet was accurately recorded and every transaction processed, Wayne's role was of a more cerebral nature. His sharp, analytical mind was the architect of the odds that adorned the Archers' blackboard, the crucial numbers that attracted the punters and ultimately determined their success or failure.

With a cheap betting shop biro between his fingers and a cigarette hanging from his lips, Wayne could juggle statistics like a magician pulling rabbits from a hat. If Wayne was the academic, the brains of the operation, Joss was undeniably the showman, the charismatic face of the business.

As soon as Joss had chalked up the prices of the six canine contestants in any given race, his voice booming across the betting ring, the banter would commence, and an ever-widening throng of punters, eager to test their luck, would circle the Archer pitch, their eyes fixed on the odds, their hopes pinned on the swift legs of the greyhounds. There was a ritual to it all now: Joss's swagger, the booming callouts, Wayne's cool recalibrations at the board, and Colin scribbling frantically as coins and notes changed hands.

Full of anticipation, their hearts pounding with a mixture of excitement and nerves, the trio had arrived at White City shortly before six o'clock, the stadium already buzzing with energy. It was the kind of atmosphere you could feel in your chest – restless, electric, and just this side of chaotic. Colin, ever the efficient and reliable driver, expertly manoeuvred their gleaming Series 5 BMW into a space in the vast, sprawling car park. The 'pilgrims' were certainly expecting to reap a rich harvest of treasure that night, their confidence buoyed by their earlier successes. The boot was crammed with kit – odds boards, betting books, extra coats, and enough chalk to supply a small school.

The first of the evening's fifteen races had commenced at 6.27 pm, a precise and meticulously planned schedule, with another following every fifteen minutes thereafter, with the notable exception of the Derby final itself. This blue-riband event, the highlight of the greyhound racing calendar, commanded a twenty-five-minute buffer on either side of its running to allow the television broadcasters ample time for pre-race analysis of the form and profiles of each contender, as well as an extended period after the main event for interviews with the winning connections, capturing the raw emotion and excitement of the moment. The buzz around the final was unmistakable – camera crews hunched under boom mics, commentators craning to glimpse the dogs as they were paraded, the smell of sausages and cigarettes hanging thick in the air.

Right from the start of the evening's sport, fortune had smiled upon the brothers, the results unfolding in a manner that exceeded even their most optimistic expectations. The fate of each favourite, those heavily backed runners that the punters had placed their faith in, turned to dust in spectacular and often dramatic fashion.

A collective groan, punctuated by frustrated boos and muttered curses, rippled through the stands as, in race after race, the heavily backed runners were 'turned over'. They were baulked at the traps, their hopes dashed before they even had a chance to race. Some were unceremoniously knocked over mid-race, their dreams of victory trampled underfoot. In the most agonising of scenarios, they were pipped at the post in the tightest of photo finishes, their noses separated from glory by the slimmest of margins.

Joss and Wayne kept their expressions neutral in public, but behind the pitch boards, they exchanged quick, knowing glances – this was their night.

The punters were reaching a point of collective despair. The temptation to abandon the stadium and head for the sanctuary of the Underground, to retreat to the familiar comforts of home and lick their wounds, was almost overwhelming, had it not been Derby night. It was a rare night where hope lingered even after wallet after wallet had been emptied. But as the minutes ticked down toward the main event, the atmosphere in the stadium crackled with a different kind of energy, a palpable sense of anticipation.

It was becoming increasingly apparent that the favourite in Trap Six, a magnificent specimen of canine athleticism, was poised to attract colossal support. Even among hardened gamblers and grizzled trainers, there was an air of reverence about this particular hound.

The creature in question was a tall and handsome black beast, his coat gleaming under the floodlights, running from his favoured outside berth, a position that gave him a clear run, and over his optimum distance of five hundred metres.

This exceptional animal had utterly dominated all opposition in the qualifying rounds over the preceding eight weeks, his performances breathtaking in their speed and agility, and possessed by far the fastest time figures amongst his five rivals.

All the major national bookmaking chains, those giants of the industry, had installed him as the red-hot 8/11 favourite earlier in the week, a price that reflected his perceived invincibility. You could feel the tension in the ring rise as his name was announced, the kind of hushed awe usually reserved for royalty or rock stars. Excitement on the track had reached fever pitch as the six dogs, their muscles rippling beneath their sleek coats, were paraded before the teeming stands, their handlers, faces etched with a mixture of pride and nerves, leading them around the track towards the starting traps, the gates that would soon unleash them into a whirlwind of speed and competition.

The noise swelled into a deafening roar as the traps drew near, bets being placed in rapid fire, voices shouting over one another, all hearts straining toward the moment of release.

"Backing odds-on favourites is not for widows and orphans!" Joss had bellowed, his voice booming across the betting ring, fully aware that the more seasoned element of his clientele, the hardened gamblers who lived and breathed the world of racing, would soon be 'piling on' the favourite, this supposed 'good thing,' with a conviction that defeat was simply inconceivable. He watched them with a showman's eye, seeing their heads turn, their lips curl into knowing smirks or muttered insults, all part of the sport.

The 'hardened' element, as it turned out, was rather larger and more intense than Joss had initially anticipated, as he observed them gathering with a palpable air of expectation, even menace, around their pitch. These were the lifers of the betting world: flat-capped pensioners clutching rolled newspapers, slick-haired spivs with wads of cash in rubber bands, and city boys in sharp suits looking for bragging rights. Still, ever the showman, he had deliberately held off quoting a price, building the tension until Colin returned from his reconnaissance mission to gauge the odds being offered by the other bookmakers, particularly the crucial price of the favourite in Trap Six.

"Okay, you lot, not long now! Ye of little faith!" Joss's voice boomed out across the expectant crowd, his eyes twinkling with mischief. "You're like whores, you lot, you're getting well and truly stuffed every fifteen minutes!" he teased, a mischievous glint in his eye.

A ripple of laughter and boos broke out, the sound rising and falling like surf against a sea wall. Some punters swore at him with affectionate venom, others just grinned and readied their notes.

"Come on, Joss, I'll get on with Dave Little if you don't 'urry up!" shouted one particularly impatient punter, his voice hoarse with a mixture of excitement and frustration, eager to place his bet before the odds changed. Joss shot him a theatrical scowl and waved him off, the whole pitch momentarily descending into good-natured jeering.

Colin eventually reappeared at the pitch, his face flushed, clutching a hastily scribbled list of comparative odds, just as the dogs and their handlers made their way to the starting traps, positioned a mere few yards away. He was puffing slightly, hair dishevelled from pushing through the crowd, but his eyes shone with the rush of battle.

The prices he handed to Wayne for the six dog were even shorter than the brothers had anticipated, reflecting the overwhelming weight of money that had been placed on the favourite. 4/6 was the most prevalent offering, a price that offered little in the way of return.

A few of the larger independent bookmakers facing the stands, those who were willing to take a slightly bigger risk, were offering the marginally more generous odds of 8/11, matching the ante-post prices set by the big national chains earlier in the week.

Wayne's brow furrowed as he read the numbers. He didn't need to speak. The little signals were all they used, a language of shrugs, winks and small gestures perfected over hundreds of tense nights.

An astute observer, someone with a keen eye for detail and a knowledge of the subtle nuances of the betting world, might have noticed Wayne exchange a quick, almost imperceptible wink with Joss, accompanied by a subtle wiggle of his right forefinger in a single, decisive up-and-down motion, a silent signal that spoke volumes.

"Alright then, you lot, not all at once!" Joss chuckled, grabbing his chalk and inscribing a small dash next to the name of Trap Six on his blackboard, the board a chaotic jumble of numbers and names.

"Evens, Trap Six!" He delivered it with the flourish of a conjurer pulling a rabbit from a hat, his grin wide and wolfish.

A moment of stunned silence rippled through the incredulous punters, many momentarily wondering if some grave error had been made, if they had misheard or misunderstood.

Evens? For the most celebrated dog in the competition?

It was like offering gold for copper prices. You could feel the disbelief hang in the air, thick as the smoke drifting over the ring. Then, as if a dam had burst, the crowd surged towards the Archer pitch, a tidal wave of humanity, literally flooding them with bets. The noise was at fever pitch as Wayne's pen danced freely over his large ledger board, recording an avalanche of bets, barely able to cope with the frenzy as Joss handed tickets out to bullish punters.

The brothers operated a £10 minimum bet policy on major nights such as this, but few of the thousand-odd wagers they recorded over the ensuing minutes were as small as that. They accepted fifties, hundreds and even thousands of pounds, the notes changing hands in a flurry of activity, the air thick with the scent of money and anticipation.

The pitch was chaos controlled by habit, the brothers' eyes scanning the crowd, the notes, the odds, every movement with predatory precision. The largest single bet was a crisp £8,000, a substantial sum, placed by an impeccably dressed, unknown customer in a dinner jacket, de rigueur for the well-heeled diners in the stadium's exclusive club restaurant on Derby night. He didn't say a word, just counted it out carefully, placed the ticket in his breast pocket and melted back into the crowd like a ghost.

Four-figure bets on the favourite were plentiful, particularly from rival bookmakers, those shrewd operators who were eager to hedge their own potentially ruinous liabilities, to offset their own exposure by placing bets with their competitors. Wayne's eyes flickered with recognition as he spotted a few of them, familiar faces, usually too proud to approach, now practically begging to spread their risk.

"Fuck me bro, we're up to our necks with this one," Wayne murmured, his voice tight with a mixture of awe and apprehension.

His fingers drummed nervously on the edge of the board, a rare crack in his usual calm. Joss hardly needed telling. His eyes, usually sparkling with mischief, were now narrowed with concentration. He swiftly produced a cloth and efficiently erased the prices of all six contenders from the board, the numbers disappearing in a cloud of white dust, his attention now fixed on the track, waiting, with a mixture of excitement and trepidation, to witness their fate. In that hush before the traps opened, the world seemed to hold its breath, every heart in the stadium beating to the same quickening rhythm.

At last, the announcer's voice crackled over the loudspeaker, the familiar words sending a shiver of anticipation through the packed stadium:

"THE HARRRRE'S RUNNING!"

Even the most hardened gamblers fell quiet, eyes locked on the track, breath held. An eerie hush descended over the stands for a few fleeting seconds, the collective breath of thousands held in suspense.

As the mechanical hare, its motor whirring, whizzed past the awaiting traps and the iron gates sprang open with a clang, releasing the six magnificent greyhounds into the race, the silence was shattered by an explosion of noise. It was like striking a match in a room full of petrol.

The dogs burst forward, a blur of muscle and sinew, hurtling towards the first bend amidst the famous Derby roar, a deafening wave of sound as the White City crowd roared their encouragement, their voices a cacophony of hope and expectation. Fists pumped the air, tickets were waved frantically, and grown men screamed themselves hoarse.

The roar was as deafening as ever that year as, swinging around the first bend a clear length in front, his black coat gleaming under the floodlights, was the seemingly unstoppable favourite in Trap Six. It was a thing of beauty: smooth, almost arrogant in his dominance. By the second bend, his lead had extended to two lengths, his pace relentless, his stride powerful and fluid. Wayne's fingers tightened around his notebook. Joss barely blinked, leaning forward like a man hypnotised.

By the time the dogs were rounding the crucial third bend, with the finish line in sight, the decibel level and the palpable excitement emanating from the crowd had reached an almost unbearable fever pitch. The stadium was a cauldron of noise, a sea of waving arms and outstretched necks, every eye fixed on the leading dog. Betting tickets were crushed in sweaty palms, prayers mumbled under ragged breath, the entire stand willing the black beast to victory or ruin.

And then, at the fourth and final bend of the track – whether it was the immense pressure of being labelled 'the champion elect' for the past eight weeks, the weight of expectation proving too much to bear, a sudden and inexplicable loss of enthusiasm for chasing a mechanical hare's backside, a moment of canine existential crisis, or simply a case of running out of steam at the most critical moment, his reserves of energy finally depleted – the unthinkable happened. It was like watching a god stumble.

The nation's darling in Trap Six, the seemingly invincible black beast, suddenly faltered. His powerful stride shortened, his legs beginning to churn without the same effortless power, his once-smooth rhythm disrupted. He was left floundering, his dream of Derby glory evaporating with every stride, as the dogs from Traps Two and One, sensing his weakness, surged forward, flashing past him in a blur of speed, a mere handful of yards from the finish line. The stadium's roar fractured into chaos—cheering, wailing and shock.

A collective gasp of disbelief swept through the stunned stadium, followed by an eruption of cheers and groans, a cacophony of contrasting emotions. It was the sound of dreams being made and shattered in a heartbeat.

For Joss and Wayne Archer, a night that had promised potential disaster, a night that had threatened to wipe them out, had miraculously transformed into an unprecedented triumph, a financial windfall beyond their wildest dreams. They didn't even cheer at first. For a heartbeat, they just stood there, slack-jawed, letting the impossible sink in.

Joss, Wayne and Colin had wasted no time in hurrying back to the car park the moment they had settled the last winning ticket after the final race, their hearts still pounding with adrenaline, the thrill of their victory tempered by a growing sense of unease.

The betting ring, once roaring with life, had fallen into a hushed, resentful quiet as punters shuffled away, licking their wounds. Under his arm, Colin carefully carried the large ledger board, a meticulous record of every single bet struck throughout the unforgettable night, a testament to their success and a potential source of evidence if anything went wrong.

Later scrutiny of that board would reveal the staggering truth: the Archer brothers had enjoyed their finest ever evening, netting a profit in the region of a hundred thousand pounds. A sum that could change lives—or end them early if they weren't careful. Joss and Wayne each had a possessive hand clamped onto the bulging leather satchel, its seams practically groaning under the weight of their unexpected bounty. Both men were acutely aware that this was a dangerously large amount of cash to be carrying around in a less-than-affluent part of West London in the dead of night, a prize that would undoubtedly attract unwanted attention. They'd been in tight spots before, but nothing like this.

The trio reached the relative safety of their four-door BMW without incident. Every footstep on the tarmac had seemed too loud, every shadow too deep. Colin, ever the responsible one, slid into the driver's seat, while Joss and Wayne settled into the back, flanking the precious satchel, their eyes constantly scanning their surroundings. Their breathing came in quick, ragged bursts as they slammed the doors shut.

As they exited the brightly lit car park and merged onto nearby Wood Lane, the tension that had gripped them throughout the evening began to dissipate, replaced by a surge of exhilaration. They started whooping with unrestrained delight, their voices echoing in the confines of the car, the sheer scale of their success beginning to sink in. Laughter bubbled up—wild, ragged and disbelieving. They were alive, rich, and for the moment, untouchable.

"Not a bad night to do that on, eh?" Wayne exclaimed, a wide grin splitting his face, his eyes sparkling with excitement. He slapped Joss's shoulder hard enough to sting.

"And we're safe with the loot," Colin added reassuringly, glancing in the rear-view mirror, his expression a mixture of relief and pride.

The car hummed along, headlights carving a path through the night as they left the stadium—and their worries—behind. For now.

Unseen in the inky blackness of the night, their celebration short-lived, a nondescript white Ford Transit van, its engine purring softly, shadowed the BMW's every move. Its headlights were dimmed just enough to avoid suspicion, the driver's hands light on the wheel as they kept a careful distance, never losing sight. It followed them through the affluent streets of Kensington and Knightsbridge, past the glittering lights of Piccadilly Circus, through the historic heart of Holborn, and across the bustling arteries of the City.

The Commercial Road followed. Finally, Colin turned right, just past Mile End station and into Southern Grove.

Southern Grove is a long, leafy road and, on this June evening, was unusually quiet, its stillness broken only by the rustling of leaves in the gentle breeze. A lone fox slunk across the tarmac, pausing to sniff the air before vanishing into the undergrowth.

The road was flanked on one sidc by thc sombre stillness of a graveyard, its ancient stones casting long shadows under the streetlights, and on the other by the more mundane reality of a council estate, its uniform blocks of flats a stark contrast to the grandeur of the earlier parts of their journey. The orange glow of sodium lamps gave everything a sickly, sepia hue, making the gravestones seem to lean conspiratorially.

Towards the far end of the road, Colin gradually slowed the car to a halt, leaving the engine idling. He reached over and handed the car keys to Wayne.

The three men exchanged high-fives and hearty claps on the back, a silent acknowledgement of their shared triumph, their bond forged in the crucible of a night of high stakes and even higher rewards.

Colin eventually disappeared down a narrow alleyway that led towards his nearby flat, his figure swallowed by the darkness. He paused once to glance back, offering a final thumbs-up before slipping out of sight, the sound of his footsteps fading quickly.

Wayne slid into the now-vacant driver's seat, with Joss remaining in the back, the satchel overflowing with their 'pilgrim's treasure' nestled securely beside him, the weight of their winnings a tangible reminder of their success. He rested a protective hand on it, feeling the solidity of the cash through the leather, his mind buzzing with plans and possibilities.

Thirty yards away, concealed in the shadows, their intentions far less celebratory, four pairs of eyes intently surveyed the unfolding scene with avid interest, their faces obscured by the darkness, their expressions unreadable.

One of them muttered something low, the words lost in the wind, and another gave a curt nod. The van's interior smelled of petrol and stale chips, the tension inside it a physical thing.

On the remainder of the short journey home, the brothers excitedly dissected the most triumphant races of the evening, reliving the moments of tension and elation, the near misses and the glorious victories. Their voices overlapped, laughter erupting in snatches as they replayed the favourite's fall from grace for the tenth time.

Joss, ever the modern man despite his slightly old-fashioned sensibilities, retrieved an extraordinary contraption from his pocket – a mobile phone. This latest marvel of scientific research and development was a Motorola, a device affectionately and accurately described as being the size of a house brick. It weighed down his coat pocket like a brick too, and it took two hands to operate it confidently.

Its sheer size and weight made it a statement piece, a symbol of wealth and status. Joss loved it, not so much for its undeniable convenience, but for the unmistakable badge of 'lairyness' – a certain ostentatious flashiness – it bestowed upon him. He liked watching people's eyes widen when it rang, enjoyed the novelty of conducting business on the move, as if he were a stockbroker in the City.

Joss also knew that his call would likely rouse his wife, Ann, from her slumber, but he had promised to call her on the way back, especially if it looked like he would be late. And late they were going to be, given the small matter of depositing over a hundred thousand pounds somewhere secure – specifically, the sturdy safe in the small office above their betting shop on Walthamstow High Street. He dialled slowly, deliberately, the keypad beeping loudly in the quiet of the car, the glow from the tiny green screen illuminating his grin.

Thirty minutes after leaving the quiet confines of Southern Grove, they arrived back on Walthamstow High Street. Wayne couldn't help but notice the stark contrast between the street's current stillness and its daytime vibrancy.

At this early hour, the market stalls were silent and deserted, their colourful awnings furled, a world away from the bustling chaos of the day, when it resembled a chaotic betting ring in its own right, with market traders bellowing their own unique 'odds' to their captive audience – the shopping public. Even now, the scent of rotting fruit and damp cardboard lingered in the cool air.

"Two pineapples for the price of one, thirteen to eight, three bar one."

Not much difference, he mused, a wry smile playing on his lips. He gave a little snort of laughter, shaking his head at the madness of it all, then killed the engine with a decisive twist of the key.

He reflected that even the betting ring at White City, usually a cacophony of noise and activity, would now be silent like this, the bookmakers gone home, the punters dispersed, the only sound the distant hum of the city. It was oddly comforting in its way, a reminder that even the noisiest places had to sleep sometime, that chaos gave way to quiet, however briefly.

Two minutes later, Wayne brought the car to a halt and managed to park just outside the betting shop, situated halfway down the hill. The shop, a modest establishment compared to the grandiosity of White City, was their base of operations, their sanctuary.

It was their fortress, their livelihood, and sometimes it felt like their prison. As was the rule in the eighties, the era of darkened glass and discreet entrances, the public were not permitted to see through the windows of licensed premises, and as such, the outside of the shop displayed darkened glass with a sign in the front that read:

Archer Brothers, Est. 1978

Joss, with his characteristic sense of irony and a touch of self-deprecation, had decided to add 'Established 1978' as befitted his sense of humour, given that the business was only five years old. He'd snickered when he first painted it on, joking that it made them sound as old and respectable as Barclays Bank.

Underneath the sign were handwritten sheets of paper displaying the odds on the forthcoming season's outright winners of the top flight. League Division One was a subject that was always a source of passionate debate amongst their customers. It read:

3/1 Liverpool, 4/1 Manchester United, 5/1 Southampton, 8/1 Nottingham Forest.

The paper was slightly yellowed, corners curling from damp, and the ink had smudged in places from careless fingers pressing up to the glass to read.

Wayne turned off the ignition, the sudden silence amplifying the sound of the city, opened the side door of the BMW, fished in his coat pocket for the keys to the shop, the metal cold against his fingers, slammed the car door shut, and inserted the keys into the latch.

The lock clicked heavily, the sound echoing in the quiet street like a gunshot. The familiar high-pitched warning signal from the burglar alarm, a piercing shriek that shattered the stillness of the night, whistled as Wayne walked briskly through the unlit shop, his footsteps echoing in the empty space. He stepped towards the counter, his hand outstretched to turn off the alarm, the red light of the keypad blinking insistently, leaving the shop door ajar and his brother outside, a silent invitation to danger. He winced at the shrill tone, muttering under his breath about getting the damn thing serviced.

Groaning as he heaved himself from the back seat of the BMW, the leather creaking under his weight, Joss cursed under his breath at the weight of the metal stand used as a frame for their betting pitch, a cumbersome and unwieldy object that he struggled to manoeuvre. It clanged against the doorframe, scraping paint as he tried to angle it through.

The satchel, heavy with its precious cargo, was clutched tightly in his other hand. He staggered towards the open door, his progress slow and laboured.

Just before he reached the entrance, his eyes momentarily drawn to the display in the window, he paused, looking at the handwritten odds on display. He squinted at them, as though seeing them for the first time that night.

"We're a bit big on Forest, aren't we, bruv?" said Joss, his voice a low grumble, his brow furrowed in concentration.

He didn't get to hear Wayne's reply.

It had all happened in a few seconds, a blur of motion and violence that shattered the relative peace of the night. There was the crunch of boots on broken glass, the whoosh of something heavy swinging through the air. As Wayne turned off the burglar alarm, the silence abruptly replaced by the soft hum of the shop's interior, he was suddenly troubled by a nagging sense of unease, a prickling feeling that something was amiss.

A shiver ran down his spine. He hadn't noticed Joss enter the shop, a departure from their usual routine. Then, his heart leaping into his throat, he heard the sickening thud outside, a sound that spoke of violence and danger.

With sudden, mounting panic, his mind racing, Wayne feared the worst. He strode stealthily yet cautiously towards the open door, his hand instinctively reaching for the heavy metal bar they kept behind the counter for protection. His fingers fumbled, slippery with sweat. He saw a figure silhouetted in the entrance, not Joss as he had expected, but a man of imposing stature, his face obscured by a grotesque mask depicting Mrs Thatcher, the Iron Lady, her stern features contorted into a caricature of menace.

The mask twisted grotesquely with each breath, its eyeholes dark and bottomless. The man in the mask made his intentions reasonably clear by the four-foot baseball bat he was carrying in his right hand, its polished surface gleaming under the dim light, a weapon of brutal simplicity. He tapped it once against the doorframe, a silent threat that needed no words.

Wayne lunged towards the intruder, his fear for his brother's safety overriding any sense of self-preservation, now petrified not only for the contents of the satchel but for the well-being of his brother.

His heart hammered so hard it hurt. He didn't see Joss, who now lay unconscious by the window, his body sprawled awkwardly on the pavement under another sign that read, with cruel irony given the current circumstances:

'Best odds in town, be on target and bet with the Archers.'

A second and third man, their faces also covered by Mrs Thatcher masks, seemingly identical in their grotesque disguise, appeared from nowhere, materialising from the shadows like phantoms. They moved with a chilling coordination, as though they'd rehearsed this moment a dozen times. Wayne later realised, with a chilling certainty, that they had most likely emerged from the narrow alleyway at the side of the shop, a place of darkness and concealment. He cursed himself for not checking it first.

A female voice, surprisingly deep and guttural and, even more surprisingly, laced with a thick Northern Irish accent, growled at Wayne, the words harsh and threatening: "Cool it, Archer. You toe-rags still have your lives, if not your money."

The accent twisted the words into something cruel and mocking, turning her threat into a promise.

Wayne stopped in his tracks, his blood running cold, and turned slowly in the direction of the voice. He instantly found himself peering down the twin barrels of two sawn-off shotguns, their dark muzzles menacing and unforgiving, one held by each of the two new assailants.

The cold steel of the weapons was a stark reminder of the deadly seriousness of the situation. He felt his knees weaken, the reality of it washing over him in a wave of dread.

"What have you..." Wayne's voice petered out, his words failing him, as he noticed his brother on the ground, his face pale and contorted, his eyes fluttering open, beginning to come round from the brutal assault. Joss let out a low groan, blood trickling from a split lip.

There was no sign of their bag of money, the satchel that had contained their hard-won winnings. It had vanished, spirited away in the chaos. Wayne's gut twisted. It was gone. All of it.

Hesitantly at first, the gunmen started edging backwards, their movements slow and deliberate, the barrels of their shotguns still trained unwaveringly on Wayne, a constant reminder of their power. Their boots scuffed against the pavement, deliberate and menacing.

Having reversed ten paces, creating a small buffer of space, the intruders finally turned their backs and broke into a sprint down the hill, their heavy boots pounding on the pavement, swiftly followed by the man with the baseball bat, his Mrs Thatcher mask bobbing grotesquely in the darkness.

Before they had covered forty yards, their escape swift and efficient, a white Ford Transit van, its engine roaring to life, screeched alongside the masked robbers, its tyres squealing in protest. The men clambered hastily in, their movements frantic and desperate.

The van screamed into a U-turn, its headlights cutting through the darkness, and sped back up the hill, passing Wayne and the now-recovering Joss in a blur of motion. Wayne flinched as the wind from its passing brushed his face.

As it sailed by, Wayne, his mind reeling, saw the large satchel, its distinctive leather gleaming under the streetlights, clutched tightly in the arms of the man in the passenger seat, who, in the surreal and terrifying circumstances, appeared to be the Prime Minister herself. The mask grinned back at him, a vile mockery of power and order.

'Mrs Thatcher', her face a grotesque parody of the real thing, managed to throw up two fingers in a defiant V-sign at Wayne as the van made its getaway, its taillights disappearing into the distance, swallowed by the darkness. It was a final insult, an exclamation mark on their humiliation.

Wayne, his mind struggling to process the bizarre and violent events, just caught sight of the registration plate, a string of letters and numbers that seemed almost meaningless in the aftermath of the robbery. He kept repeating it out loud, his voice hoarse and strained, trying to retain it in his mind, a desperate attempt to cling to some shred of hope before he could write it down. He didn't hold out much hope of it doing any good.

The van, he knew with a sinking certainty, was probably stolen anyway, a disposable tool in their audacious crime. The thought left a sour taste in his mouth.

"Who the fuck has just ruined our big night, bruv?" croaked Joss, his voice weak and groggy, clutching his head, his fingers gingerly probing the swelling bruise. His eyes were glassy with pain and confusion.

"Dunno," said Wayne, his face buried in his hands, his shoulders slumped in defeat, the weight of their loss pressing down on him. The adrenaline drained from his body, leaving only exhaustion and anger.

"I'm even money we find 'em. Let's go and have a drink," said Joss, ever the optimist, though even he couldn't quite muster his usual bravado. His voice cracked, the bravado a thin veneer over raw bitterness. The bravado would come later.

CHAPTER 2

— *August 1986*

Sir Marcus Holderness still took the Central line into the City each day. He often chuckled to himself, recalling Thatcher's rather infamous pronouncement in the early eighties, when she declared, "Anyone who still uses public transport in their thirties hasn't made it in life."

It was a sentiment that might have rung true for some of his peers, but for Marcus it was nothing more than political bluster, a relic of an era long gone. He had always believed there was quiet dignity in routine and simplicity, especially in a world obsessed with luxury and excess.

Watching tired commuters clutching their coffees and newspapers, he often wondered how many of them knew a knight of the realm stood among them, disguised in a wool coat and cashmere scarf.

Marcus, however, wasn't in the least bit bothered. The Central line station was a mere two-minute stroll from his rather substantial residence in Notting Hill, and it whisked him from his front door to the London Stock Exchange in a comfortable thirty-five minutes.

Notting Hill Gate to Bank by tube was far more convenient than relying on his chauffeur, and what's more, it afforded him a quiet sense of satisfaction that he still possessed the common touch.

He also enjoyed the stillness of those morning rides. The rumble of the train and the rustle of papers provided a strange comfort. Occasionally, he would spot headlines that mentioned names he knew – sometimes friends, sometimes rivals – and smile to himself. The City was a small world when you'd been around long enough.

In any case, Marcus had most certainly made it in life. Following his time at Eton, he'd spent a brief period working on a sheep station in Australia before taking up his place at Cambridge to read Economics.

A 2:1 – "a gentleman's degree," his mother had proudly announced, quite unaware that the term referred to third-class honours. National Service had duly followed, after which he'd respectfully disagreed with his barrister father about pursuing a career in law, and had instead opted to join a small firm of stockbrokers, Edwin James & Co.

That decision had raised a few eyebrows among the Holderness family, but Marcus had never been one to blindly follow tradition. There was something about the pulse of the markets, the high stakes, and the ever-shifting nature of finance that excited him far more than dusty legal tomes ever could.

Here, he'd started at the very bottom, as a 'blue button'. Despite his somewhat privileged background, he was perfectly content to carry bags, chalk up stock prices on Edwin James & Co.'s board at the Exchange, deliver messages, and, most importantly, take the partners' breakfast orders each morning.

Marcus was invariably the first to arrive in the 'box', the room within the Exchange where the dealing staff at Edwin James spent the trading hours when they weren't actually on the floor itself. They would typically return to their office in Moorgate shortly after half past three in the afternoon, the official close of the London market each day.

That cramped little room, full of barked orders, frantic scribbles, and the smell of bacon sandwiches, became his training ground. He listened more than he spoke, learned more than he revealed, and slowly earned the trust of even the most cantankerous partners.

Marcus proved to be a most diligent junior. A fundamental respect for his fellow men, regardless of their social standing, had been firmly instilled in him during his National Service at Catterick Barracks.

While he had been fortunate enough to miss the Second World War by only a handful of years, his Regimental Sergeant Major, a stern and unforgiving Welshman, had pushed Marcus to the very limits of his mental and physical endurance. This experience stood Marcus in good stead, enabling him to earn respect, make friends readily, and work with unwavering diligence.

It was also during those barracks days that Marcus had come to understand the difference between leadership and command. You didn't need to shout to be respected. You just needed to show up, do the work, and never ask of someone what you weren't willing to do yourself. Those principles carried him through every rung of his career.

After two years working in the box, Marcus was presented with a choice. He could either progress to become a 'yellow button', an authorised dealer permitted to take orders directly from clients, or he could move away from the intense atmosphere of the dealing environment and become more involved in the research side of his employer's business.

Marcus opted for the latter, and it wasn't long before his sharp analytical mind was producing research papers that not only drew envious glances from his colleagues but also brought him to the attention of some of the larger City institutions.

Each report was meticulously crafted, not just with numbers and trends, but with narrative and insight. He had a knack for seeing beyond the data, for weaving context into his analysis. Within the industry, his name began to quietly circulate – not as a loud mover, but as a thoughtful mind who could spot market currents before they became waves.

His reputation soon outgrew Edwin James & Co., and in his early thirties, Marcus made a move, both in terms of company and job, joining a prestigious merchant bank, Sinclair's, in their Corporate Finance department. It was a bold but calculated step, one that many of his peers quietly envied.

The atmosphere at Sinclair's was markedly different – brisk, cut-throat, and humming with ambition. Marcus took to it with the same measured discipline he had applied throughout his life, quickly establishing himself not just as a reliable mind but as a leader capable of delivering under pressure.

Despite receiving numerous enticing offers from rival merchant banks and venture capital firms, Marcus remained loyal to Sinclair's, staying there for the entirety of his corporate finance career. He valued stability, and Sinclair's had offered him the space to grow, fail, learn, and ultimately succeed on his own terms.

Over the years, he witnessed various economic booms and recessions come and go, each one leaving behind new rules, new players, and fresh cautionary tales. He navigated them all with considerable skill, advising acquisitive companies on their intended takeover targets or, equally, vulnerable companies on how to maintain their independence when caught in the glare of an unwelcome suitor.

The 1970s had provided a particularly volatile period for world markets. In 1970, there had been a thirty per cent drop in prices during monetary tightening, a forty per cent collapse in 1974 amid the oil crisis, and another twenty-six per cent dip in 1978 as inflation accelerated.

Throughout, it was Marcus who remained calm when others panicked, helping clients stave off disaster and reposition for recovery. He was the steady hand warning against over-leveraged plays into volatile start-up stocks. His counsel wasn't always popular, but it was usually right – and that built him a reputation as not only a strategist, but a sage.

Marcus retired shortly after his fiftieth birthday, having been awarded a knighthood for services to business. Some of the nation's most distinguished captains of industry attended his retirement dinner, hosted by Marcus, his wife Diana, and their two sons.

The venue – an exclusive private dining room overlooking the Thames – buzzed with laughter and reminiscence. The accolades and speeches continued late into the evening as Marcus reflected with gratitude on a successful career and looked forward to a long and happy retirement. There were toasts, vintage wine, and heartfelt anecdotes from peers who had once been rivals.

It was, by all accounts, the kind of send-off most professionals only dream of.

Retirement, however, did not come easily to Sir Marcus. He had never had much time for golf, and his shooting was decidedly poor, regardless of the number of lessons he took. His enthusiasm was genuine, but his coordination less so. He had never really acclimatised himself to the countryside or its associated sporting pursuits, and apart from spending a month with Diana at their villa in the South of France, where he spent most mornings reading financial newspapers and annotating margins with sharp pencil notes, Marcus's time was predominantly spent at their Notting Hill residence, diligently studying global market movements and preparing for numerous company meetings where he held board positions.

Within two years of his new 'idyllic' existence, Marcus was bored stiff and beginning to fray the nerves of his family. His sharp mind, used to the pace of boardrooms and trading floors, was left untethered. He became restless, pacing from room to room, tinkering with spreadsheets, and reading company reports with the fervour of a man still on the clock.

His sons were driven to mock despair whenever Marcus sighed heavily, "There's simply no way I can go back now. I'm far too old, and nobody in their right mind would have me."

Diana, ever patient, took to suggesting long walks or cultural outings, but Marcus would inevitably steer the conversation back to regulatory frameworks or global interest rates.

One day, a letter plopped through the letterbox at his spacious Notting Hill abode. The envelope was crisp and formal, embossed with the crest of the London Stock Exchange. Upon receiving an invitation to luncheon from the Chairman, he immediately suspected a hidden agenda.

"No such thing as a free lunch, you know," he announced to his long-suffering family with a raised eyebrow and the ghost of a smile.

He was quite right. Throughout the meal, three unhurried courses served with quiet efficiency, the Chairman of the Stock Exchange extended an invitation to Marcus to take up an appointment as head of the Regulatory and Supervision Committee.

It was an offer cloaked in flattery and framed in national duty. Marcus protested that his experience was hardly befitting of such a role (it was rather akin to a poacher turning gamekeeper, he mused), but the Chairman harboured no such doubts. He explained that what he sought was a figurehead, a sharp mind capable of adapting to any of the myriad circumstances that could lead to breaches of Stock Exchange regulations. There had been a recent surge in cases of insider dealing, and the government was putting pressure on the Stock Exchange to implement preventative measures by securing evidence that could lead to successful prosecutions.

Sir Marcus listened carefully, his expression unreadable, but something stirred within him—an old sense of purpose. It was a challenge, and though it came dressed as oversight and protocol, he recognised the deeper call to service. He didn't say yes right away, but he also didn't say no. And as he sipped the last of his claret, he realised, with a flicker of anticipation, that perhaps retirement wasn't quite the end to his story after all.

To the undoubted relief of his family, Marcus accepted the role and was bestowed with a magnificent office on the twenty-third floor of the London Stock Exchange. A breathtaking panorama stretched out over Threadneedle Street and beyond. The view, with its mix of gleaming modern towers and historic rooftops, gave Marcus a renewed sense of purpose. Each morning, the city below unfurled like a map of ambition and enterprise.

Marcus swiftly settled into his new position, familiarising himself with his department by inviting the entire twenty-person team for drinks in his office one evening. The informal gathering was more than just a meet-and-greet; it was a strategic move.

Over sparkling wine and nibbles, Marcus listened more than he spoke, noting interpersonal dynamics, shared frustrations, and whispered gossip that never made its way into official reports.

The members of the team were primarily made up of chartered accountants, solicitors, and Information Technology specialists, but also included a couple of retired police officers, several former compliance officers from various financial institutions, and two young members of Stock Exchange staff who otherwise performed general administrative duties.

Despite their varied backgrounds, there was a quiet competence to the team, a sense that each individual brought something essential to the whole. Marcus, with his innate sense for talent, could already see who might rise to greater responsibility.

Marcus wasn't entirely sure at first precisely what 'general duties' entailed, but he soon discovered that their discreet role within the Regulatory and Supervision department was to act as intelligence officers, operating under the guise of their administrative jobs on the market floor. This subtle network of internal eyes and ears fascinated Marcus. It felt like a game of chess being played behind the curtains of the Exchange, a quiet war against corruption where every pawn had purpose.

Marcus made his customary journey from Bank Station into Throgmorton Street and through the grand double doors of the Stock Exchange, offering greetings to old acquaintances as he went, mainly stockbrokers and stockjobbers about to embark on another day's trading battles on the floor. These brief exchanges, often accompanied by a firm handshake or a knowing glance, reminded him of the camaraderie and competitiveness that had always defined life on the floor.

The stockbrokers took the 'orders' from their clients, while the stockjobbers facilitated those orders, quoting a two-way price—one price at which they were prepared to buy, and another at which they were prepared to sell—on either of which the stockbrokers could execute their trades. It was a system that had withstood the test of time, a delicate balance of risk and reward choreographed with precision every trading day.

There was a significant new issue on the cards today, an offering of stock in a newly listed public company that had recently been denationalised by the government, preceded by a substantial television advertising campaign designed to encourage the general public to invest in shares. It had been impossible to miss; the adverts were everywhere, from prime-time television to bus shelters, promising average citizens a chance to own a slice of Britain. It was, Marcus mused, capitalism wrapped in patriotism.

Share volumes were on the rise, and widespread share ownership was strongly advocated by the Conservative government. Today's trading was certain to attract considerable media attention and witness a degree of pandemonium on the floor of the Exchange, as jobbers were almost bowled over in the rush while eager brokers jostled to deal at the most favourable prices. The energy was palpable even in the corridors above; tension buzzed like electricity in the air, and every screen flickered with anticipation.

Share prices were generally booming, and the press were speculating that this 'bull market' still had a considerable distance to run.

Analysts were optimistic, hedge funds aggressive, and the cocktail of political confidence and public enthusiasm stirred a potent brew of investor mania. Marcus had seen this before, of course, but it never failed to stir a flicker of excitement in him.

Sir Marcus felt a fleeting pang of nostalgia as he walked past the bustling floor and stood by the lift, his mind drifting back to those happy early days as a 'blue button' at Edwin James & Co. He remembered the rush of his first trade, the tremor in his fingers as he chalked up prices, the subtle nods of approval from his seniors.

He heard the opening bell ring, followed by a crescendo of noise as the brokers surged onto the floor towards the waiting jobbers, who stood firm at their designated pitches like soldiers defending their ground. These pitches were large hexagonal enclosures that protruded slightly from the floor, with constantly updated prices displayed alongside the name of each stock traded there.

The floor transformed into a hive of human energy – shouts echoed, papers rustled, phones rang in rapid succession. It was chaos with a rhythm, and Marcus, despite his elevated role, still felt the familiar pulse of adrenaline as he watched it all unfold.

The morning unfolded in its usual predictable manner. The sun cast a pale golden light across the skyline, its rays filtering into Marcus's office and reflecting off polished surfaces and framed accolades.

Marcus received his customary coffee and the morning newspapers from his secretary. The aroma of the fresh brew filled the room, grounding him in the familiar ritual that started each day. He accepted the bundle with a nod of thanks, already scanning the front page of the *Financial Times*.

As he perused the financial news, he made the occasional note of any unusual share price movements and press commentary that alluded to 'speculative buying or selling' that had precipitated any sharp increases or declines in stock values. His annotations were quick and concise, a legacy of years spent analysing such data with a critical eye.

Even now, his instinct could often spot a questionable trade before the algorithms did – a sixth sense that age had sharpened, not dulled.

At eleven o'clock, he attended a meeting that provided an overview of the progress the department was making with its ongoing investigations. The boardroom was cool and quiet, the air dense with the low hum of projectors and murmurs of anticipation. He was made to feel rather antiquated as one of the bright young IT wizards demonstrated the sophisticated new technology his team was employing to detect subtle price anomalies.

The screen lit up with cascading data, glowing graphs, and digital fingerprints no naked eye could detect. Marcus watched with a mixture of awe and discomfort; while impressed, he couldn't shake the feeling of being an analogue man in a digital world.

Following the meeting, Marcus returned to his office and returned Diana's call, reminding him that they were scheduled to attend the Royal Court Theatre in Sloane Square that evening for Caryl Churchill's latest play, *Serious Money*.

He smiled to himself during the conversation, the cadence of Diana's voice always bringing a trace of warmth to his day.

Marcus couldn't help but wonder if it would contain any depictions of financial skulduggery. He imagined the characters: greedy traders with manic eyes, fast-talking brokers, whispers in corridors, and the click of closing deals echoing like gunshots across the stage. It would be, if nothing else, an entertaining change of pace.

He was just about to depart for luncheon when his secretary knocked on the door before entering the room and placing a substantial brown folder on his desk. The thud it made as it landed seemed to carry weight beyond paper. There was a quiet pause, the kind that often preludes significance.

Lunch that day was with Brian Perry, a long-standing partner of one of the major jobbing firms on the floor, a veritable market legend, and a very old and dear friend of Marcus's. Their lunches were never simply meals – they were events, heavy with reminiscence, gossip, and the occasional trading secret slipped between courses.

Affixed to the folder was an envelope bearing the words '*London Stock Exchange, Strictly Private and Confidential*'. The lettering was bold, unmistakably formal, and its message clear: this was no ordinary correspondence. It was further marked *For the attention of Sir Marcus Holderness'.*

A curious chill crept up Marcus's spine as he gently removed the envelope, noting the texture of the thick paper beneath his fingertips.

Marcus opened the envelope and was rather taken aback to see that the note inside was handwritten and from one of his senior accountants. The neat cursive slanted slightly to the right, as though written in some haste but with care. It read simply:

"Dear Sir Marcus,

I do hope that one of the names on the enclosed list doesn't cause you any unnecessary embarrassment. We are merely at an exploratory level of investigation at this stage anyway.

Kind regards,

Alan."

Marcus read the note again, slower the second time. His pulse quickened, but his face remained composed. Years of training had taught him not to react visibly. He reached for the folder with a steady hand, though his thoughts were already racing.

What name could possibly provoke such a warning?

With growing curiosity, and a not insignificant degree of concern, Marcus carefully placed his umbrella back on his desk. A soft clink echoed off the polished mahogany surface, punctuating the sudden shift in his morning. Brian could certainly wait a few more minutes. Their long-standing friendship offered him that grace.

From the folder, he extracted a thick computer printout containing itemised records of hundreds of trades and their corresponding counterparties. The weight of the stack was telling – weeks, perhaps months, of data compressed into endless streams of numbers, columns, and abbreviations.

They initially made little sense to him as he flicked through the green and white sheets, the computer paper crinkling slightly between his fingers. Rows of dates, transaction codes, quantities, and buyer-seller identifiers blurred before his eyes.

A more forensic examination would be needed, of course, but for now, he was searching for something that stood out – something human amid the numerical tide. His attention was then drawn to an unattached memo featuring a list of individual names, alongside the name of the bank, stockbroker, or stockjobbing firm that each person was associated with.

These were listed in alphabetical order. A rather clinical presentation – deliberate, emotionless, designed to shield the reader from the implications that might lie beneath the surface.

None of the names immediately rang any bells as he scanned down the list: Davis, Drysdale, Fuente, Grossmith,

Henderson, Hill, Jackson, Johnson, Michaels, Norris, Perry. His eyes continued down the list before doubling back.

"Perry?" Marcus murmured the name almost inaudibly. It lingered in the air like the tail-end of a whispered secret.

Marcus noted with a sense of relief that the initial was not 'B'. He exhaled, unaware he'd been holding his breath. However, the potential culprit's employer was a matter of very real concern. The unease that had started as a faint twinge now took root. He looked again, his eyes focusing on the letters before him: *Perry, D. Sinclair Bank.*

"Daniel Perry?" The words left his mouth in disbelief. Brian's son.

The very same Daniel Perry for whom Marcus had secured a position in his final year at Sinclair's. A favour extended in good faith. A nudge into the right circles. That this name should now appear in such a context felt like an affront, a sting of personal betrayal mingled with professional alarm.

Having lunch with the lad's father today was, to say the least, an unwelcome coincidence. The timing, Marcus reflected grimly, could hardly have been worse.

Marcus decided against mentioning anything to Brian for the time being. A confrontation now, without substantiated facts, would be premature and potentially damaging. It was far too early, in any case, to be making any accusations, and besides, Marcus didn't yet fully comprehend the precise nature of the alleged offences. His experience reminded him that finance could be murky, but ambiguity wasn't guilt.

All he knew for certain was that they appeared potentially quite serious.

He would simply have to endeavour to make the best of lunch and steer the conversation towards more light-hearted topics. Despite the tangle of thoughts clouding his mind, Marcus straightened his tie, composed his expression, and headed out.

They had arranged to meet in The Long Room', a popular grill in Throgmorton Street much favoured by brokers and jobbers. The very name carried echoes of an older, louder era: elbows on the table, voices raised over pints, deals spoken in shorthand and sealed with a handshake. Marcus's rather more refined fellow committee members wouldn't have been seen dead there, but he had always enjoyed the vibrant atmosphere that permeated the place.

The restaurant buzzed with chatter and laughter, the sound of cutlery on plates, the clink of ice in tumblers, and the occasional whoop of triumph when a lucky punt paid off. The air smelled of chargrilled meat, tobacco from the outdoor terrace, and the faint tang of gin and lime.

The unique brand of humour shared by the majority of the regulars who congregated there, some on a daily basis, for gin and tonics, followed by steak and chips, cheese, red wine and, for some, a glass of port or a measure of calvados for 'afters', gave the place a kind of defiant charm.

Brian was in typically high spirits as he boasted about the successful trading positions his dealers had enjoyed that morning. He slapped Marcus on the back, chuckling with that booming laugh that turned heads at other tables.

"The market smiled on us today, my friend," he declared, raising his glass. Marcus forced a smile in return, even as a knot of unease settled deeper in his chest.

"We were five million quid long of stock coming into this morning, doubled that by elevenses, but now those pikey brokers can't get enough of it. Every time I mark a price up, even more buyers appear."

Brian's eyes sparkled with the thrill of the game, his booming voice resonating off the dark wood panels of The Long Room. The room around them bustled with animated conversations and the clang of cutlery, but for Marcus, the edges of the world had slightly blurred.

The banter, the laughter, the high-octane rhythm of city trading life—it was all familiar. Comforting, even. But today, it felt like a fragile veneer stretched over something far more troubling.

Marcus chuckled along with his old pal. He and Brian had been blue buttons together in the early days and shared a great many mutual Stock Exchange friends.

There was a time when the two of them had worn out shoe leather running between brokers' boxes, shouting out quotes and relaying orders in a language only traders truly understood. Their camaraderie had been forged in the furnace of floor trading, under pressure, noise and sleepless ambition.

He wondered, with a slight unease, if that had played any part in his appointment to the regulatory committee. Perhaps someone had assumed he would turn a blind eye, or worse, offer leniency when faced with familiar names and faces. Not that he had any reason to feel awkward in Brian's company.

Marcus couldn't recall a single instance in their long acquaintance where Brian had acted with anything but total professional integrity.

Brian Perry may have come from less privileged beginnings, but integrity and honesty were his defining characteristics, and Marcus trusted him implicitly.

There was a certain grounded decency to Brian, an unpretentious directness that many of their contemporaries lacked. Marcus possessed an excellent judgement of character, a valuable quality that had served him exceptionally well throughout his career. And it was this very instinct that now sat uneasily in his gut, because for the first time, he felt it falter.

He listened attentively as his friend recounted his latest anecdotes: how he had "cleaned up in Cable and Wireless," the time he'd told Alan Sugar that he would "do all right with

Amstrad," and the amusing tale of Sweaty Betty wandering around the trading floor all day with a duster mischievously attached to the back of her skirt by some blue button.

The humour was brash, old-school and unmistakably of the world they both came from, a world that was fast vanishing amid reforms, regulation and electronic trading.

Still, it warmed Marcus to hear it, to remember the ease and simplicity of those earlier years. And yet, even as he smiled at the stories, a shadow lingered behind his eyes.

As he listened, Marcus felt a profound sadness at the potential pain his old friend might face if the Regulatory Department pursued his son on charges of insider dealing.

There were few things more devastating than seeing one's child ensnared in scandal, especially for a man who had worked so hard to build a reputation founded on trust. It struck Marcus as especially cruel that a man like Brian, so far removed from duplicity, might be tainted by association.

He would need to give considerable thought to how best to handle this deeply uncomfortable situation. Marcus knew that objectivity would be expected of him—required, even—but objectivity didn't come with instructions on what to do when the lines between friend and professional blurred.

Back in his office, Marcus meticulously examined the contents of the file. His office, once a place of calm efficiency, now felt like a battleground of conflicting responsibilities. The documents lay splayed across the desk like pieces of a jigsaw with no clear picture. He pressed the buzzer to summon his secretary, already dreading the chain of actions this day might set in motion.

CHAPTER 3

— *May 1986,*

Three Months Earlier

Dan Perry was not in a good mood that Friday morning in May. A dull ache throbbed behind his eyes as he slumped into his chair, exhaling heavily.

With a series of tired gestures, he turned each of the screens in front of him on, eyes blinking at the harsh glow of charts and figures. Numbers spilled across the monitors in relentless waves: overnight markets, currency ticks, futures, indices – but none of it lifted the weight in his chest.

He turned away briefly and rubbed his temples. Another day, another race, though these days, not always the kind that ended on turf.

His routine hadn't changed in months: leave his flat in Fulham at 7:00 am sharp, pick up his copies of *The Sporting Life* and *The Financial Times*, then catch the number 14 bus to South Kensington before disappearing into the Underground and taking the Circle Line to Liverpool Street. It was a dance he knew by muscle memory now, a solitary commute with papers folded neatly under one arm and eyes fixed on nothing in particular.

By the time he arrived at Liverpool Street, he could usually be at his desk at Sinclair Bank a few minutes later – well before the strict 8:00 am deadline required of all traders.

But today, punctuality was the least of his concerns.

Dan felt the dryness in his throat and the sick feeling in his stomach. It wasn't just the lingering effects of the alcohol he'd guzzled the night before – although that certainly hadn't helped – it was the pit in his gut that came from knowing just how much he'd lost to those wretched bookmakers. Again.

The afternoon before had been a quiet one in the financial markets and appeared to present a good opportunity to get stuck into the racing on an above-average weekday meeting at Newbury. That was how he justified it to himself, anyway. But Dan knew, inwardly and with mounting dread, that the quality of the fare didn't really make much difference anymore. He was in deep now, and it was no longer about form or strategy. He needed the rush. He craved the chase.

He had even started having large bets on greyhounds – an act of growing desperation masked as a casual flutter.

And then there were the Friday nights. The rituals. The unravelling.

He and his mates would crowd into The Crispin after work, a slightly run-down pub just around the corner from Sinclair Bank, and lose themselves in lager and a game they called *shoot pool.* It involved flipping the tops of coins and betting on whether it would be heads or tails. That was it.

No skill. No edge. Just blind chance and blind faith.

The stakes always spiralled. Always.

With each round, the pile of coins grew and the laughter got louder – fuelled by bravado and bitterness in equal measure – until someone would write a cheque they had no business writing, chasing an impossible comeback, hoping the next flip would somehow set it all right again.

Dan had been that someone more than once.

Maybe tonight would be different. Maybe he'd recover some of his recent gambling losses. He told himself that often. He felt he was owed it, as if the universe had been conspiring against him and surely, surely, his luck was due a turn.

In the background, Dan heard an analyst droning on about Marks & Spencer's figures, which had just been released. The voice was nasal, dry, full of economic jargon that washed over him like static.

Dan was a trader. He didn't care for the academics who forecast the imminent destination of companies' share prices. In his world, decisions were made on gut, momentum and timing – reflexes honed over time, not by theories but by blood, sweat, and sometimes, blind risk.

"I'm recommending going overboard on the shares on the back of this statement," he heard the analyst say.

Dan smirked to himself, the corner of his mouth twitching without warmth. That wasn't how it worked – not really.

As a trader, Dan's skill was to study changing share prices and act, often on instinct, speculating heavily with the bank's money. He lived for the thrill of decisive moments, the adrenaline that surged when you risked everything and came out ahead. But today, even that thrill felt dulled – overwritten by too many bad bets and the gnawing worry that he was starting to lose more than just money.

This morning, Dan's mind was certainly not focused on the direction of Marks & Spencer's share price. His thoughts kept drifting back to the previous night – slow, sticky memories that clung to him like the remnants of smoke and lager.

After losing more than he felt comfortable admitting during the previous day's racing, it had seemed like a perfectly reasonable idea to round up some of his hardcore betting chums and head to Walthamstow dogs. That was their escape hatch, a fallback when the stock tickers felt too slow and the world too sharp.

The usual pattern unfolded. As soon as they could slip out of the office – usually around 5:30 pm – they piled into a minicab and made the forty-five-minute journey from the City to the track. The moment they arrived, it was straight to the bar.

Over a few drinks, they'd huddle around the race card with a kind of reverence reserved for far more noble causes. That sort of analysis, at least, Dan respected. It was familiar, instinctive.

One of them might suddenly exclaim, "Oh my God, have you seen this three-dog in the 7:29?"

Or another would chime in, "Do you remember that dog's early pace last time?"

The usual reply followed like clockwork, often accompanied by laughter: "Yeah, plenty of early but not enough late!"

Dan always felt a faint thrill as the cab rounded the final corner and the bright red neon sign came into view:

WELCOME TO WALTHAMSTOW,
THE HOME OF GREYHOUND RACING

Just beside it blinked another, smaller sign:

CHARLIE CHAN'S

The latter was a nightclub popular with Essex girls and lads, along with the occasional group of young City traders who stumbled in after the races, adrenaline still surging and wallets lighter than they'd hoped.

That evening, Dan had made up his mind—he was going to up the stakes. He was chasing.

He set his sights on a major bet towards the end of the night. As usual, he planned to place it with the Archer Brothers, who held the prime pitch right in front of the stand.

The brothers, grizzled, sharp-eyed, and always sharply dressed, were in their late forties and, while they gave off a slightly hard edge, they had a certain charm about them. Dan had never once seen them refuse a bet, no matter the size.

They knew how to work a crowd and had built a rapport with the regulars, especially with Dan and his lot.

Loud, theatrical, and always with a grin, the Archers had figured out early that the best way to separate these City boys from their money was to shout the loudest, offer the flashiest odds, and make sure they were always the ones holding the biggest bets.

It worked.

A couple of months back, Joss Archer had even offered to buy the 'yuppies', as he called them, a drink and encouraged them to open credit accounts. Dan had hesitated. He remembered asking how much credit he was being offered and feeling a faint unease when Joss gave him a knowing wink and said, "You don't have a credit limit, son. We always get our money back in the end."

That line had stuck with Dan. It still echoed now, though he had tried to laugh it off at the time.

At twenty-five, Dan had never had a credit account before—not like that. His love of betting went back to his final years at Lancing College in Sussex. There had been a day boy in his house who brought him a copy of *The Sporting Life* each day, and through that paper, Dan discovered a whole new world. It was there that he first noticed the advertisements from bookmakers offering deposit accounts.

Even then, he had always bet bigger than his friends. Much bigger.

Especially during their illicit schoolboy visits to courses like Brighton, Plumpton, Goodwood, and Fontwell. He still remembered the thrill of standing at the rail, heart thumping, eyes locked on the track.

But back then, access to cash had been a problem.

Now, the access was easier. The habits, however, had only grown harder to break.

He had opened a deposit account with a firm called Guntrips and, during half-terms or holidays, topped it up by sending Guntrips the cheque he was inevitably given by his parents.

Eight years later, his circumstances had significantly changed. His father's friend, Marcus Holderness, had helped him get a foot in the door at Sinclair Bank. Given that he hadn't gone to university, Dan had done remarkably well, rising from tea boy to trader in just three years.

As his seniority within the bank increased, so too did his salary. They even paid him substantial bonuses. Dan decided that, with his newfound status, it was time to have a proper credit account.

With the Archer Brothers' account—unlimited—Dan no longer had to concern himself with restricting his bets to whatever cash he happened to have in his pocket, or the funds lodged with his three existing deposit accounts: Mecca Bookmakers, Heathorns, and Guntrips. Those accounts came with the added hassle of posting off a cheque, then waiting for it to clear before he could place further bets. No, an unlimited credit account was ideal. It suited his elevated position as a senior trader at Sinclair Bank.

With his mind now fixed on the first race, Dan thought back to the £2,400 he had lost to the Archers while betting from the office the previous day. He had backed one favourite after another, and they had all been beaten. He already owed them a further £1,800 from earlier that week, so it was crucial he clawed back a couple of grand that night.

Unlike his mates, Dan fancied himself as a shrewd punter. Everyone knew that 'shrewdies' didn't go big on every race. So, he resolved to keep his bets to £200 per race—just for interest—until his big fancy of the evening ran in the 8:47. He'd decided that he would back that dog to win whatever amount he owed the Archer Brothers. Chasing losses didn't bother Dan in the slightest.

By the time the ninth race rolled around—the 8:47 at the Stow—Dan was feeling increasingly uneasy, not to mention drunk. He and his mates had been downing a pint of lager between every race, and the only food they'd had all night was the occasional packet of cheese and onion crisps or some dry-roasted peanuts. He had only placed small bets on the earlier races for interest's sake, but things had already gone badly.

Eight losing wagers of £200 each—£1,600 down on dogs he hadn't even fancied that much. Worse still, it now meant he owed the Archer Brothers a total of £5,800. And he knew their statement would be waiting for him come Monday.

The only way out was to lump it all on Trap Three—the hot favourite in the 8:47. Dan stood a few steps up in the stands, gazing down at the row of bookmakers' pitches spread out in front of him. It was an 'open' race, meaning the runners had come in from tracks across the country.

Tonight was a good example: the Trap Three dog was from Hove, a course he'd visited not long after leaving Lancing. Hove wasn't far from home, and he had returned several times—each time, to his surprise, turning a profit. He tried to convince himself this was a good omen.

Dan was preparing to place the biggest bet of his life on the Hove runner in Trap Three. Not because he had any real confidence in the dog, but because he had no choice. He was already struggling to cover his mounting debt to the Archer Brothers.

If he didn't act fast, they might freeze his account altogether. He also knew that only the Archers would be willing to accommodate the size of the stake he intended to place.

One of the bookies down the line, directly in front of where Dan stood, began chalking up the odds for each of the six runners—the first to do so. Others quickly followed suit. Soon, with just one surprising exception, every pitch was displaying prices.

Trap Three was a very short price – generally 8/11.

With only a couple of minutes to go before the "Hare is running" announcement rang out over the tannoy, Dan was starting to panic.

The floodlights dimmed – a sure sign the race was about to begin. He shoved past a few racegoers and marched straight up to Joss Archer. Irritated, he demanded, "Why aren't you showing prices?"

Joss took a drag from his Cuban cigar and smirked at Dan. He glanced at the chunky gold watch on his wrist and replied, "You're first in my queue, son."

Then he chuckled.

Dan lost his temper. "You're the only bloody bookie I've got credit with – and you don't want to lay a bet?" he snapped.

At that, Joss picked up a piece of chalk and casually marked a dash next to Trap Three.

On course, that meant even money.

Dan was stunned. His anger vanished, replaced by a wave of apprehension. Why would Joss lay this particular dog at evens when every other bookie was odds-on?

As the thought crossed his mind, he was suddenly caught in a surge of punters, all charging past him, waving tenners and twenties – scrambling to grab the generous price now on offer. Joss Archer wasn't interested in laying any of the other dogs. He was fully in the swing of things now, bellowing:

"LAY EVENS THREE! LAY EVENS THIS GOOD THING!"

A man in a duffle coat, his East End accent thick as smog, shouted, "'Ere, Joss, an even monkey?" – meaning a straight £500 bet.

"AN EVEN MONKEY DOWN TO BRIAN! WHERE ARE YOU YUPPIES WHEN I NEED YOU?" Joss bellowed, his voice booming across the pitch.

The moment had arrived. Dan pushed his way back through the swelling crowd around Archer's stand and stammered, "Any chance of an even six grand, please, Joss?"

"AN EVEN SIX BAGS DOWN TO BOY!" Joss roared to his brother Wayne, who was scribbling frantically in the betting ledger. Wayne raised his eyebrows slightly as he recorded the wager.

Dan climbed back up the stairs into the stands, unsure whether to feel proud or foolish for having just placed a six-thousand-pound bet – without even being given a ticket.

The lights dimmed. The announcer's voice cracked through the tannoy: "THE HARE'S RUNNING!"

The six greyhounds burst from the traps. Trap Three broke in fourth, swung into third around the first bend, and surged forward, chasing the leader as the crowd erupted around him with wild cheers.

Dan couldn't bear to watch.

Seconds later, he knew.

The cheers turned to groans. Trap Three – once looking every bit the winner around the penultimate bend – had tangled with another dog at the final corner, lost momentum, and crossed the line a close second.

Moments later, one of his mates – well aware of Dan's staggering loss – clapped him on the back. It wasn't just to console him; he was also suggesting that they were off for a curry, and Dan should come along.

Curry and company were the last things Dan wanted.

Still, he walked with his friend towards the stadium exit, past Charlie Chan's, and into the car park where the minicab waited. His mates were huddled nearby, no doubt whispering about Dan's disastrous gambling habits.

The cab ride to the nearby Pride of Punjab curry house was quiet. Nobody spoke. When they arrived, his friends piled out of the car, but Dan, despite their protests, told the driver to take him home.

As the cab pulled away from the neon-lit chaos of Walthamstow Stadium, a wave of shame swept over him. The fluorescent buzz faded in the distance, but the weight of his losses settled deeper than ever.

He stared out of the window, watching the familiar streets of London slip by – each one a reminder of the life he had built, and how close he now stood to the edge. The financial markets had always been a gamble, but this – this was different. This was personal. The thrill of the punt, the adrenaline of the bet – it had all curdled into something else entirely.

A darkness was gathering.

And it was beginning to close in.

As the cab navigated through the streets, Dan's mind raced. He thought about the Archer Brothers and their seemingly endless patience with him. They had been friendly, almost familial, but he knew that their kindness had limits. They weren't the sort of men who gave second chances freely – not without a price. He could almost hear Joss's voice in his head, that cheeky grin as he had laid down the odds.

"We always get our money back in the end." The words echoed ominously, a reminder of the precariousness of his situation.

Dan leaned his head against the window, the blur of headlights and shopfronts casting fractured patterns on his tired face. That single phrase haunted him. We always get our money back in the end. Was it a promise, or a threat? He couldn't be sure anymore.

Arriving at his flat, Dan paid the driver and stepped out into the cool night air. He fumbled with his keys, his hands shaking slightly as he unlocked the door. His heart pounded – not from fear, but from the toxic mixture of anxiety and regret that had rooted itself deep in his chest. Inside, the silence was deafening.

The flat felt empty, devoid of the laughter and camaraderie that usually filled it after a night out. Even the television, usually humming in the background, remained off, as though in mourning.

He dropped his bag on the floor and sank onto the sofa, staring blankly at the wall. The muted ticking of the wall clock only heightened the stillness, reminding him that life continued to move on – even as his own world had screeched to a halt.

The reality of his situation began to sink in. He had lost more than just money; he had lost control. The thrill of gambling had morphed into a desperate need to win back what he had lost, a cycle that seemed impossible to break.

A sickness, really – a compulsion dressed up in adrenaline and dopamine. He thought about his friends, their laughter, and their carefree attitudes towards money. They didn't seem to understand the weight of the losses he had incurred, the pressure that came with being obsessed by odds and risk.

To them, a bet was just a bit of fun. To Dan, it was survival.

Dan picked up his diary and leafed through his contacts. He hesitated, contemplating whether to reach out to his friends or to the Archer Brothers. He knew he needed to talk to someone, to confess the extent of his losses, but the fear of judgment held him back. What would they say? That he was reckless? Addicted? Weak?

Instead, he found himself scrolling through Ceefax, a new digital service available on modern televisions, the familiar rush of excitement creeping back in. His eyes hovered over forthcoming races, his pulse quickening like it always did when he saw the available odds.

"No," he muttered to himself, pressing the 'off' button. He tossed his phone aside. The sound of it landing on the carpet was dull, unsatisfying – just like the false thrill of the chase. He considered whether he could break the cycle, to step back from the edge before it was too late. But the allure of the next race, the next big win, was a siren call he found hard to resist.

The remorse was a heavy cloak, the depression a deep current pulling him under, and the idea of stopping a fleeting thought rather than a firm resolve.

There was no grand epiphany, no dramatic moment of decision – just a man slipping further into a pattern he no longer controlled. He was deep in the mire, but not yet at rock bottom. That was still to come.

As the night wore on, Dan wrestled with his thoughts, the internal battle raging within him. Logic versus compulsion. Fear versus desire. He knew he had to make a choice: to continue down this path of self-destruction or to consider seeking help, to confront the demons that had taken hold of him. But making that call felt like climbing Everest barefoot.

The decision weighed heavily on his heart, and as he finally drifted off to sleep, he knew that the morning would bring with it a new set of challenges, a new day to face the consequences of his actions.

His dreams offered no refuge – just fragmented images of flashing numbers, running dogs, and disappointed eyes.

The sun rose the next day, casting a warm glow over London, but for Dan, it felt like a new beginning shrouded in uncertainty. He awoke with a sense of dread, the memories of the previous night flooding back. The sunlight that filtered through the blinds felt too bright, too honest.

He had a choice to make, and he knew that whatever path he chose would shape the course of his life moving forward.

Would he continue to gamble, chasing the high of a win, or would he take a step back, reassess his priorities, and contemplate a way out of the cycle that had ensnared him?

He sat on the edge of the bed, staring at the floor, waiting for the courage to arrive.

As he prepared for work, Dan felt a flicker of determination ignite within him. He would not let this define him. He would confront his issues head-on, whether that meant facing the Archer Brothers or simply considering what steps he could take.

The journey ahead would be difficult, but he was determined to at least think about taking a first step towards reclaiming his life.

With a newfound unease, Dan left his flat, stepping out into the bustling streets of London, ready to face whatever challenges lay ahead. The world was still spinning, and he was determined to navigate it, one uncertain step at a time.

CHAPTER 4

Potential new employees at Sinclair Bank had to follow a thorough interview process. These were initially conducted by the Personnel department (later known as Human Resources), situated on the top floor of the bank, and subsequently by the candidates' prospective line manager.

The offices on the top floor were tastefully furnished, quiet, and carried an air of expectation; hopeful applicants sat outside the meeting rooms rehearsing answers, straightening ties, or nervously glancing at their watches. Should the candidate emerge successfully from those first two meetings, it was usual practice for other senior members of the department to conduct further interviews on a slightly less formal basis.

Often, these informal sessions took place over coffee or during a casual walk through the trading floor, designed not only to assess the candidate's technical skills but to judge how well they might handle the pace and culture of Sinclair's frenetic environment. Candidates who showed exceptional insight into the financial markets and had a personality to match would be referred to one final meeting with the head of trading before a final decision was reached on whether an offer of employment would be made.

That final meeting was considered the true test, an unspoken rite of passage that separated the truly exceptional from the merely competent.

It was now mid-morning, and Dan perused a number of CVs that had landed on his desk from Personnel. He flipped through the pages with the seasoned eye of someone who had seen hundreds before. Education, experience, internships – it all blurred together unless something unusual caught his attention.

The trading department at Sinclair Bank was not just limited to the large dealing room in Liverpool Street, as it also had a significant presence on the floor of the London Stock Exchange. Whilst the dealing room itself buzzed with life – multiple rows of desks laden with monitors, voices overlapping in a symphony of transactions, and the constant cheering and groaning as price action unfolded – transactions were traded by telephone. The Stock Exchange, however, provided human interaction and face-to-face trading between the hours of 9.30 am and 3.30 pm.

To the side of the main trading floor, where brokers and jobbers plied their trade, was the London Traded Options Market. This comprised what were known as options traders, traders similar to Dan and his peers but specialising in the trading of financial 'bets' that forecast where a share price might be in a specified amount of time. It was a world of calculated risk and sophisticated strategy, where a well-timed decision could yield incredible returns or catastrophic losses.

The Traded Options Market had been formed in the early 1980s and, within a short time, was trading in huge daily volumes. Speculators could buy or sell at a fraction of the price of the underlying shares. The prices of these options fluctuated violently, and the potential for huge gains or losses was an ever-present concern for the risk committees at the world's banks.

One of Sinclair's rivals, Barings, was a London-based merchant bank that had been established in 1762. For over two centuries, Barings had enjoyed a reputation for prestige and prudence until that reputation was shattered in a matter of months. In the mid-nineties, the bank collapsed after suffering losses of £827 million, resulting from poor speculative investments in futures and traded option contracts executed by their employee Nick Leeson from the trading floor in Singapore. The shockwaves of that failure reverberated across global markets and served as a cautionary tale of overconfidence and under-supervision. Risk management had become an extremely important business even before the Barings disaster, with banks desperately wary of such a catastrophe befalling them. Since the mid-1980s even the most aggressive trading desks were under constant scrutiny from management. Internal risk committees kept a much closer eye on trading activity, demanding more detailed reports, stricter controls, and transparent accountability.

Whilst Dan was not one of the option traders on the floor itself, he did have a certain amount of influence on the positions that Sinclair Bank's floor traders entered into, and it was part of his job to monitor the size and risk of the positions involved. He was not merely a passive observer but a strategic filter, one whose calm judgement often determined whether a trade went ahead or was pulled back.

If concerned, he was required to inform the head of trading and the bank's risk committee. Such responsibilities carried immense pressure, especially when millions of pounds were on the line. Dan interacted throughout the trading day with the traders on the floor and knew them all well personally. Some were brash, some meticulous, but all respected the tightrope they walked. He would visit the floor daily, walking down to the Stock Exchange in Throgmorton Avenue, staying for about twenty or thirty minutes.

During this time he would discuss the positions of the bank's traders and their outlook on the future direction of share prices and markets in general. These meetings were often fast-paced but rich with insight, Dan's quick mind parsing through complex theories and strategies in real time. He had a good relationship with them overall and held their respect, as he was regarded as a wise head on young shoulders, at least when it came to trading in stocks and options. That respect, however, was always conditional; one mistake, one misjudged call, could undo years of credibility. And Dan knew that all too well.

That morning his attention was less on risk and the CVs in front of him, and more on the looming arrival of the Archer brothers' account. Despite holding a position of real responsibility at the bank, Dan felt his compensation hardly matched the pressure.

Forty thousand pounds a year plus a decent year-end bonus might sound respectable, but it was only just over three times what he'd earned when he first joined Sinclair Bank as a tea boy. Between the sky-high rent for his Fulham flat and his relentless gambling habit, he had barely managed to save a penny in nearly eight years.

His father had rescued him more than once but had made it crystal clear there would be no next time. And now, with £11,800 owed to the Archer brothers, Dan was staring down a financial abyss.

He sifted through the remaining CVs, discarding most with little thought, until a photograph caught his eye – an attractive young woman named Ciara Rogers. She had dark shoulder-length hair, defined cheekbones, and a subtle, confident smile that lingered just enough to draw him in.

"She's alright – definitely alright," he murmured to himself, amused.

But he knew better than to be swayed by a photograph. The real measure lay in the details.

"*An ambitious graduate with a first in applied mathematics from Trinity College Dublin, with internships at Allied Irish Bank and Société Générale, seeks entry-level position with a leading UK bank.*"

"Well, Ciara," he said under his breath, "today might just be your lucky day."

He pushed the other CVs aside and slid hers into the top drawer of his desk. She was getting an interview.

Rising from his chair and slipping on his suit jacket, Dan made his way out to check in with the traders on the Stock Exchange floor.

The Exchange was unusually frenetic that day. British Telecom had posted better-than-expected figures, and fresh rumours of a General Electric Company takeover were causing a surge in electrical sector shares. Prices were soaring.

Dan scanned his team's positions and gave a satisfied nod. He offered a few minor suggestions – cut back slightly here, increase exposure there. One position caught his eye: they were still holding an unusually large bullish stake in Standard Electric. Fortunately, the stock had continued to rise steadily since they'd taken the position.

The trader responsible for the electrical sector position was someone Dan had personally recommended to Sinclair Bank's management. Mark O'Brien had only been with the bank a few months, having previously worked at a rival firm on the floor. An Irishman two years Dan's senior, Mark had dark curly hair, a stocky build, and a calm, measured way of speaking with a thick Irish accent.

Dan sometimes wondered what Mark really thought of him. Dan was less experienced, yet his superior, and on a considerably higher salary. Still, they maintained an amicable working relationship, even if they weren't exactly mates.

That's why Dan was caught off guard when Mark asked if they could grab lunch together. It was just past midday, and the restaurants on Throgmorton Avenue were already filling up with brokers and traders. Dan had no plans, and curiosity got the better of him. He agreed.

They settled on the Long Room Bar and Grill, a near-exclusively male hangout, thanks to the few women working on the Exchange floor. The place was lively but cosy enough for private conversation, and Dan had a particular fondness for it. He had first dined there with his father and Sir Marcus Holderness to celebrate landing his job at Sinclair Bank.

They glanced through the menu, then ordered pints, steak and chips, and a bottle of Côtes du Rhône. But Dan's patience was wearing thin.

"All right, mate," he said, leaning forward. "We're not here to chat about Amstrad or General Electric. What's this really about?"

Mark finished the last of his pint, lit a cigarette, and glanced discreetly around the room. His tone lowered, his accent more pronounced, as if he were a racehorse trainer giving a post-win interview.

"Listen, Dan. Everyone knows you like a flutter. And if you don't mind me saying," he paused, "you've not exactly got a lot to show for it. Even though you're one of the bank's top traders."

Dan flinched inwardly. The £11,800 owed to the Archer brothers sat heavy on his mind.

Mark continued, his voice slow and deliberate. "Thing is, I've got a friend in Corporate Finance at Wade Bank. He's told me they're advising on a takeover. The twist? It's for one of the stocks I cover. Geneva Electric is planning a bid for Standard Telecom. Announcement goes public Monday morning."

He leaned back slightly, his eyes searching Dan's.

"You see where I'm going with this?"

He went on, "When we left the floor, Standard Telecom were trading at £1.39. Geneva are going to pay £2.00 in cash, and the whole deal has been agreed by both parties. If you've got money troubles, and I hear that you have, this could be your way out."

Dan gulped.

The mention of £2.00 in cash rang in his ears like a fire alarm in a quiet building. It wasn't just a jump in share price, it was a hard, definite figure backed by a confirmed agreement. The kind of inside scoop traders dreamt of. The kind of scoop people could go to prison for. Yet, in Dan's world, reality was growing darker by the day, and temptation was starting to look a lot like salvation.

He had his own stockbroker but had only ever used the firm to buy public share offerings in new issues such as British Gas and British Telecom.

It was all straightforward until now. He was comfortable with the safe bets, the retail-friendly moves that didn't make headlines or rattle nerves. He had never crossed into the world of whispers and winks, where profits were made before the news ever hit the press.

Maybe this was the way out, but at what risk?

The word "risk" echoed in his head, but it was drowned out by the louder, more urgent drumbeat of debt. Numbers had already started rolling around in his head. Figures flashed through his thoughts—calculations made on instinct rather than logic.

How many lots did he need to buy? Would twenty be enough? Fifty? He had no idea. The maths was quick, but the consequences were murky. How much did he need to make to get the Archer brothers off his back?

That question came with a specific, terrifying number: £11,800. He had memorised it like a phone number, burnt into his memory by sleepless nights.

The great thing about buying options was that he could gain greater exposure for a smaller risk. That line kept repeating itself.

More exposure. Less upfront.

Big wins with small stakes. It almost sounded harmless. He considered that if someone in the know gave him a tip for a horse at 10/1 right now, he'd have twelve or fifteen hundred pounds on in a flash.

He wouldn't hesitate, he'd throw it down and wait for the race to end. That was gambling. This felt different.

This was different though. A certainty, a real one.

Not hope. Not chance. This was numbers and timing and access guaranteed. All the pieces were lined up. All he had to do was say yes.

Mark was in full flow now. "Get onto your broker and tell him to come into the Electricals crowd this afternoon and ask him to quote the September £1.40 calls in Standards."

Mark's voice grew more animated, like a coach laying out a winning play in the final seconds of a match.

"The other guys will probably offer to sell them at 15, but I'll call them lower by a bit, say 14."

That subtle tweak, that fraction of a point—Mark made it sound so easy, so routine.

"Then get your man to buy 50 lots."

Dan's throat tightened. That was big. That was bold.

"I'll sell them to your broker, and next week you sell them back and we'll share the profit."

Clean, simple, fast. Like passing a baton in a relay—just one hand to another, no questions asked.

"So long as your guy keeps his mouth shut about who he's dealing on behalf of, it's safe as houses."

A slight grin touched Mark's lips. He spoke with the confidence of someone who had done this a dozen times before and never once been caught.

"It's not like we're defrauding Sinclair's anyway."

Mark raised his hands slightly, as if fending off an invisible accuser.

"As you saw earlier, I've been buying call options in these for weeks, so the bank won't lose out."

That was true. Dan had watched him do it. This wasn't a sudden gamble, it was a move weeks in the making.

"In fact, the bank will also clean up."

'Everyone wins,' Mark seemed to say. No victims here. Just smart men making smarter moves.

"When the announcement comes that the bid is agreed at £2 per share, our calls will be worth 60p, and we will have paid 14p."

Dan could feel his heart rate rising. That was a massive jump. The kind of profit that turned sleepless nights into champagne evenings.

"That's a profit of 46p times five hundred pounds per point, twenty-three grand between us."

His breath caught slightly. Twenty-three thousand. Just like that.

"Even better, you won't even have to pay upfront for them, as we'll trade out of our position as soon as the announcement comes out."

No money down. No real exposure. It was almost too good to be true. Dan considered his options. He sat back slightly, weighing the invisible scales between his instincts and his desperation.

Insider dealing was not something he had contemplated before. He had always assumed it was the kind of thing other people did – rich people, reckless people. But the chances of getting caught were negligible. And with the kind of returns being whispered over wine glasses and steak tartare, it was easy to see why. He knew this practice was rife on the floor and had only been outlawed a few years earlier; it was even still legal in Holland.

A different country, a different rulebook. It all felt arbitrary when money was on the line.

'Yes,' he thought, 'everyone else is at it, why not me?'

That was the thought that finally broke through. The door he'd been holding shut swung open.

"You're a bad man, Mark, but count me in," Dan said.

A grin crept onto his face, part amusement, part adrenaline. They stayed at lunch rather longer than he had expected.

The deal might have been quick, but the weight of what he'd agreed to needed to be drowned in a few more glasses of wine.

The lot size is the number of options traded. A 50-lot represents an investment of £500 per point, a 100-lot £1,000 per point, etc.

CHAPTER 5

— *Monday Morning*

She certainly looked the part.

There was a poise about her that morning, a polished assurance in the way she walked, the set of her shoulders, the subtle confidence behind each glance. She had woken up early, not from obligation but from a surge of anticipation.

Her alarm had gone off at six, but she had already been lying there awake, eyes fixed on the ceiling, rehearsing her answers and imagining how the interview would go.

She'd bought an expensive Armani suit with money lent to her by her parents and had taken a considerable amount of time that morning making herself look like the professional she expected to become.

Every detail was intentional. The charcoal grey fabric fell perfectly against her frame, tailored just enough to look sharp but not flashy. Her blouse was cream silk—elegant but understated—and her shoes, freshly polished, clicked softly on the pavement as she walked. She'd even styled her hair twice that morning, unsatisfied with the first attempt, before finally pinning it into a sleek, businesslike twist. Her make-up was minimal, just enough to conceal the nervous sleeplessness under her eyes.

Whilst nervous inside, she appeared more like an experienced barrister interviewing for a role at a new chambers than the graduate intern she really was.

She had practised her composure for weeks. It was a mask she had worn before, during debates at university, during internship panels, but this time it felt more consequential. More real. Her heart fluttered slightly in her chest, but outwardly she carried herself with the air of someone who belonged.

Ciara had taken the Tube to Liverpool Street, and as she emerged, she saw that she was over an hour early for her interview.

The morning crowd bustled around her in waves—suits, newspapers and coffees clutched in tired hands. The familiar smell of warm pastries from nearby vendors mingled with the scent of city rain evaporating from the pavements.

She'd planned this deliberately, as she wanted to get as close as she could to the Sinclair Bank building and catch up with all the latest financial news as quickly as possible.

There was no room for error today. She wanted to feel prepared, to immerse herself fully in the world she was about to step into. Knowledge was armour, and she intended to walk into the interview clad head to toe in it.

She found a branch of WH Smith, a large newsagent within the concourse of the train station at Liverpool Street, and bought a copy of the *Financial Times* before finding a café.

The newspaper felt crisp in her hand, still cold from the metal rack. She held it tightly, as if its pages might steady her nerves. She moved towards a nearby café tucked behind a corner of the station—quiet, with a few scattered tables and the soft hum of conversation.

She ordered a black coffee, found a table, and put her handbag aside.

The aroma of roasted beans filled the air. As she took her seat by the window, she carefully set down her handbag—her mother's vintage leather tote, something borrowed for luck—and unfolded the pink-hued broadsheet in front of her.

She glanced at the newspaper's headline.

Geneva Electric expected to announce takeover of Standard Telecom.

The words hit her with the force of a jolt. This was no ordinary morning headline. This was the kind of news that echoed through the halls of financial institutions and dominated boardroom discussions.

She digested the headline article and turned to the markets column of the paper to catch up on the current levels of the FTSE, Wall Street, and Far Eastern markets.

She scanned each line with the precision of someone decoding a puzzle. The figures rolled past her eyes—percentage gains, commodity shifts, confidence indices.

She noted the price of sterling and the dollar, then turned to the back page, where she read the widely acclaimed commentary on the day's most important financial news in the *Lex* column.

The *Lex* column was her favourite. More than just facts—it offered insight, analysis, the kind of commentary that made her feel a step closer to understanding the power games behind the money.

The title of the comment read:

GE Bid Better than Standard For Telecom Shareholders.

Her eyes narrowed, drawn in by the elegant sting of financial language.

It continued:

"It is reported in this paper today that an agreed takeover of Standard Telecom by electrical giant Geneva Electric has been agreed by both parties."

A confirmed deal. This wasn't speculation anymore—this was movement. Big movement. She underlined the phrase with her fingernail as if to pin it in place in her mind.

"It is likely to be announced on the London Stock Exchange as early as this morning."

Right now, she thought. Right this moment, suits in glass towers were preparing statements, press officers were drafting releases, and traders were making calls with shaking hands.

"If the reported price of the offer of £2 per share is accurate, it will prove to be a huge tonic for long-suffering shareholders of Standard Telecom."

The phrasing made her smile. A tonic—as if money could cure wounds. And maybe, for many, it could.

"Standard's shareholders would have no doubt been delighted with an offer of only half that price under a year ago."

She remembered reading about the dip back then, buried in a financial column she followed. Everyone had written them off.

"It was merely last October that the company reported dire revenue and earnings, together with a warning that trading conditions remained difficult, culminating in the share price reaching a three-year low of 78p."

What a climb, she thought. From 78p to £2—who wouldn't be delighted? It was a turnaround fit for case studies.

"The current offer, if accurate, however, does not underestimate the net worth of Standard, which has undergone a transformation since the appointment of David Haine as Chief Executive at the turn of the year."

David Haine—she'd studied him. A risk-taker, a reformer. His interviews were sharp, dry, and strategic. He didn't speak often, but when he did, markets listened.

"His shareholders should be grateful for the fine job he has done, if not frustrated that £2 per share may not reflect the true future worth had Haine been left without the attentions of a predator as mighty as Geneva."

She paused. There it was—the subtle tension in the dance of power. She folded the paper slowly, letting her mind turn over the implications. This was no longer just headline reading. This was real insight into the market world she was about to step into. The timing couldn't have been more perfect. Her nerves were still there, but now they were buzzing with energy.

She took a sip of her coffee, closed her eyes for a moment, and told herself, *You belong here.*

The official announcement had come out in pre-trading hours on Reuters. Dan Perry had seen it the moment he turned his screens on at 7:30 am. He'd punched the air with delight and shouted, "Oi oi oi!" to the slight bemusement of some of the analysts already in the office a few rows down from his desk.

One turned to his immediate colleague and joked, "Dan's clearly had a winning bet on the Japanese golf."

Little did they know that he'd made £11,500 trading on the breaking story of the day, let alone the means by which he'd achieved it.

He sat there, a grin spread wide across his face, basking in the afterglow of what felt like divine intervention. Everything had aligned perfectly. He glanced once again at the profit/loss ticker on his terminal, the green digits blinking back at him like a personal applause.

For the first time in a long while, Dan felt like he was ahead of the game—not scrambling to stay afloat, but flying. He swivelled his chair back and forth slightly, drumming his fingers on the desk, letting the sense of victory settle over him like warm sunlight after a storm. There had been risk, of course there had, but now it seemed almost poetic how well everything had panned out.

Ciara entered the bank through the sliding doors of Sinclair Bank and approached the reception desk.

"Ciara Rogers for an eleven o'clock meeting with Mr Dan Perry, please."

The lobby of Sinclair Bank exuded the kind of clinical professionalism one would expect from an institution that moved billions before breakfast. Glass walls, metallic finishes, and a faint scent of lemon polish made the environment feel both intimidating and invigorating. Ciara, still slightly jittery despite the coffee and the *Lex* column, felt herself straighten up as she spoke, forcing confidence into her posture. She was ready, or at least she told herself that repeatedly in her mind.

The elderly receptionist checked his clipboard to view the appointment list and picked up the telephone to dial. A minute later, he replied,

"Aye, luv, Mr Perry will be down shortly. Please take a seat."

Ciara smoothed her skirt down and took a seat in reception. She placed her handbag neatly on her lap, then repositioned it on the chair beside her, not entirely sure what the protocol was but desperate to look composed. The clock on the far wall ticked steadily, though to Ciara, every second felt heavier than the last. She reviewed the names of the executives displayed on the corporate plaque mounted nearby, mentally rehearsing the key points of her pitch one last time.

Shortly afterwards, a well-dressed young man with a very broad smile extended his hand to her.

"Dan Perry," he beamed. "Welcome to Sinclair Bank."

Dan was not usually the easiest of interviewers, but that day he was charm personified. The good mood radiated from him like heat from asphalt in July. His handshake was warm and confident, his smile genuinely disarming. He'd earlier written out a cheque to Archer Brothers Bookmakers for £11,800.

Aside from the fact that he'd finally got the bookmakers off his back—at least for the time being—given his niggling feeling that he might have an issue with gambling and future losses that could be awaiting him, he felt a huge weight had been lifted from his shoulders. Not only had he and Mark O'Brien made a killing, so had the firm, and he knew that from the day's events, only good could come career-wise for both him and Mark.

It was a clean slate, a new chapter, and the world was, for once, on his side. He had gone from a man calculating survival to a man measuring opportunity. His movements carried a spring of confidence, and even his tone had a lighter, friendlier cadence.

"Now tell me, Ciara, why do you really want to join this ghastly profession?" he said.

"Well, I have a degree in applied mathematics and a massive interest in all financial markets. If I could combine the two, it would be my perfect job to work in traded options, especially at an institution as prestigious as Sinclair Bank," was the well-rehearsed reply.

It was a pitch she had fine-tuned for weeks, said with a calm poise that belied the thudding of her heart. She locked eyes with him, determined not to falter. Her voice was crisp, clear, and slightly melodic—intelligent yet humble.

Dan liked her, not just for her obvious intellect but from a purely male perspective. He struggled to distract himself from staring at her nyloned legs and perfect cleavage.

The photograph on her résumé didn't do her justice. He didn't have a girlfriend at the moment but thought to himself, *You never know.*

The thought came from out of the blue but lingered in his mind like a background hum. He wasn't proud of it, not exactly, but in a world as cut-throat and impersonal as high finance, human instinct had its own persistent rhythm. Still, he made a mental note to keep things professional—at least for now.

The interview lasted for about an hour, though to both of them it felt like time had sped up. If anything, by the time the meeting neared its end, it seemed as though the roles had reversed—Dan was the one being interviewed by Ciara. Her questions were sharp, well-informed, and impressively relentless. She asked about every single aspect of the business, from the intricacies of arbitrage strategies in volatile markets to how Sinclair Bank managed its derivatives exposure during economic downturns.

It was clear she had done her homework. Dan found himself, more than once, having to bluff his way through answers he should have known cold but didn't. He offered vague generalities, peppered with buzzwords, and hoped his charm and confidence would carry the rest.

In truth, he wasn't trying to impress her merely out of professional obligation. He genuinely wanted her to think well of him. He admired her tenacity, her ability to stay composed, and her perceptiveness—traits rare even among seasoned professionals, let alone graduate interns.

But even more than that, he felt something stir—a glimmer of connection, or at least fascination. There was something magnetic about her, and though he struggled to separate professional interest from personal curiosity, he already knew she'd left an impression on him.

The truth was, he had probably already made his decision back in reception when she'd stood up to greet him—poised, confident, and with eyes that spoke of both ambition and awareness. He'd thought, *She's going to be on my team*, before she had even said a word.

As the interview began to wind down, an idea started forming in his mind—one that had been building in the background all morning. He had wanted to speak with Mark O'Brien ever since the market opened. He was practically itching to exchange a knowing glance, to confirm that everything had unfolded the way Mark had predicted.

But they'd both agreed on Friday that Monday would be a silent day.

No contact, no loose words.

Sinclair Bank's phone lines were all recorded – every call archived, every conversation scrutinised for potential breaches. Any deviation, even a single careless sentence, could spell disaster. The consequences weren't abstract; they were terrifyingly real. He could picture it all too vividly – an internal enquiry, legal hearings, the disgrace, thc inevitable press coverage, and worst of all, prison. It would only take one slip-up.

Just one.

And yet, there was a way to communicate – indirectly, safely. That's when it struck him.

"OK, Ciara, I like what I've heard," Dan said, shifting slightly in his chair, his tone suddenly more decisive. He could see the spark of hope in her eyes, and it made him pause for half a second longer before continuing.

Ciara may have been young and relatively inexperienced, but Dan sensed a unique combination of raw intelligence and emotional poise in her that made her stand out. Bringing her in as a 'blue button' – the entry-level position in the trading hierarchy – seemed like a minimal risk to the bank and potentially a long-term asset to his own team.

"I think you could make a decent blue button on our floor trading team," he continued, leaning forward slightly. "But before we go any further, I'd like you to meet some of the team. See the environment, the pace, the energy. We'll take a walk down to the Stock Exchange. That'll give you a proper look at where the action happens."

Ciara nodded, clearly delighted. "I'd love that," she said, her voice bright, though she tried to keep her composure. She quickly gathered her things, slipped her handbag onto her shoulder, and followed him out into the city streets.

The sun had broken through the August clouds, casting sharp reflections off the office windows as they made their way through the financial district.

Twenty minutes later, they stepped onto the vibrant, chaotic floor of the London Stock Exchange. Though quieter than usual that day, there was one exception that stood out immediately.

A crowd of over a hundred traders had amassed in the electricals section, a thrumming hive of bodies and voices. The roar was deafening – brokers were shouting over one another, urgently calling for prices on Standard Telecom and Geneva Electric. It had been like this since the opening bell, the announcement setting off a frenzy that hadn't let up.

Dan and Ciara paused at the edge of the crowd, careful not to disturb the rhythm of trading. They remained on the periphery, observers in a theatre of controlled chaos. From a distance, Mark spotted them – his eyes sweeping across the floor until they landed on Dan. He raised his hand in a casual wave, a grin spreading across his face.

But then he saw her.

His grin froze, then slipped. He blinked and looked again, this time focusing on the dark-haired woman beside Dan. She was wearing a Stock Exchange visitor's badge and standing calmly, almost regally, next to Dan as though she belonged there. His stomach clenched. A name formed in his mind, unbidden.

Ciara.

Mark's expression tightened. He felt a jolt of something unpleasant – surprise, unease, maybe even guilt. He muttered something under his breath, his mood visibly changing. Dan caught the shift instantly.

"Well, well, well," Mark said at last, forcing a chuckle that didn't quite reach his eyes. "Ciara, as I live and breathe. What in God's name are you doing here?"

Dan turned, intrigued. Something in Mark's tone wasn't quite right. There was tension, a history perhaps, hidden beneath the surface.

"You two know each other?" he asked, raising an eyebrow.

Ciara smiled lightly, though Dan noticed it wasn't her usual bright smile – it was more cautious, almost rehearsed.

"We knew each other as children. Dublin feels like a lifetime ago now, but yes. Mark and I go way back," she said, meeting Mark's eyes for just a moment too long.

She tried to shift the energy back to something light. "I'm trying to persuade Dan here to give me your job," she joked, nudging Mark playfully with her shoulder.

But Dan was watching them both now with a sharpened curiosity. Something had passed between them – something subtle, unspoken, but real. And he wasn't entirely sure he liked not knowing what it was.

Dan decided that this was not the ideal opportunity to have a discussion with Mark about their illicit gains and left Ciara with him while he went to examine his other traders' positions. The air buzzed with activity and low-level chatter from the surrounding pits, and Dan found it oddly calming. The familiarity of the routine – check positions, recalibrate strategies, note the spreads – helped centre his focus, even while his mind remained half-occupied with the events of the morning.

He planned to let her observe Mark trading for another half an hour or so, then introduce her to a few others before sending her home. That was the script forming in his mind: Ciara would leave with a solid first impression, a story to tell, and a clear indication of her future within Sinclair. As far as he was concerned, subject to dealing with the personnel department, Ciara Rogers was Sinclair Bank's new blue button. There was something about her – poise, intelligence, charm, and an air of quiet confidence – that made her appointment seem not just appropriate but inevitable.

However, he would need to ask Mark about her before placing them together in the electricals crowd. Something in Mark's expression earlier hadn't sat right. That flicker of recognition, followed by a stiffening of posture, was subtle but telling. Dan wasn't sure whether it meant history, tension, or something deeper. Perhaps an old flame? Or maybe just a coincidence that caught him off guard. Either way, due diligence was called for – not just for team dynamics but to protect himself.

When Dan had finished commenting on his other traders' positions and advising on forthcoming trading strategy, he walked back to the electricals pitch with an expectant glance. He felt a slight bounce in his step, anticipating how Ciara might have impressed Mark in action. She had the kind of mind that could dissect a derivatives trade the way a surgeon dissects tissue: precise, analytical, and with a natural curiosity. It would have been interesting to see her pick apart one of Mark's strategies, or better yet, challenge one.

Somewhat to his annoyance, there was no sign of either Mark or Ciara. Not a single glimpse of her black blazer or Mark's distinctive navy pinstripes. His brow furrowed. That wasn't part of the plan. He scanned the floor, eyes darting across the crowd, catching glimpses of familiar faces, arms raised, tickets waved – but no Mark, no Ciara.

He asked an old colleague, now trading electrical options for Hoare Govett, if he had seen them, only to be told that they had left the floor half an hour earlier.

"Left together?" Dan asked, trying not to sound too surprised or bothered.

"Yep. Seemed in a bit of a hurry, if you ask me," came the reply. "Looked like they had somewhere more important to be."

Dan gave a tight nod and forced a smile, though inside his thoughts were churning. Where had they gone? Why hadn't Mark waited, or at least left word? Was there something going on between them that he didn't know about? Or worse – something he should have known about?

It was after 1.00 pm now. Dan decided to return to the office. The morning's adrenaline had finally begun to wear off, replaced by a low-grade tension he couldn't quite place.

He would call Mark after trading on one of the bank's telephones to suggest meeting for a drink after work.

A casual chat, sure, but there would be questions embedded carefully beneath the pleasantries. He needed to gauge Mark's mood, his confidence, and perhaps squeeze out a little more clarity about what had gone down.

He knew that he had bought 50 of the September 140 calls on Friday, as by prearrangement, he had called his broker on his mobile phone the following day, Saturday, and had it confirmed.

"Bought you 50 at 14, Dan. Your bank sold them to me."

Those words had played like music in Dan's ears at the time. Confirmation of the first part of their delicate manoeuvre.

But the true payoff, what mattered most, was whether the exit had gone through. Whether Mark had executed his end of the play cleanly, precisely, without drawing attention or leaving fingerprints.

Dan still wanted confirmation that the sale side of the trade had gone through that morning, though. That was the last box to tick, and he wasn't comfortable relying on assumption.

In this game, assumption was just a slow-moving disaster in disguise.

He had another idea. If Mark had gone temporarily AWOL, he would find the broker himself. He left the floor and went to one of the payphones (unrecorded) near the entrance to the floor and dialled the number of Edwin James & Co., fingers tapping rhythmically against the plastic casing while he waited for someone to pick up.

He was told that his broker was currently executing an order and might be found on one of the equity jobbers, Pinchin Denny's Oils pitch.

Dan thanked the receptionist tersely and hung up. Without missing a beat, he made his way to the pitch. He weaved through clusters of traders, past raised voices and clattering keyboards, until he spotted the man in question.

The broker was in his forties, definitely not a public school type, but he had worked in the market all his career and could spot the difference between a coincidence and a dodgy trade in his sleep. He carried the kind of confidence only years of survival on the floor could give: unflappable, worldly, and always two steps ahead of whatever scandal might be brewing.

The broker winked at Dan the moment he caught sight of him.

"You old bastard!" said the broker jovially, voice low but laced with amusement. "Sold your 50 lots at 60p. Drinks on you, son. Hope you don't get into the shit, though."

Dan gave a tight laugh, equal parts relief and anxiety. The numbers were good, very good. But the comment hung in the air between them, heavy with implication. *Hope you don't get into the shit.* Because in this line of work, profit was only ever as clean as the silence that followed.

Dan shuddered and returned to the office. A sudden chill rippled through him, not the kind born of cold, but of creeping uncertainty. Surely, he would be OK? Twenty-three grand was nothing, after all. In the grand scheme of the City, that was pocket change, a forgettable figure on a screen filled with millions. It wasn't the kind of sum that turned heads or invited investigations. It was the big-time crooks the authorities were interested in. The real players, the ones pulling strings behind shell companies and offshore accounts. Not him. Not Mark. Not over this.

And yet, a seed of doubt had planted itself deep in his gut, taking root and refusing to be ignored. Because if there was one thing Dan knew about the financial world, it was that things could spiral out of control with terrifying speed, from whispers in bars to headlines in the *FT*.

A misplaced trade here, a loose word there, and suddenly your entire career was on the line.

Back at the office, he called Mark again. The dial tone rang in his ear like a metronome of rising frustration. Still no reply. His jaw tightened. This was beginning to feel deliberate.

After several more attempts, each more impatient than the last, he called one of the lads in the retail sector, whom he had earlier advised on trading strategy, only to hear that Mark hadn't been spotted all afternoon.

"Nothing," the trader said. "Hasn't been seen since late morning. Maybe he pulled a sickie?"

Dan muttered something vaguely agreeable, though his thoughts were racing. Mark didn't take sickies. Not without a reason. Not without telling someone.

He called the Long Room Bar & Grill in case Mark had taken Ciara to what would have been, by then, an extremely long lunch, but again, to no avail. The girl on the line checked twice, even asked the bartender.

No sign. No booking under either name. No familiar faces fitting the description.

Dan stared at the receiver in his hand for a long moment after hanging up, the dial tone replaced by a persistent ringing in his ears. Something was off. This wasn't just Mark being flaky. This wasn't normal.

By now, the clock hands had crept mercilessly forward, dragging the day towards its close. The late afternoon sun had shifted, casting golden lines across his office wall, but they brought no comfort. His computer screens still glowed with graphs and tickers, but the data blurred in his vision, numbers without meaning, moving too fast to register. His focus was shot.

At 6.00 pm, feeling exasperated and slightly nervous that something might not be right, Dan finally switched his screens off, left the office, and headed home. The metallic click of the screen shutting down echoed louder than it should have.

The office was quiet now, emptied of its earlier buzz, shadows growing in the corners as the day surrendered to dusk.

He walked the hallways with heavier steps than usual, his mind still chasing possibilities. Had Mark panicked? Had Ciara seen something she shouldn't have? Was it possible—no, surely not—that they had planned something behind his back? The thought clung like a thorn.

Dan pushed the door open to the street and stepped into the evening air. It was warm, but he barely noticed. For the first time in a long time, the city felt unfamiliar, like it was holding its breath, waiting for something to happen.

CHAPTER 6

— *Late November 1986*

Sir Marcus was in a quandary. A genuine and deeply unsettling one. The kind that kept a man of his stature pacing silently in his office long after everyone else had gone home, his tailored suit creasing slightly as he ran a hand over his neatly combed hair.

Realistically, he knew that he should avoid speaking to Dan Perry altogether and report him directly to the Securities and Futures Association for further investigation. That was the protocol. That was the law. And Marcus was nothing if not a man of procedure, usually.

That would entail Dan being summoned to the Securities and Futures Authority offices in Queen Victoria Street for an intense taped interview in front of SFA officials and a detective from the Serious Fraud Office of the Metropolitan Police.

The process was rigorous and designed to shake the truth loose from the most seasoned of traders. It was not a place for the faint-hearted. Men had emerged from those sessions pale and broken, their careers in tatters before they had even stepped outside.

On the other hand, he liked the boy and had enjoyed a career-long friendship with his father. Brian Perry had always been a man of integrity, known and respected throughout the industry. They had shared countless boardroom meetings, charity dinners and golf games over the decades.

The thought of potentially ruining Dan's future weighed heavily on Marcus's conscience. Could he really do that to Brian's son? The image of Brian, laughing warmly across a glass of wine just last week, flickered across his mind. How could he tell a man he admired that he had sanctioned his son's downfall?

He studied some of the other names on the list. Typed out cleanly in bold font, they stared back at him with quiet accusation. To be fair, the twenty-three thousand pounds that Dan had made was towards the lower end of the scale. Practically a rounding error in the world of high finance. Still inappropriate, yes, but not egregious.

All the names on Marcus's list were market professionals who worked under the scrutiny of the Securities and Futures Association, and he knew that profits of fifty thousand pounds and over were automatically reported to Queen Victoria Street.

The implications of this were significant; he wondered if it was ethical of him to warn Dan that he might be in a great deal of trouble. His moral compass spun wildly. After all, the offence of insider dealing, if convicted, carried an unlimited fine and a maximum jail sentence of seven years.

Seven years.

It was a phrase that echoed sharply in his mind, a stark contrast to the bustling office floor Dan had once roamed with such promise. Could he live with himself if Dan ended up behind bars?

He had only had lunch with Dan's father, Brian Perry, the previous week and had chosen not to mention the matter until he had had some more time to consider his options. They had talked about old times, reminisced about the early days of the market when things had been simpler, if not always cleaner. Brian had spoken of Dan with pride, unaware of the shadow creeping at his son's heels.

Marcus made a note of the five names on the offenders' list, those that had made varying profits of between fifty and one hundred and seventy-five thousand pounds on the Geneva Electric takeover of Standard Telecom. Those figures were not just unethical, they were brazen. He picked up the phone and asked his secretary to furnish the Securities and Futures Authority with the five names. It was the correct decision, the clean decision, but it gave him no sense of triumph.

The remaining names, including Dan's, would be placed on a watchlist and monitored constantly in the future for any other instances of insider dealing. Perhaps this was an impending disaster that might be averted? Maybe Dan could be spared a public humiliation, this time. It was with this in mind that he asked the secretary to contact Hamdan.

There was still time to manage the fallout, he hoped. Still time to prevent the whispers from turning into headlines.

Hamdan was the elderly superintendent who presided over the waiters on the Stock Market floor. A familiar figure in his crisp red and blue jacket and calm demeanour, he moved through the chaos of the trading day like a lighthouse in a storm.

The waiters were responsible for assisting any of the dealers on the floor with anything from organising the delivery of newspapers to mending broken telephones and general security within the Stock Exchange building. But Hamdan's role extended far beyond the mundane.

Over the years, he had become something of an unofficial guardian of the trading floor, a silent witness to countless deals, betrayals, breakdowns and breakthroughs.

He had seen many young traders come and go, some rising to great heights while others fell from grace, and he had developed a keen sense for the undercurrents of tension that often accompanied such dealings. It was in the way they walked, the abrupt change in tone, or how they avoided eye contact. Hamdan's intuition, sharpened by decades of quiet observation, had rarely failed him.

Hamdan put down the phone. It was not often that Sir Marcus Holderness's secretary called him, so it must be something important, he mused to himself, stroking the edge of his neatly trimmed moustache as he stared at the receiver. She had asked him to find Dan Perry from Sinclair Bank and requested that Hamdan ask him to visit the twenty-third floor and ask for Sir Marcus Holderness, who wanted to have a "brief conversation" about "a certain matter."

Brief conversation. Certain matter.

Hamdan had heard it all before. Polite phrases that thinly veiled a disciplinary summons, career-ending confrontations, or worse. In Hamdan's long experience as a waiter, he knew that to be summoned to the twenty-third floor was usually a sign that someone was in trouble. Nobody got called up there for a chat and a biscuit.

The weight of this knowledge hung heavily on him as he made his way through the bustling trading floor. The din of voices, the buzz of tickers and the mechanical rhythm of phones ringing created the usual symphony of chaos. Yet Hamdan moved through it all with quiet grace, his footsteps purposeful, his expression unreadable.

He spotted the lad on the side of the electricals crowd, talking to the pretty Irish girl, Ciara. Ciara was gorgeous, thought Hamdan to himself, nice with it too, unlike some of the stuffy old stockbrokers who looked down their noses at him.

There was a softness about her that reminded him of his own daughter, and he often found himself quietly rooting for her in a world that could be ruthlessly cold.

He walked over to Dan and respectfully ventured, "May I have a word with you, Sir? In private," smiling bashfully at Ciara, who looked on with curiosity.

Her eyebrows lifted ever so slightly, sensing something was not quite right, but she said nothing. Hamdan's tone, as always, was courteous, but there was an undertone of finality in it that did not escape her.

Hamdan and Dan walked the few yards to the entrance of the floor, where the head waiter was situated throughout the trading hours of the working day. The atmosphere was charged with the frenetic energy of traders shouting orders and the flashing of phone lights from the Jobbers' hexagons, but Hamdan's focus was solely on delivering the message. Every second, a deal was being made or lost, fortunes shifting hands as casually as coffee orders.

"Sir, I have been asked to inform you that Sir Marcus Holderness has requested that you visit him in his office on the twenty-third floor at some stage this morning. You will need to take the lift up, and the receptionist will be expecting you." His voice was soft, measured, but the words landed like a hammer blow.

He'd anticipated the reaction and instantly recognised the look of the condemned man. That familiar moment of confusion followed by dawning dread. He'd seen the same look each time he'd performed this unenviable task over the past twenty years or so that he'd been head waiter. They always did the same thing. They'd frown and look utterly indignant.

They'd say, "What? Me? Are you quite sure?" as all semblance of colour drained from their faces.

The disbelief. The fragile hope that maybe, just maybe, it was all a mistake. Sadly, he thought, this was no different. Another ruined career. Another bright spark snuffed out by the sharp blade of accountability.

Dan had reacted exactly as expected, like they always did. The denial. The twitch of the jaw. The slight tremble in the hand. Hamdan watched as Dan walked slowly off the trading floor and turned the corner to the lifts, beginning the unenviable climb towards the dreaded twenty-third floor. It was a walk Hamdan had witnessed many times. Each step seemed to echo through the years.

The march of the condemned man, he thought, feeling a pang of sympathy for the young trader. He hoped, quietly, that this wouldn't be the last time Dan walked these halls—not with purpose, not with promise.

But in the world of finance, one wrong move could eclipse a thousand good ones.

"I have a meeting with Sir Marcus," Dan said confidently to the receptionist, though he feared what the topic of convcrsation would bc.

He was quaking inside, a feeling he'd never experienced when due to meet anyone, least of all his father's close friend, but he knew he needed to start acting, and acting well.

"Confidence," he thought. "Confidence without arrogance."

The receptionist gave a small, professional smile and gestured for him to follow. She led him down a long corridor, the heels of her shoes clicking rhythmically against the polished marble floor.

The corridor seemed unusually long, the kind of hallway that stretched out in dreams—calm on the surface but heavy with foreboding. Dan swallowed. Each framed oil painting lining the wall, each tall plant in a glossy ceramic pot, seemed to echo with judgement.

She knocked on a heavy oak door at the end. "Come in," said Sir Marcus. "Thank you, Jane."

Dan found himself in Sir Marcus's office, an office unlike any he had ever seen. It was more like the living room of a very wealthy man. Deep-pile carpet, four comfortable and expensive-looking sofas, oil paintings adorning the walls, and a large mahogany desk that exuded authority and power.

Everything in the room smelled of power, wealth, and influence. The scent of old books and faint cigar smoke lingered in the air, creating an atmosphere that was both refined and intimidating. It felt like stepping into the inner sanctum of the establishment itself, a room where reputations were made and unmade.

Sir Marcus smiled at him kindly and clasped his hands together, not offering to shake Dan's hand. "Dan, my boy, how nice to see you again. How are things?" he said, beckoning him to take a seat in front of his large mahogany desk.

"I had lunch with Dad only last week."

Dan, determined not to show how fast his heart was pumping, routinely replied that things were going well at Sinclair Bank. He'd recently been promoted again and asked politely about Marcus's wife, Diana.

Small talk was a welcome distraction, but he wished that Marcus would get to the point. Perhaps he was wrong? Maybe this was about some forthcoming social occasion?

As if.

Sir Marcus gave a slight nod, as if acknowledging the niceties before leaning forward. The light caught the rim of his glasses, hiding his eyes momentarily.

"Dan, I'll come straight to the point. I'm most concerned about you," said Sir Marcus, his tone shifting to one of gravity.

Dan's stomach clenched involuntarily.

Marcus let his spectacles run down his nose as he viewed the list of names in front of him. He paused, allowing the weight of his words to settle in the air. Dan felt sick for a moment. A cold sweat began to collect at the back of his neck, and he shifted slightly in his chair, trying to mask the discomfort.

Marcus continued, "I have in front of me a list. As you will no doubt be aware, my position within the Stock Exchange is Head of Regulation and Compliance. From time to time, I am sent, by members of my department, lists of people who have fallen under our scrutiny. It's our collective responsibility here to spot suspicious dealing activity."

Dan's throat felt dry. He resisted the urge to clear it. His mouth was suddenly full of questions he dared not ask.

Marcus had deliberately decided not to be specific by mentioning the Geneva Electric/Standard Telecoms deal. He wanted to see Dan's reaction, to gauge the young man's understanding of the gravity of the situation.

He continued, "Unfortunately, Dan, your name is on one of these lists, which concerns suspicious dealing activity. Now, I must tell you that I have not, and will not, mention this to Dad, but I would advise you to possibly tell him yourself. I don't want to frighten you in any way, Dan, but I've seen how these situations can develop, and it can become expensive legally to defend oneself if things manifest in the wrong way, not to mention the severity of the consequences if found guilty. Someone in my department has been monitoring your personal trading activity recently, and it frankly doesn't look very good. I'm not going to be any more specific than that at this point, but I will say this: whatever you have done or are thinking of doing again, you must stop it right now. Furthermore, I have the names of others at your bank on this list. I strongly suggest that you speak to them in private."

Dan's world had just turned upside down.

He hadn't quite expected this. He'd guessed that he was in trouble; there had been little doubt about that, but Marcus hadn't mentioned the others on his list. He wondered if Mark O'Brien's name was there and had no idea who the others from Sinclair Bank were. He thought wryly for a split second that those creepy analysts who sat in front of him in the office, with their Oxbridge degrees and Hermes ties, had probably been involved too, but how would they have known?

His thoughts tumbled one over the other, a silent storm behind a carefully neutral face. He was calculating, recalculating—had he left a trail? Had someone spoken? Were his trades too obvious? Had they seen a pattern?

He felt bewildered, lost, like being back at school facing the headmaster.

Only this wasn't school. This was real. This was serious.

And the stakes were higher than he had ever imagined.

"Well, Marcus, to be honest, I'm completely shell-shocked," said Dan, his voice steady but his heart racing. He had to make the best of what was now a very bad situation. Every second felt like a minute, and the room, though elegantly furnished, suddenly seemed to close in around him like a vice. "I must confess that I made a few quid out of buying some options in Standard Telecom before the takeover, but I certainly had no inside information, assuming that's what you're implying."

His words were carefully measured, rehearsed silently in his mind before spilling from his lips. "It was an innocent but highly fortunate punt, no more, no less."

Dan felt his self-confidence rising, despite his lies. Somehow, the act of confessing to a small transgression made the bigger truth feel less daunting. Telling a tiny part of the truth surely made him more believable than an outright lie?

At least, that's what he hoped.

His mind began to spin scenarios of how others might perceive his explanation—reasonable, rational, even plausible. He wondered if Marcus might see him as just another ambitious young man who'd got a bit lucky. And maybe, just maybe, this whole thing would blow over.

"And who exactly would you like me to speak to about this?" he continued, with just a hint of aggression laced in his voice.

It wasn't full defiance, but enough edge to suggest he wasn't going to let himself be railroaded. Sir Marcus noticed the sarcasm in Dan's tone, a defensive mechanism that was all too familiar in such conversations.

Over the years, he'd seen many young men squirm under the weight of scrutiny, clinging to their pride like a shield.

Sir Marcus replied calmly, his tone devoid of judgment but firm nonetheless. "Dan, I've been a close friend of your father for many a year now, and I'm incredibly embarrassed that I find myself in this situation with you." He sighed gently, removing his glasses and placing them on the desk.

"You're a top chap, and I'm delighted to hear how well your career is going, although slightly concerned that your dad tells me he's worried you have a gambling problem. That's none of my business though. This is."

There was a long pause.

Marcus's eyes locked with Dan's, as if attempting to read the truth straight from his soul.

"This dealing thing will most probably come to nothing," he continued, "but I am already breaching my professional standards by even having this conversation with you."

His fingers interlocked, knuckles tight with restraint. "The fact is that you had never bought any traded options for your personal account in any company before Standard Telecom. Perhaps it's unfortunate that the first time you've traded in options, it was in them. Furthermore, it's unfortunate that when my team questioned your stockbroker at Edwin James about it, he said that the trade was effected at a cheaper price than was available from the other market makers, by your own dealer at Sinclair Bank, something that our records had already confirmed."

Dan sat frozen, caught between denial and fear. It felt like being on a precipice; one wrong word or expression could send him over the edge.

"If you've done nothing wrong," Marcus continued, more gently now, "I'm sure you won't hear of the matter again. I'm just warning you to be extremely careful going forward, as next time, if there is a next time, I won't be able to prejudice my position by speaking to you first. By that, I mean if we need to take things any further."

He paused again, his expression softening. "Now, off you go, and regards to your Pop." But then Marcus corrected himself mid-thought, as though reconsidering the implications of everything he'd just said. "Actually, forget that; it might be better, ahem, for him not to know we had this conversation, despite my earlier advice, but I'll leave that decision up to you."

Dan gave a respectful nod, feeling like a schoolboy who'd just been caught cheating on an exam. The entire conversation had lasted less than fifteen minutes, but the impact of it lingered like a storm cloud.

In the lift back down to the floor, Dan's mind was working in overdrive. His reflection in the elevator's brass mirror looked pale, ghostly, like someone aged years in a few moments.

What had Marcus meant when he said, "If the situation develops the wrong way"? "How things can manifest," and the talk of legal fees for a potential defence?

On the other hand, he recognised that his father's friend had been trying to help him. That much was clear. Marcus could have easily let the system run its course and left Dan to face the full brunt of investigation without a word of warning.

There was a degree of mercy in the way this was handled—quietly, privately, and with just enough ambiguity to give Dan a way out. He was partially comforted to recall Marcus saying that things probably wouldn't go any further. He clung to that hope like a lifebuoy in turbulent waters.

But uncertainty gnawed at him. What if others in the department wanted to pursue it further? What if someone leaked the details to the press or, worse, to his father?

He'd just have to wait. And pray it was the latter.

Hamdan spotted him as he walked from the lifts. The young man didn't return to the trading floor. They rarely did. Instead, he stood at the edge of the bustling market, feeling the weight of uncertainty pressing down on him. The vibrant chaos of the trading floor felt distant, as if he were watching it through a foggy window.

The reality of his situation began to sink in, and he knew he had to tread carefully. The stakes were higher than ever, and the consequences of his next moves could alter the course of his life forever.

CHAPTER 7

— December 1986

Tower Bridge is not only one of the most recognisable bridges in the world, but it also provides a unique venue for corporate events and weddings. Overlooking the River Thames with stunning views of the metropolis, it houses three beautiful venue areas, each offering a unique setting for celebrations of every kind.

The panoramic high-level walkways and the majestic Victorian Engine Rooms were in high demand that Christmas, offering the perfect venue for office parties, and that year they were the chosen location for the Sinclair Bank Trading Department.

The choice of Tower Bridge, with its old-world grandeur blending with the modern London skyline, was clearly an attempt to make a statement—a statement of power, tradition, and affluence. It wasn't just a party venue; it was a signal, a reminder that Sinclair Bank still stood strong amidst market chaos, regulatory pressure, and internal politics. The directors wanted their team to feel proud. To Dan, however, it all felt performative. A coat of glitter over something dull and obligatory.

Much to Dan's chagrin, attendance at the office party was mandatory this year. The previous year, the bank had hired a huge function room at the Dorchester Hotel, only to find that the event was somewhat undersubscribed by a large portion of the seventy-strong trading department. These occasions were not inexpensive, and aside from the grand room being sparsely occupied by the staff who attended, a great deal of fine food, beer, wine, and champagne had gone to waste.

Yet, in the eyes of management, extravagance was fine—so long as it was appreciated. The leftover drinks, particularly the unopened crates of vintage champagne and the rare Scotch selections, were quickly claimed and distributed under the guise of 'client entertainment'.

Everyone knew that meant directors' offices and boardroom fridges, but no one said anything aloud. It was, after all, how the game was played.

One of the absentees had been Dan, who was of the opinion that he should be entitled to party and drink with his own friends in his own time, rather than spend a dreary evening talking to the directors, settlements staff, and anyone else he generally disliked among his colleagues.

To him, socialising with most of the people from work was not only a chore, it was draining—an exercise in politeness where false smiles and business jargon dominated the room. He preferred the pub, the banter, the thrill of the high-stakes shoot pool games, and the company of people who didn't wear two faces.

He'd also heard a rumour that the Compliance Officer had been invited this year. As far as Dan knew, the Compliance Department wouldn't have been made aware of his little indiscretion earlier in the year. He still hadn't heard anything back from his meeting with Sir Marcus, which at least he considered good news, but he really didn't want to be making polite conversation with a man who evidently took great pleasure in catching staff members breaking Stock Exchange rules, let alone the law.

There was something about the Compliance guys that made Dan itch. They walked with the air of silent hunters—blending into departments unnoticed, listening, taking notes, always a step behind but never out of reach. He imagined the Compliance Officer smiling too broadly, asking vague questions, fishing for clues. The very thought made Dan's jaw tighten.

Even worse was the fact that they had to wear black tie, which meant a tedious visit to Moss Bros, the formal attire outfitters, after work—a considerable waste of good drinking time, or even worse, on a Saturday. That would have been time misspent when he could be reading form for the day's racing.

For Dan, racing form was more than a hobby; it was a discipline, a thrill. He could read the names, the conditions, the odds—and feel a pulse of intuition about who would take the win. Losing time on that felt like losing a part of himself.

A memo had been sent to everyone in the department the previous month informing staff of the location and time of the party, with a sinister warning at the bottom saying:

'ATTENDANCE IS MANDATORY.'

The capital letters weren't just stylistic. They screamed obligation, and more importantly, they made it clear that excuses would not be tolerated.

Dan looked at himself in the mirror of the Sinclair Bank men's lavatory on the second floor as he adjusted his bow tie. He'd lost his elasticated one and was disappointed that they only had those self-tie ones in Moss Bros. He scowled slightly at his reflection.

This whole black-tie nonsense felt like putting a leash on a wolf. Artificial. Stifling. He preferred his suits sharp but casual, his style more Bond-in-the-field than Bond-at-the-ball.

He looked at his watch: six fifteen. He'd arranged to meet some of his peers in The Crispin, the pub around the corner in Broadgate, where he played shoot pool on Friday nights for large amounts of money.

The Crispin had become something of a second office for Dan—a sanctuary where numbers mattered in terms of gambling but only on the outcome of heads or tails. No spreadsheets, no performance reviews, no directors.

Today, being a Friday, he knew his gambling pals—mostly traders from rival banks—would be there as usual, expecting him to play. The thought was comforting. There, he was known for his nerve and his willingness to put up big pots, and shooting for the lot when someone else was Banker and the stakes were high.

No form or logic required here—just nerve and a big wallet.

But tonight, he thought he'd probably leave it and socialise with his Sinclair Bank peers. Yes, he thought, just a few pints, then off to the Tower Bridge nightmare. He told himself he'd smile, nod, make conversation, and leave as soon as it was respectful to do so.

He exhaled, straightened his shoulders, and gave himself one last look. Tonight, he'd play the part. Again.

It was six thirty pm when he entered the pub. Being a Friday evening, it was packed. The air was warm and thick with the mingling scents of beer, aftershave, and the subtle sharpness of office-worn cologne. Laughter echoed off the wooden beams, and the din of clinking glasses and loud voices merged into the familiar, almost comforting chaos of the end-of-week ritual.

The first person he saw whom he recognised was Mark O'Brien, who was buying a round of drinks. Mark, as usual, looked entirely in his element—his dinner jacket slightly wrinkled already, grinning confidently as he shouted orders across the bar like he owned the place.

Ciara was there too, standing just behind him, chatting with a colleague and smiling faintly. Along with her were a dozen or so other traders, both from the floor and the office, all dressed to the nines but maintaining that easy swagger unique to financial men who thrived in fast-paced environments.

He'd found himself increasingly thinking about Ciara recently. It wasn't just casual interest anymore. It was the sort of fixation that crept into the quiet moments between trades and lingered in his mind late at night when he stared at the ceiling in his flat. She could have fronted any television advert or magazine cover, but she had a natural beauty that Dan felt was more attractive than the look of an airbrushed model.

There was no artifice about her—none of the exaggerated effort you saw in so many women in the City. There was something about her: a shyness, hesitation in her body movements, and a softness in her Irish lilt.

That gentle, unassuming tone had a way of disarming him, making him feel, oddly, like a schoolboy again. Her cream dress had a tailored look that contrasted boldly with her dark bobbed hair. The cut was simple, but elegant—timeless rather than trendy.

She was strikingly tall too, and in her heels, considerably taller than Dan's six feet. That, oddly, made her all the more appealing—intimidating, yes, but magnetic in a way that made it impossible for him to look away.

He pictured her in stockings and suspenders with her legs astride him.

It wasn't just lust, though that certainly played a part; it was a deeper craving for something thrilling, something elusive. Standing just a few feet away, he realised at that moment that he was hooked. This wasn't a passing attraction. This was dangerous. The kind of attraction that led to trouble.

He had considered asking her out for dinner, but this would no doubt have got out and been embarrassing for him professionally. Office gossip travelled faster than lightning, and if she rejected him—God, if she rejected him—he'd be the butt of jokes for weeks. And even worse, as her boss, how embarrassing might that prove to be? He was curious about her relationship with Mark too.

Was it strictly professional, or was there another element to their relationship? Were they just old colleagues, or was there history there—romantic, messy history? They'd clearly known each other from before their Sinclair Bank days. Perhaps they had worked at the same firm, or maybe they'd even studied together. Whatever it was, there was a familiarity in the way they stood together, spoke together, laughed together.

Dan cursed himself for having placed her in the electricals crowd on the floor as Mark's blue button. It was a decision made quickly and now, in retrospect, it felt like a gross underutilisation of her potential. She was wasted there—too intelligent, too composed, and frankly too good for it. It was something he'd address in the new year, he decided. She could be transferred to the stores sector.

He'd call it "widening her horizons".

That would at least allow him to interact with her more professionally—an excuse to speak, mentor, and observe without raising suspicion.

"What are you drinking, Guv?" shouted the dinner-jacketed Mark, spotting his boss. Dan requested a pint of lager and moved over to the group. He slipped into the circle of conversation with the ease of someone used to managing personalities, blending in with the crowd of sharp suits and louder laughter. They talked about the party, the Tower Bridge location, and what time they could leave.

Everyone was already calculating how long they'd need to stay to be seen as "present" before making a tactical exit. Dan was in earnest conversation with one of his colleagues about the future direction of Wall Street when he noticed one of his Friday night gambling pals at the bar, looking in his direction. The man gave him a subtle nod and lifted a pint, as if calling him over like a magnet.

Dan excused himself and scrambled through the Friday night throng to his friend, where another pint of lager was handed to him. The pub was packed tighter than a racecourse grandstand on Derby Day, and every inch of floor was contested by moving feet or swaying bodies. Elbows brushed, pints sloshed, and laughter cut across conversations like short, sharp blasts of music.

"We're in the far corner over there," the friend said. Dan looked over to see another four of his usual Friday night crowd in the far corner of the pub, looking impatient to start the dealing again as they awaited their next round of drinks. Their eyes lit up as they saw him—recognition, challenge, and expectation all wrapped up in a single glance.

Dan secretly wished he were with them. There was something almost haunting about the brutal honesty of these bets, the bravado, the occasional swearing, the clatter of coins and pint glasses. He longed for that adrenaline rush—the kind that came not from financial markets but from being on the edge, just barely in control.

But he explained that tonight was the night of the Sinclair Bank Christmas party, and with his colleagues there, he'd best duck out of the proceedings that night. He didn't relish the idea of splitting his loyalty, but the optics of playing the shoot pool coin game with a bunch of rival traders instead of making small talk with his own team would be disastrous.

"Come on, mate, you lost your bottle?" one of them teased, smirking.

"OK, just a couple of rounds, and I want to be banker for one of them," said Dan, and walked over to the corner of the pub.

As he made his way across the room, the crowd parted for him slightly, and he allowed himself a grin. Just one or two hands wouldn't hurt, would they? He'd be in and out before anyone from the office even noticed. After all, what was Christmas without a little risk?

Shoot pool is a very simple but highly dangerous gambling game. It involves seven one-pound coins being stacked on top of each other by the banker. Each player in the group takes it in turns to be the banker. The chosen banker then specifies a "pot", a sum of money that he is prepared to lose. The lads usually played with pots of fifty pounds, typically increasing as the evening went on. The game, deceptively straightforward in appearance, had become a Friday night ritual—one that brought with it a mix of thrill, tension, camaraderie, and occasional regret.

The pub would always hum with laughter, clinks of pint glasses, and the subtle clatter of coin stacks being handled with the reverence of a sacred rite. Dan and his companions had developed their own language for it—quick calls, raised brows, and amused curses when luck turned. It wasn't just about money; it was about pride, intuition, and guts, and holding your nerve when it mattered. You always had a fifty-fifty chance.

The banker would then turn to the player on his immediate left, who was required to predict heads or tails for the upward-facing coin after the one at the top of the stack had been turned.

Prior to this, he had to declare the sum he wished to bet on the outcome. There was little or no skill in calling—no timing, no bluff, no observation, no reading the room. These were just random guesses. Players sometimes watched the banker's body language, the way he stacked the coins, to see if they could spot an edge.

At least, that's what they convinced themselves.

The player could only stake up to the amount in the pot. Should the player win, the value of his win was deducted from the pot; conversely, it was added to the pot should he lose, before the turn of the next coin and the next player's chance to call. It was this back-and-forth of adding and subtracting that gave the game its name—coins shot out, money shot up, and tempers sometimes flared when losses piled up unexpectedly.

The round ended either when the sum of the banker's pot had reached zero, with the banker having to pay out the full stake of his original pot, or when the last remaining player had had his call, whichever outcome came first. Dan always kept a sharp eye on the pot.

A game could flip dramatically in the last seconds. He'd seen cool-headed players lose everything in a single miscall. Others walked away smug, having cleaned out the pot without blinking twicc. It was this unpredictability that made the game feel alive.

At any time in the round, a player could "shoot for the pot". That meant he could back heads or tails for everything that was remaining. It was the bravest move, the riskiest by far. Not many did it unless they were confident, drunk, or both.

When someone shouted "Shoot for the pot", all conversations at the table ceased. All eyes focused on the coin, the banker's fingers, the tension in the air.

Whilst the banker could never lose more than the size of the original pot—in this case, fifty pounds—several losing calls by the players could push the size of the pot up considerably. The pot, sometimes swelling to many multiples of its original size, could tempt even the most cautious into a reckless shot. In those moments, it wasn't about the fifty quid anymore—it was about shooting for the pot.

Once each player had had a call, the round was finished, and the banker retained all the money, if any, left in the pot.

Dan took his seat at the table and placed his pint down. He exhaled slowly, the weight of the working week evaporating with the familiar scent of lager and pub woodwork. The guys were already grinning, their sleeves rolled, anticipating events getting out of hand. They usually did.

"Right, lads, I'm only staying for two rounds, and I'll be banker for one of them. You know I'd prefer to stay here all night rather than go to this stupid party, but that's life." He tried to sound casual, but a part of him itched to stay, to forget obligations, to drown in the banter and thrill.

Nobody seemed to mind. They nodded, muttered approval, and gestured towards the coins. This was familiar territory. He reached for the seven one-pound coins in the middle of the table, shuffled them in his hands, and made a neat stack of them in front of him. The metallic sound of the coins clinking together was oddly satisfying, almost ceremonial.

"There's a hundred quid in the pot, gentlemen," he said.

Eyes lit up. That was a solid start. Not too small to be boring, not too big to be terrifying. Just enough for things to get interesting.

At seven thirty, and after ten rounds, they had been playing for an hour. The time had flown by. As was entirely usual, the stakes had increased as more beer was consumed. Laughter was louder, calls bolder, and the air was thick with anticipation. Dan had been losing. Unlucky calls, bad staking, and poor timing had all piled against him like a relentless tide.

Having started as banker and promptly losing his first hundred pounds, he'd decided to quickly get his money back and "shoot" for the pot whenever the bank was up to high stakes. It was a move he often warned others about. And yet, here he was, gambling instinct overriding his usual caution.

Shortly before he'd reluctantly had to retire and head for Tower Bridge, he'd found himself eight hundred pounds down after shooting for pots of one hundred, another for one hundred and fifty, and on his final round, a tasty four hundred and fifty pounds.

The sound of cheering and groaning from the lads still echoed in his ears. It had been brutal. One loss had led to another, like a cascade he couldn't stop.

If only he'd stuck to just the two rounds he'd planned to play. He muttered the words silently, scolding himself. It was classic Dan, making bold moves, then regretting the fallout. Disgusted with himself, he reached for his chequebook and wrote out several cheques to the friends he owed his losses to before making his excuses and leaving. Signing away nearly a grand felt like punching himself in the gut.

Back in the main part of the bar, he was further annoyed to see that none of his Sinclair Bank colleagues had waited for him.

The pub felt colder somehow, less inviting. He half expected to see Ciara at the bar, laughing over a drink, her dress catching the light, but she was gone. Everyone had gone.

He cursed himself for losing so much at that ridiculous game when he should have been showing off in front of Ciara. She would've been impressed by confidence, not by reckless coin flips and losses. He imagined her arriving at Tower Bridge, elegant, laughing at someone's joke, while he trudged there late, frustrated, and out nearly a thousand quid.

Another poor gamble, only this time it wasn't just money he feared he'd lost.

Alone in the cab, he decided to keep a very close eye on Mark and Ciara. He'd recently asked Mark if there was anything going on between them, which Mark had denied.

Dan was not sure that he believed him and decided to earnestly monitor the body language between them that night. If he could be convinced that they weren't shagging, he'd ask Ciara on a date after all.

He leaned back against the worn leather seat, the low hum of the engine mingling with the intermittent crackle of the radio in the driver's cabin. The warm interior of the cab clashed with the cool tension brewing in his chest. His thoughts circled around Mark's casual denial, trying to pick it apart—had there been a flicker in his voice, a pause too long? Had his eyes darted away just a little too quickly?

Dan clenched his jaw and turned to stare out the window. Neon reflections from pubs and kebab shops splashed against the glass, momentarily distracting him. He told himself to calm down, to stop overthinking, but something deep within refused to settle. He hated feeling this way—suspicious, possessive, unsure. Yet the thought of Ciara, radiant and warm and intelligent, choosing someone else—Mark, of all people—made his stomach churn.

The Friday night traffic ensured that the short distance between Broadgate and Tower Hill took longer than it should, and it was after eight when Dan found himself in the conference room within the bridge.

The party was in full swing by now. A low throb of music pulsed through the room like a heartbeat, mixing with laughter, footsteps, and clinking glasses. He accepted the glass of champagne proffered to him by a waiter as he entered the room, before finding himself talking to a crowd of analysts discussing the oil price. One was droning on about the oil price:

"The US dollar has been caught up in a price war orchestrated by Saudi Arabia, which will inevitably lead to the collapse of the US oil industry, triggering many years of production declines."

Dan made his excuses and moved on. He had heard the same speech in different suits dozens of times.

During the course of the next couple of hours, he worked the room efficiently, ensuring that he spoke to everyone he should, feigning interest and bonhomie. His smile was fixed; his nods were polite but calculated. He made the rounds like a seasoned performer, laughing when appropriate, inserting clever asides when the moment called for it, and all the while keeping one eye scanning for Ciara.

Yet something was bugging him. Where were Ciara and Mark? All the other Sinclair staff who had been drinking earlier in the Crispin were present. He'd seen Mark and Ciara in their finery, so why on earth weren't they here? Ciara's absence, especially, was bound to be noticed, as men outnumbered women at Sinclair Bank by about twenty to one.

A couple of people had already asked him, "Seen Ciara?" in passing. He'd shrugged, played dumb, but each query turned the knife a little deeper.

"Dan, great to see you, buddy," said the compliance officer, interrupting Dan's train of thought.

"Great to see you, Eddie," replied Dan, lying.

"Well, you guys have had another good year, I see. How do you make so much money when one company takes over another?" asked Eddie.

"I suppose that's why you're in compliance and why we're traders, you asking questions like that," joked Dan, somewhat nervously.

Dan was keen to finish this conversation immediately. He didn't want to get into a discussion with this man about takeover bids. There was a subtle change in Eddie's tone—half-teasing, half-prying—that Dan didn't like. He felt his bow tie coming loose and seized the opportunity to extricate himself before making his way to the men's toilet.

Away from the noise of the party now, he relieved himself before setting about the arduous task of fixing his bow tie in front of the mirror. The bathroom's fluorescent lights buzzed overhead, stark and unflattering, making his reflection look tired and older than he felt. He pulled at the stubborn fabric, fumbling slightly, hands not quite steady—whether from the alcohol or nerves, he couldn't tell.

A few minutes later, tie situation saved, he looked at his watch: ten thirty. This wouldn't take much longer, he thought. He'd leave at midnight and take a cab home. Maybe swing by that late-night Chinese takeaway near his flat, drown his misgivings in noodles and soy sauce.

As he shut the heavy door of the toilet behind him, he was surprised to hear that the level of noise emanating from the party further down the corridor had considerably reduced. The closer he approached the room, he suddenly realised that there was no noise at all.

Not a murmur. Not even distant laughter.

He wondered if he'd gone the wrong way and if this was a different room. He'd had a fair amount to drink, sure, but in no way was he drunk.

He stepped inside the room. It was most certainly the same one, but there was not a single person there. He noticed a number of broken glasses and food that had tipped onto the carpet.

A woman's handbag lay on the floor, unopened. He was feeling distinctly uneasy. The decorations still hung neatly. Music equipment and speakers were still powered on, humming faintly, but no one manned them. Wine was still slowly dripping from an overturned bottle on a white tablecloth. The scene looked abandoned—hurriedly and silently.

His seventy-strong department of colleagues had vanished. There must have been a fire scare and they'd been evacuated, he thought. But then where was the alarm? Why hadn't anyone knocked on the bathroom door? Why hadn't Mark, or anyone, texted him?

He knew he needed to get out of there, and fast. He turned back to the entrance, rushed through the door, and made for the stone staircase that led down to street level. It was then that he heard a man shouting at him from a long way down the stairs.

"Dan, where the fuck are you?" screamed an Irish accent. It was the unmistakable voice of Mark O'Brien. "There's a fucking bomb scare. Get down here."

The explosion was enormous. It was as if a wall of orange flame had decided to engulf the conference room. The corridor disintegrated, and windows shattered. Smoke and fire rushed into the corridor and staircase. Thousands of shards of glass and nails, the deadliest of combinations, rained down.

The fire alarm, shrill and deafening, erupted into life. The force of the blast had literally lifted Dan off his feet as he'd started his descent of the wide stone staircase, and he fell down about twenty steps.

Feeling terror that he'd never experienced before in his life, he just managed to pick himself up and run down the remaining steps. His throat burned. His ears rang with the roar of the blast. The weight of the smoke was suffocating, clawing at his lungs with every breath.

At the bottom of the staircase, he collapsed, choking from the fumes of the smoke. Coughing violently, he clutched the marble floor with scraped hands, heart pounding like a war drum inside his chest. His clothes were scorched at the edges. The smell of chemical fire filled his nostrils.

Then there was silence and nothing but darkness.

CHAPTER 8

Dan, with a discernible jolt, regained a tenuous hold on his consciousness, the very air around him now a thick, suffocating blanket. In a clumsy, almost disjointed fashion, he tried to raise himself to his feet, each struggling breath a painful, rasping intake. He choked profoundly on the acrid, dense smoke that had, with alarming rapidity, engulfed not only the immediate entrance to the historic bridge but also the intricate, sprawling Victorian engine rooms nestled at the very bottom of the expansive staircase.

Every inch of his lungs screamed in protest. His throat was raw, burning with every gasp, as if razor blades lined the very path of his breath. The world had become a blur of heat and noise: metallic groans from the structure, the distant shriek of alarms, and the eerie crackling of flames chewing through everything in their path.

Meanwhile, Mark had managed to extricate himself from the raw chaos that had unfolded within the very heart of the structure. He had, in the immediate aftermath of the explosion, seized the fleeting opportunity to gulp down several much-needed breaths of the biting, icy night air found just outside the immediate blast zone.

The cold, while shocking, grounded him in the here and now, a stark contrast to the chaos he had just fled. His heart pounded against his ribcage, each beat reminding him he was still alive. His momentary relief was short-lived, as he returned with a swiftness bordering on the instantaneous.

Less than a minute after his initial escape, a gnawing realisation dawned upon him that there had been absolutely no discernible sign of Dan since he had shouted his warning up the stairs. A cold dread spread through his chest. He had not seen Dan emerge. He had not heard another voice behind him. That silence was deafening.

With a renewed sense of purpose and a fresh, deep inhalation of the frigid atmosphere, he burst back into the swirling vortex of chaos and destruction, his determined entry closely pursued by two uniformed officers of the Metropolitan Police force. Their boots pounded the pavement, urgency etched into every movement. Sirens blared outside, but inside, the silence was unnatural, broken only by the occasional creak of a structure that no longer felt safe.

It was, at this moment, barely possible to properly discern anything within the immediate vicinity. The swirling, dense, black smoke now took its insidious, suffocating toll on visibility. The lights overhead flickered, some of them broken, others obscured by the churning clouds.

Mark and the two constables required only a matter of seconds to locate the precise source of the tormented, groaning body.

Dan, it became painfully clear, had fallen back down onto the debris-strewn floor. Shards of glass surrounded him like tiny daggers, and smouldering remnants of tablecloths and party decorations littered the ground. He could, with a growing sense of desperation, distinctly hear his various rescuers calling out his name, their voices muffled by the surrounding pandemonium.

However, the profoundly asphyxiating and debilitating nature of the fumes that permeated the air rendered any attempt at coherent shouting utterly impossible. His lungs were on fire. His limbs were heavy.

Consequently, the very best he could manage, in his current dire predicament, were a series of weak, almost helpless moans, tinged with an undeniable sense of pain and vulnerability. These proved, remarkably, to be entirely sufficient. His voice, though frail, was enough to draw them to him, like a beacon in a smoky abyss.

Now, having reached him with a collective surge of effort, the policemen each firmly took one of his flailing arms, exerting a steady, determined pull to bring him back to his feet. Mark, with considerable strength, simultaneously lifted his legs, providing crucial support.

Together, they stumbled awkwardly, almost ungainly, but with a shared purpose. They moved towards the welcoming egress, effectively carrying Dan to the relative sanctuary of the outside world and the waiting, fully equipped emergency ambulance. Dan's head lolled back slightly, eyes fluttering, the distant flicker of blue lights reflecting off the glass shards in his hair. His suit was torn, his shoes scuffed, his skin smeared with soot and blood, but he was alive.

Outside, a state of utter chaos raged unchecked, a mix of urgent shouts, flashing lights, and the bewildered murmurs of onlookers. Pedestrians crowded behind makeshift barricades, some numb with shock, some hysterical.

Others prayed silently, frozen in stunned silence. The police force, acting with well-trained swiftness and professionalism, had cordoned off the entire thoroughfare on both sides of the bridge within twenty minutes of receiving the initial telephone call at Bishopsgate Police Station. Yellow police tape flapped violently in the breeze as officers directed traffic and cleared the area.

Whilst they had grown accustomed to receiving a high volume of hoax bomb threats since the early 1970s, there was no room whatsoever for doubting the grim, terrifying authenticity of this one.

The distinct Irish voice emanating from the other end of the line had, with chilling precision, used the appropriate pre-arranged code word when he had communicated with the duty desk sergeant at Bishopsgate. He had left no room for misinterpretation or doubt. It was not a drill.

This was real.

The threat had materialised, and the consequences had unfolded in horrifying clarity.

The attending paramedic, exhibiting a calm demeanour amidst the chaotic scene, diligently performed a series of routine yet thorough diagnostic checks. These included assessments for potential internal bleeding, a comprehensive examination for any signs of a head injury, careful monitoring of his blood circulation, and a precise measurement of his pulse rate. Every movement was deliberate, measured, efficient.

Dan's face and hands were smeared with a considerable amount of blood, a stark testament to the traumatic events he had just endured. His knuckles were cut, his left cheekbone beginning to swell, and his collar was soaked in both sweat and soot. Despite this disquieting sight and the significant volume of smoke he had inhaled, his rescue had been swift and commendably efficient.

As he lay upon the standard-issue stretcher, an unexpected wave of awareness washed over him. With a growing sense of surprise, he perceived Ciara's concerned face peering intently down at him. She was kneeling beside him, her coat draped over her shoulders, hair dishevelled, and eyes glistening in the blue ambulance lights.

Even in his precarious state, he could tell from the look on her face that she had been crying. The redness around her eyes, the faint tremble in her jaw, all pointed to a woman who had feared the worst.

"How are you feeling, Danny boy?" she enquired, her voice laced with profound concern, clearly reflecting the depth of her anxiety. Her hand brushed his, fingers trembling slightly, as if needing to confirm that he was indeed real and still breathing.

Dan, to his slight astonishment and Ciara's evident relief, actually managed to conjure up a faint, weary smile. His facial muscles protested the movement, tight and sore from both the strain of the night and the smoke still lingering in his lungs, but the gesture was sincere, if small.

"I probably lost more of the vital fluid playing shoot pool in the Crispin," he croaked, his voice still somewhat hoarse and rough from the smoke, attempting a light-hearted joke. He winced immediately after speaking, both from the physical effort of talking and from the dryness that clawed at his throat like sandpaper.

Ciara, ever perceptive, caught the fleeting grimace but chose not to dwell on it. Her fingers, already clasping his hand, gave a reassuring squeeze, as though to remind him that humour, however feeble, was still a sign of hope.

"When things in life as ghastly as this happen, it just puts everything into perspective. Gambling, trading, risk, all the things you consider the most important in your life... they mean nothing at times like this," she whispered.

Her voice was filled with an underlying gravity. Her eyes searched his face for reassurance. Concerned not just for his physical state, she wanted assurance that his mind had not been shattered by the trauma. The events of the night had left their invisible fingerprints on everyone present, and she feared the long-term cost.

The attending paramedic, clearly operating under a pressing imperative to transport Dan for a more comprehensive doctor's examination at the nearby Guy's Hospital, was evidently in a considerable hurry. He was checking his watch almost by instinct now, even though the flashing lights and distant sirens made time feel surreal. Nevertheless, he still managed to offer a cheerful quip of reassurance to Ciara.

"I think he's going to be just fine, love. Maybe a complimentary, albeit involuntary, stay overnight at the rather less than five-star 'Hotel Guy's' and a somewhat uninspiring hospital breakfast, and he should be back out and fit enough to play tomorrow."

His tone was calm and breezy, a studied professionalism that suggested he had seen far worse in his time, and that, compared to others, Dan had escaped remarkably lightly. His bedside manner, although quick and clipped, carried the comforting rhythm of routine.

Dan, with a renewed spark in his eyes, looked upwards once more and, in response, managed to produce another faint yet genuine smile. The comfort of hearing something vaguely normal, like bad hospital food or jokes about hotels, brought him some sense of grounding amidst the haze.

"Perhaps I shall still make it to Newbury Races tomorrow, after all," he tentatively ventured, a flicker of his characteristic optimism returning.

In truth, the thought felt absurd given his condition, but even entertaining the idea of normality felt like a triumph. The idea of returning to a world where horses ran and crowds cheered was somehow life-affirming.

Dan awoke with a quiet start in the sterile confines of his hospital bed the following morning. The rhythmic beeping of monitors and the soft, muffled footsteps of nurses in the corridor blended into a strange symphony of calm. For a moment, he lay there, disoriented, trying to piece together where he was.

A young staff nurse promptly provided him with a dose of paracetamol to alleviate the dull, persistent ache in his head. Her presence was both warm and reassuring. Dan found her soft-spoken professionalism oddly soothing.

He certainly felt thoroughly bruised and battered, a testament to the ordeal of the previous evening. Still, apart from these superficial discomforts, he was, quite remarkably, in good and serviceable order. His body ached with every movement, but it was the clarity of his thoughts, sharp and hyper-aware, that surprised him most.

His mind, however, spun with a dizzying, relentless replay of the harrowing events of the preceding evening, the vivid images and sensations swirling without cessation. Sounds, sights, and even the acrid taste of smoke haunted his senses in a looping, nightmarish montage. Each time he blinked, he saw flashes: the explosion, the dark stairwell, the confusion, Mark's voice echoing somewhere in the distance.

With a conscious effort, he reached for his mobile phone and placed a call to his parents. His hands trembled slightly as he dialled, more from adrenaline fatigue than fear, but the need to hear their voices was overwhelming.

"Darling, we've been so incredibly worried about you," his mother exclaimed, her voice thick with both anxiety and relief. It sounded like she had barely slept, her words tumbling over one another in a rush of emotion. "We saw it unfold on the news, and I said to your Dad I had a distinct feeling your firm was holding its Christmas party in rooms within Tower Bridge. We've had a completely sleepless night, just fraught with concern. We rang you countless times at home, but there was no answer, and we... we were simply in utter despair."

Her voice cracked near the end, a barely contained sob escaping through the line. Dan closed his eyes, the guilt of having caused them such worry sinking in like lead.

"Look, I'm absolutely fine, Mum, really," Dan reassured her, attempting to inject a calming certainty into his voice. "I'm here in the hospital, just a bit battered and bruised around the edges, but there's no real, lasting damage. I'll be out of here in a mere couple of hours, I anticipate. I'll recount the full, exhaustive story later when I'm safely back home."

He tried to sound upbeat, inserting casual inflections where he could, though his voice still rasped from the smoke and strain.

He proceeded to furnish his parents with a brief yet concise résumé of the night's extraordinary events, ensuring to emphatically reassure them that his overall health and well-being were, more or less, entirely satisfactory. As he spoke, he noticed that recounting the events, even briefly, brought a certain catharsis. Putting words to the chaos helped make it real, helped him begin to process what had happened.

On the other end of the line, his mother was quiet now, listening intently. His father occasionally interjected with a low, gruff word of agreement or concern. It was, Dan realised, the start of a long recovery—not just of body, but of confidence, normality, and trust in the world.

Another nurse, her movements brisk and purposeful, entered the ward, pushing a trolley laden with the comforting paraphernalia of morning refreshments: an assortment of tea and coffee, along with a selection of newspapers, which, somewhat restrictively, were limited to only *The Mirror* and *The Daily Mail*. She moved with the efficient grace of someone who had repeated this task countless times before, her shoes squeaking faintly against the linoleum floor as she weaved between the beds, her trolley rattling gently.

When politely asked about his preference, Dan requested a strong black coffee and a copy of *The Mirror*, having been informed, with a note of unmistakable disapproval, that no, they regrettably did not stock either *The Sporting Life* or the more recently established *Racing Post*. The nurse, perhaps sensing his mild disappointment, offered him a sympathetic smile before handing over the paper and retreating to continue her rounds. The coffee, though not of the highest quality, had a bitter strength that grounded him slightly more in reality as he sipped it cautiously, still feeling the lingering weight of fatigue pressing on his shoulders.

The headlines emblazoned across the front page of *The Mirror* screamed with a raw, visceral urgency:

CHRISTMAS HORROR AS IRA BOMB CITY CHRISTMAS PARTY.

The black print seemed to throb on the page, each word striking his brain with fresh reverberations of shock and disbelief. It felt surreal to see his night, his trauma, summed up in bold typography, reduced to a headline that the rest of the country might read over breakfast before turning to the crossword. The accompanying news report then followed, detailing the grim facts with clinical precision:

"Last night, Christmas revellers from the leading City investment house, Sinclair Bank, were abruptly evacuated under terrifying circumstances from their festive office party. Being staged at London's internationally famous Tower Bridge function rooms, this followed a precisely coded warning from whom police now believe to be the Provisional IRA. A devastating explosion followed the evacuation, causing extensive, widespread structural damage to the bridge itself and inflicting a maximum degree of disruption throughout the immediate local area. Crucially, there are not, at present, believed to be any fatalities. One member of Sinclair Bank's staff is understood to be in hospital undergoing treatment for what

are described as minor injuries. Police are, at this crucial juncture, particularly interested in hearing from any witnesses who may have observed two men running directly away from the scene of the bombing incident at approximately 9:45 p.m. last night. Both individuals are understood to have been of a similar height, around six feet tall and dressed casually. According to an onlooker, they wore distinctive masks resembling the Prime Minister, Mrs Margaret Thatcher."

Dan exhaled slowly, the weight of the moment settling once again on his chest. He read and re-read the article, absorbing every word. It felt both personal and distant, his own nightmare now documented for public consumption. The factual tone of the report did little to capture the chaos, the dread, and the rush of adrenaline that had surged through him the previous evening. He thought of his colleagues, of Ciara, of the panic that had broken out, of the eerie calm before the blast, and how lives, his own included, could have ended in that instant.

Dan was, as anticipated, officially released from Guy's Hospital in the afternoon, though his discharge occurred a little too late for him to make it to the Newbury races, much to his slight, albeit understandable, disappointment. He had so looked forward to that outing, the thrill of the turf, the chatter of the crowd, the hopeful buzz before a race began. But now it seemed trivial, overshadowed by the night that had left him with ringing ears and a rattled soul. Still, he held onto the small hope that normality might resume soon.

Outside the hospital entrance, he hailed a black cab, instructing the driver to take him back to his flat in Fulham. The familiar smell of the city—the sharpness of diesel, the cold breeze funnelling through the narrow streets—felt oddly comforting as he leaned back against the cab's cracked leather seat, watching the world go by in a blur through the rain-flecked window. The driver, sensing his exhaustion, or perhaps simply aware that he was driving home a recently released hospital patient, didn't make conversation, which Dan silently appreciated.

As he fumbled clumsily within his pocket for a crumpled five-pound note with which to settle the driver's fare, his fingers brushed against a piece of paper that he did not, at first, immediately recognise. It was a sheet of letter-writing paper folded in two. Upon extracting it from the rest of the clutter in his coat pocket, he soon realised it was a handwritten note from Ciara. The sight of her handwriting stirred something within him. His mood lifted as he read.

"Please call me, Dan, whenever you find a good moment, to let me know how you are," the neatly written script implored. *"I can, of course, visit you if you are still confined to that wretched hospital. Get well soon. Ciara."*

He read the note twice, then folded it slowly and placed it carefully back into his inside pocket, close to his chest. Her words meant more than she could have known. Amid the fear and noise and smoke, there had been a quiet moment of connection—one he was now determined not to let slip away.

She had thoughtfully left her telephone number at the very bottom of the note. He was, of course, already aware that she resided somewhere within the bustling confines of central London. Though they hadn't yet discussed exact addresses, he had gleaned from snippets of conversation that her flat was somewhere near Notting Hill—leafy, charming, and unmistakably her—although he remembered that she was considering a move to Fulham, nearer to him. The thought of seeing her again, outside the nightmare of the past two days, brought with it a lightness he hadn't felt in some time. A rather intriguing idea suddenly materialised in his mind.

He let himself into the familiar comfort of his flat and, with a sense of quiet contemplation, lit a cigarette. The sharp flare of the match caught his eye as he inhaled deeply, allowing the familiar taste of tobacco to momentarily ground him. The flat was exactly as he had left it—slightly dishevelled, papers on the table, a forgotten tea mug on the windowsill—but today, the ordinary mess felt strangely comforting. This, he mused, was an opportunity simply too good, too compelling, to miss.

He picked up the telephone receiver and, with a quickening pulse, carefully dialled the number she had provided.

"Hi Ciara," he announced with a playful yet confident tone, "London's finest trader here, calling you from the comfortable confines of home. They kindly let me out just after two o'clock."

"Oh, Holy Jesus, thank God you're really okay, Dan," she exclaimed, her voice brimming with palpable relief. "We've all been worried sick."

"No, I'm entirely fine, really I am," he reiterated, seeking to fully assuage her lingering concerns. "It was, admittedly, all a hell of a shock, a bloody nightmare, but I'm nothing worse than a bit sore in places, just a collection of aches and minor bruises. Physically intact, mentally shattered—that's the real summary. The whole night feels like a half-remembered shambles soaked in adrenaline. Since I didn't manage to have any lunch today, I'll most certainly be needing a decent dinner tonight, but sadly I've got no food whatsoever in the house. I don't particularly feel up to going out to play with the lads tonight. I know it's terribly short notice and a bit spontaneous, but how about din-dins? I desperately need to give you your end-of-year appraisal," he joked, a hint of his usual charm returning.

Ciara, now genuinely relieved that he sounded so much better despite the previous evening's traumatic events, playfully indulged him in his jest. There was a brief pause—one of those fleeting silences that settle before a decision—and then she laughed mischievously.

"You're London's finest trader, eh?" she retorted, a hint of amusement in her voice.

"Well, I wouldn't necessarily, perhaps not entirely accurately, say I was London's finest, but I'd most certainly be in the top one," he affirmed with mock seriousness, copying the comments of the leading football manager Brian Clough. "And why on earth are you asking such a leading question anyway?"

"Because it's mighty flattering, exceptionally so, for a mere blue button—a humble junior—to be asked on a date by such a star trader, London's top stock and options trader, as you self-describe yourself," she replied with just a touch of irony, her voice soft but clear. "Yes, I'd absolutely love to."

Dan felt his spirits soar dramatically, a surge of exhilaration coursing through him. It was the kind of buoyant, unexpected high he hadn't known since that perfect market day the previous spring when everything had gone his way. He instinctively pumped his fist in the air—a familiar gesture he employed whenever he'd secured a large, significant winning bet or had illegally landed a coup in a stock, however much a clandestine financial manoeuvre. The walls of his flat seemed to brighten with the very idea of a shared evening—good wine, maybe laughter, perhaps even the beginning of something real, something lasting.

He then suggested, with a confident air, that they meet at the highly acclaimed and ever-popular Italian restaurant Il Pontevecchio, located on the well-known Old Brompton Road, at eight o'clock.

The deal with Ciara now sealed and mission accomplished, he turned on the television set, its low hum briefly filling the otherwise quiet room. With a flick of the remote control—a motion now so well-practised it was nearly automatic—he tuned into Channel 4. This particular channel had only recently, and to some controversy, acquired the exclusive television rights for broadcasting live horse racing, having taken over from ITV in what had been widely regarded as a landmark deal within the industry. The transition had been met with a mixture of scepticism and cautious optimism by racing fans, but Channel 4, to their credit, had handled the responsibility with both professionalism and flair. The racing public loved it.

At that very moment, the programme was providing its usual thorough and entertaining coverage of the racing from both Newbury and Ayr, complete with articulate commentary, vivid camera work, and regular interviews from trackside correspondents. Normally, this sort of content would have sparked an immediate and irresistible flutter of anticipation in Dan's gut—that familiar, almost electric itch in his fingers to place a bet, to study the odds, to weigh up the form and conditions and make a snap decision that might, just might, lead to a rewarding payout. But this afternoon the fire wasn't there. For once, and in a rare departure from his usual inclinations, he found that the prospect of gambling simply didn't carry its usual pull. The thrill was absent. His mind, it seemed, was elsewhere.

With a slow, considered sigh he knew that he just didn't have the urge. The prospect of his forthcoming date being spoiled because of another afternoon's losses did not appeal. He reached forward and switched off the television. The screen faded to black, the silence that followed somehow soothing. He stood for a brief moment, glancing around the walls of his flat, before allowing his body to sink back into the comfort of his well-worn sofa. There, he allowed himself to simply breathe, the tension in his shoulders gradually easing. And then, with no further ceremony, he drifted off into a deep, undisturbed, restorative sleep—the kind of sleep that feels like a warm cocoon after a storm. His mind, unburdened by odds or racing papers, wandered gently into a dreamscape where the central figure was unmistakably Ciara—her voice, her smile, her beauty dominating his subconscious thoughts.

The snow had continued to fall steadily throughout the late afternoon, its persistent descent transforming the usually grey, bustling city into something almost magical. The roads were slick with slush and the pavements lined with footprints, yet, remarkably, Dan had no difficulty securing a taxi when he stepped outside later that evening. Perhaps it was good fortune, or perhaps the city, usually so impatient and relentless, had been temporarily slowed by the snow's quiet insistence.

By the time the taxi dropped him off, he found himself outside the restaurant at precisely seven forty-five—a full quarter of an hour ahead of their agreed meeting time. He brushed a few snowflakes from his coat collar and took a quick glance at the glowing façade of Il Pontevecchio. The restaurant lay on the right-hand side of the Old Brompton Road, a mere stone's throw from Earl's Court. The exterior was hidden by leafy green trees, perhaps so that diners could be spared from witnessing the goings-on at a somewhat gauche pub opposite. Beyond the trees was a conservatory with an ample awning that could be removed on hot summer days. The interior of the dining area itself exuded a kind of discreet opulence: polished wood, dimmed lighting, and the faint aroma of garlic, basil, and freshly baked bread hanging in the air like a promise.

He moved to the bar and, with an air of quiet confidence, ordered a large, generously poured gin and tonic. As the barman prepared his drink, Dan pulled out a cigarette, lit it with a deliberate flick of his lighter, and leaned back slightly, watching the flame momentarily dance before it died. He inhaled deeply, exhaled slowly, and allowed himself a few quiet moments of thought. His mind, predictably, returned to Ciara—how she might look tonight, what sort of mood she'd be in, how the evening might unfold. He carefully mapped out a conversational strategy, mentally rehearsing charming responses, readying himself for humour, flattery, and just enough flirtation to keep the energy light yet promising.

And then, just as the clock ticked towards eight o'clock, the restaurant doors opened—and there she was.

Ciara entered with a grace and poise that seemed to momentarily suspend the room's activity. She looked breathtakingly different from how he was used to seeing her at work—the neat professional attire, the restrained make-up, the hurried air of someone constantly under pressure.

Tonight, she was transformed. She wore a luxurious mink coat in a rich, chocolate-brown hue, which caught the subtle lighting and shimmered faintly as she moved. Beneath it, a sleek black dress clung with precision to her tall figure, cinched perfectly at her waist, creating a silhouette that was both refined and arresting. Her dark hair had been swept up and away from her face, revealing those sharp cheekbones and the curve of her neck.

As their eyes met, her face lit up with a radiant, completely disarming smile. Her oyster-white teeth caught the light, and for a brief, breathless second, Dan felt something tighten in his chest. An electric jolt surged down his spine. He had to fight the very real, very present impulse to walk over and kiss her immediately. Instead, he summoned his restraint and settled for the more socially acceptable 'mwah mwah' kiss on each cheek—though his eyes betrayed the fire he was attempting to contain.

A polite waiter appeared beside her and helped her off with her coat, revealing more of the stunning dress beneath. She thanked him with a smile, and then turned her full attention to Dan.

They took their seats, ordered a robust Tuscan red recommended by the sommelier, and allowed the conversation to flow.

Naturally, the topic turned quickly to the events of the previous night. The tension, though slightly dulled by distance, still lingered like an unwelcome shadow.

"I have to ask," Dan began, his voice low, "why on earth did you and Mark show up so late to the party? You nearly missed the whole damned thing—though I suppose, in hindsight, that may have been a blessing."

Ciara chuckled faintly, her fingers lightly tracing the rim of her wine glass.

"We ran into some of the opposing traders from the floor by the taxi rank outside Broadgate," she explained, her voice rich with irony. "And somehow—I'm still not entirely sure how—we got swept into a spontaneous drink at Corney and Barrow's in Broadgate Circle. The atmosphere was electric. Everyone was in high spirits. It was one of those unexpected, oddly perfect evenings where time just... disappeared. We honestly hadn't realised how late it was."

Dan gave a wry smile. "And there was I thinking that punctuality was an Irish virtue."

"Oh, it is," she replied, raising an eyebrow with playful defiance. "We were just... momentarily distracted by good company."

His next question, while offered casually, carried a deeper interest beneath the surface. "So... you and Mark. How far back do you two go?"

She took a sip of wine, then answered with the frankness he had come to admire. "We were part of the same gang back in Ireland during our late teens. You know the scene—pubs, discos, the usual mischief. I didn't know him that well, truth be told, but he was always one of the lads. Loud, confident, always had a story to tell."

"And now?" Dan asked, tilting his head. "How do you get on working together?"

"He's a bright man, undeniably intelligent, and a particularly good teacher," she affirmed with genuine appreciation. Her voice carried an undertone of admiration, and as she spoke, her eyes momentarily drifted upward, as if recalling specific lessons or conversations that had genuinely impressed her. "He's taught me a considerable amount about the intricacies of traded options." She took another sip of her Brunello di Montalcino.

"And that, please tell me, is really as far as it goes?" Dan probed, a subtle but unmistakable hint of hopeful anxiety in his voice. His gaze lingered on her expression, seeking the faintest trace of hesitation, a flicker of ambiguity, but found none. There was something almost childlike in his question—earnest, searching, quietly vulnerable. It was not jealousy exactly, but the raw and human need to know where he stood in a situation rapidly becoming more complex than he'd anticipated.

"Dan, I sincerely hope you're not suggesting something entirely inappropriate..." Ciara began, a fleeting flicker of annoyance momentarily crossing her elegant features. Her eyebrows arched slightly, and her lips tightened for the briefest instant. However, this very display of irritation paradoxically made Dan feel an extreme, almost profound sense of relief. It was, without question, crystal clear that absolutely nothing untoward was going on between them. Her indignation, he realised, was precisely the reaction one might expect from someone wholly innocent and above reproach.

"How would you feel," Dan ventured, seizing the moment, "if I were to consider moving you to an entirely different sector within the bank, perhaps the stores, for instance?" His voice was measured, casual even, though his heart was thudding as he studied her face for a reaction.

Ciara carefully considered the proposition in silence for a few reflective seconds. She tilted her head slightly, as if weighing the idea on an invisible scale, considering not only the professional implications but also the unspoken personal motive behind the suggestion. "I think that's not at all a bad idea, actually," she responded, her expression softening. "Having a bit of a change, a fresh challenge, wouldn't be a bad thing in the slightest—so long as, of course, you're not doing it purely because you're jealous of Mark."

She uttered this last remark with a knowing smile, specifically designed to ensure that Dan wouldn't feel even the slightest bit embarrassed by the suggestion. There was a teasing glint in her eyes, the kind that implied she was fully aware of her effect on him and not at all averse to it. It was a calculated kindness—playful, but not cruel.

"Nothing, my dear Ciara, could be further from the unvarnished truth," Dan lied smoothly, a perfectly executed deception. His smile didn't waver, and his tone remained light, but somewhere deep down, he knew she saw right through him. With these rather delicate home truths now gracefully cleared out of the way, they spent the remainder of dinner discovering an increasing amount about each other, delving into the more personal facets of their lives. The tension that had hovered between them like an invisible veil now dissipated, replaced by the warmth of genuine connection.

They discussed their respective brothers, sisters, and parents, sharing intimate details. She spoke engagingly about her time at the prestigious Trinity College Dublin and recounted her valuable internships at both Allied Irish Bank and Société Générale. Dan, in turn, candidly shared anecdotes about his own life and meticulously recounted how he had originally secured his coveted position with Sinclair Bank. His storytelling was animated, laced with wry humour and the occasional self-deprecating remark, which made Ciara laugh in a way that made her eyes crinkle at the corners.

He considered that talking to Ciara socially and outside work was on a different plane. He felt at total and unburdened ease in her company, and she, in turn, listened with rapt attention to his every word. There was an unspoken understanding blooming between them, a sense that this was more than just polite conversation—it was connection in its truest form. He didn't even, to his surprise, mind confessing to her that he had, in fact, never attended university, and that his father's influential friend, the venerable Sir Marcus Holderness, had effectively arranged for him to be hired without his even having met him personally.

They also exchanged genuine goodwill, paying each other sincere compliments in a mutual display of admiration. She remarked, with compelling conviction, that a university education in Dan's specific case would have been entirely irrelevant, given his extraordinary acumen and innate talent as a trader. He, in kind, returned the compliment by highlighting the amazingly rapid progress she had made during her first five months at the bank. Her cheeks coloured slightly at the praise, but she accepted it graciously.

They had been eating, drinking, and chatting earnestly for well over two hours, the time seemingly dissolving into the conversation. The hum of background chatter, the clink of cutlery, and the low murmur of music in the restaurant faded into a gentle backdrop to their unfolding evening.

Ciara declined to have a pudding, but Dan, in a subtle yet deliberately romantic move, ordered the rich tiramisu. He suggested that they should perhaps share it, a gesture that she found endearing, despite only taking a small teaspoonful herself when it finally arrived. The gesture spoke volumes—it was more than dessert; it was a symbol of something tentatively beginning, a definite sign of the affection quietly taking root between them. When the spoon brushed her lips, Dan found himself wondering, with a sudden intensity, what it might be like to kiss her in that moment. But he held back, just as he had before, savouring the slow burn of possibility. Public displays of affection were not his bag in any case.

It was, by all accounts, fast approaching that nerve-racking juncture in the evening, the awkward and delicately poised moment that men in particular have come to recognise as the inflection point. Was it time to either gently wind down proceedings or progress thrillingly into uncharted territory? For Dan, it was a moment soaked in anticipation, marked by a mixture of rising confidence and nagging doubt, a balancing act between restraint and boldness. The dinner had gone splendidly, the conversation had flowed like a fine vintage wine, and by now the two of them had partaken in several rounds of expensive brandies and rich, velvety coffees, each sip adding a layer of warmth and relaxed intimacy to the night.

Dan found himself genuinely impressed—and, truth be told, just a touch intrigued—by Ciara's ability to imbibe a fair amount of alcohol while still retaining a composed, sophisticated air, without so much as a flicker of slurred speech or impaired poise. She sat across from him like a woman entirely in control of herself, her faculties sharp, her charm intact. At last, bolstered by the slowly building chemistry between them and a growing desire not to let the moment fade into anticlimax, he inhaled quietly, gathered his courage like a gambler about to place the final, decisive bet, and voiced the next, fateful suggestion.

"Do you fancy going on to a club?" he asked, forcing a casual tone but instantly regretting the phrasing.

Almost as soon as the words left his lips, he berated himself inwardly. A club? Was that really the best he could come up with? What was he thinking—a loud, strobe-lit environment with pounding music and sticky floors? Hardly the setting for a sophisticated continuation of the magical rapport they'd built over dinner. He winced inwardly at the sheer lack of imagination. What he really wanted to say, and say boldly, was that he didn't want the night to end. That he wanted her to come back with him, not to some sweaty dancefloor, but to the quiet, ambient warmth of his flat. But the courage to voice that desire directly had, at the final hurdle, deserted him.

To his great relief, however, Ciara saved him. She responded not with confusion or judgement but with that intuitive finesse he was beginning to realise was one of her defining traits—the ability to cut through the clutter of a situation and get to the heart of it.

"I'm simply not a nightclub type of girl anymore," she said, her voice calm, clear, and utterly self-assured, tinged with the gentle amusement of someone who had, in her past life, danced that dance too many times already. Then, with a tilt of the head and a slow smile that sent a pleasant heat rushing to his ears, she added, "You could, however, always show me precisely where a star trader such as yourself lives, though."

It was the perfect invitation. Simple. Decisive. Intimate.

Dan wasted no time. His flat, fortunately, was just a short cab ride from the restaurant—a quick journey that afforded just enough time for them to engage in a light, slightly flirtatious exchange of small talk. Their words were more placeholders than actual conversation, gentle markers of time passed while, beneath the surface, a shared anticipation thrummed between them. They both knew, in that unspoken way that only emerges when two people are quietly attuned to one another's desires, that this was the continuation—perhaps even the culmination—of something they had both been silently hoping for.

When they arrived, Dan unlocked the door with a smooth, familiar motion, flicked on the hallway lights, and ushered her inside. "I'll just pop into the kitchen and get some champagne," he said, his voice softer now, tinged with a different kind of energy—not nervousness exactly, but a gentle reverence for the moment. "Do feel free to show yourself around."

Ciara stepped gracefully into the large, softly lit living room. Her eyes took in the modern layout, the carefully curated art pieces on the walls, the sleek, tasteful furniture that blended comfort with understated class. Most notable was the massive bookcase—a towering testament to eclectic taste and intellectual curiosity. She walked slowly around the space, her fingers brushing over the spine of a hardback novel, then paused to examine a striking abstract painting that hung near the window. She removed her mink coat with languid precision, folding it and draping it neatly over the armrest of the nearest sofa before continuing her silent exploration of the room.

Back in the kitchen, Dan expertly located a chilled bottle of vintage champagne, popped the cork with a discreet flourish, and grabbed two delicate crystal flutes. When he returned to the living room with everything in hand, a faint smile on his lips and *Water Music* by Handel already playing in his mind, he was momentarily taken aback—the room was empty.

He glanced around. No Ciara.

Perhaps, he reasoned, she had stepped into the bathroom to freshen up. He set the champagne down and moved toward the corridor, the familiar opening strains of Handel now floating gently through the flat from the speakers he'd just switched on. There was a heady tension in the air, the kind that prickles at the edges of your awareness, preparing you for something unexpected or unforgettable.

And then he saw her.

She was there, sitting on the edge of his bed with the quiet confidence of someone entirely at home in her own skin. Her posture was relaxed yet poised. Her expression, softly lit by the hallway light spilling in, was equal parts mischief and invitation. She wore nothing now but a bra, panties, stockings, and a pair of sleek black stilettos that accentuated the smooth curve of her legs.

"I'm moist already, Dan," she murmured, her voice low and sultry, each word coated in a husky drawl that sent a pulse straight through him.

Her eyes met his—steady, gleaming, alive with anticipation—and in that electric second, Dan knew with absolute certainty that he was entering a realm where desire, intimacy, and connection would entwine into something unforgettable.

Dan, at this point, needed absolutely no further encouragement. He reached for her outstretched hand and, with a gentle yet firm pull, guided her gracefully to her feet, before embracing her with the full, unbridled force of all the pent-up passion he had felt for her over the preceding five months, a raw, powerful desire finally unleashed.

Breathing deeply, drawing in the intoxicating scent of her perfume, he felt the adrenaline building rapidly within him, surging through his veins just as it had always, without fail, done since his teenage years, when he first began to experience the profound stirrings of sexual arousal. His clothes, as if by some unseen force, virtually fell off him, shedding with an almost effortless ease.

Ciara, the junior blue button in the bustling electricals crowd, was, in her exquisite lingerie, the very epitome of femininity. Her tall, remarkably slender figure, yet possessing curves that inspired in him such an intense, almost overwhelming attraction that he felt, for a fleeting moment, almost dizzy with desire. He gently laid her across the bed, and she, with an instinctive, almost primal grace, arched her back, subtly yet unmistakably inviting him to undo her bra, an action for which he, once again, required absolutely no encouragement whatsoever to perform. She then, with a languid, sensual movement, slid her silk panties down her long, elegant legs, and he, with an appreciative gaze, admired her thick, neatly trimmed pubic hair, whilst she, in turn, admired his now rock-hard, unyielding cock.

Their lips, with an unspoken yearning, finally met, intertwining in a deep, passionate kiss. He placed his hands firmly yet tenderly on her waist, whilst his tongue, with an insatiable hunger, devoured her mouth. She wrapped her long, stockinged legs firmly and possessively around his thighs and groaned audibly in raw pleasure as he delved deep inside her, a profound, fulfilling penetration. They sighed together, in perfect, synchronised unison, as he finally entered her.

His strokes were, at first, slow, deliberate, and remarkably considerate, and there were even moments when he would ease off slightly, simply drinking in her exquisite beauty, allowing the moment to truly register. They flowed together in perfect, effortless unison, a harmonious dance of bodies. There seemed to be no requirement whatsoever for elaborate sexual positioning, nor, for that matter, any need for explicit oral stimulation; their connection was purely intuitive.

Her gasps, as the intensity mounted, became progressively shorter and noticeably louder, and her face, taut with burgeoning sensation, hardened in concentration as she inexorably approached the precipice of orgasm.

Dan, too, was now rapidly nearing his climax, and with one final, urgent flurry of rapid, powerful pumping movements, she screamed aloud, a guttural, uninhibited cry of sheer release, and as he came long and hard inside her, a deep, forceful culmination, she simultaneously experienced what was, without question, the most excruciatingly intense orgasm of her entire life.

CHAPTER 9

— March 1987

Sir Marcus Holderness had bought a racehorse. It had been his wife Diana's idea after they had attended a race meeting one Saturday afternoon at Sandown Park. The air that day had been filled with electric excitement: gentlemen in tailored suits sipping champagne, women in elegant hats whispering odds, and the unmistakable thunder of hooves striking turf. For Marcus and Diana, the experience was intoxicating, the sort of afternoon that stirred forgotten dreams and sparked new ambitions. They had gone down to the paddock after each race to see the horses returning, flanks lathered with sweat, nostrils flaring, muscles twitching beneath gleaming coats. They had witnessed the beaming expressions on the faces of the winning connections—owners, trainers and jockeys alike—basking in the glory of success.

For Diana, always a lover of both beauty and competition, the moment stirred something profound. She had leaned close to Marcus and whispered, "Why not us?" At first, he had laughed, amused by the spontaneity of it. But the idea took hold, and the more they talked, the more it felt not only feasible but inevitable. Knowing that they could comfortably afford to buy something decent, they had decided to go ahead and buy one of their own.

Marcus hadn't had a great interest in the sport before. He had always considered it the realm of eccentric aristocrats or thrill-seeking gamblers, not City men with structured portfolios and firm handshakes. But, like so many others before him who had stumbled upon the world of thoroughbred racing by chance, he was now captivated. He had started reading the racing pages of the newspapers each day with growing interest, marking names, noting form, absorbing terminology that once sounded like a foreign language—going, handicaps, bumpers, novices and hurdles. It was a steep learning curve, but he found it exhilarating.

Soon, he realised that, to have a horse likely to win at the highest level, they would probably need to invest in a jumps horse. The economics of the sport made this approach far more practical. This way, they could avoid having to compete with the world's richest tycoons and Arab oil sheikhs, who mostly frequented the winners' enclosure at Royal Ascot on the Flat, where the price tags were astronomical and the margins for success brutally slim. Jump racing, by contrast, still retained a sense of noble grit, a sport where pedigree mattered, but heart and tenacity often meant even more.

One evening, as Marcus sat reading *The Racing Post* over a quiet drink in his study, he saw a trainer, Captain Neville Taylor, interviewed on television. The man had just trained a big-race winner and was speaking with calm authority, giving nothing away, yet radiating competence. A flicker of recognition passed through Marcus. He knew Captain Taylor from their National Service days, when they had both served at Catterick, although their career paths had subsequently led them in very different directions. Marcus had gone into the

City, building a life of finance, mergers and numbers, while Taylor had remained in the army, continuing to rise through the ranks.

He remembered him back then—always first on parade, boots polished to a mirror shine, a crack shot on the range, and a stickler for detail. There was a discipline to him that never wavered, and a work ethic that drew the respect of both his peers and senior officers. Captain Neville Taylor was an all-rounder, an achiever. He didn't just complete tasks—he dominated them. Marcus painfully remembered stepping into the boxing ring with him one day as part of their unit's sports rotation. The match had been short and bruising; Marcus left with two black eyes and a cut lip, a bout that was heavily one-sided but oddly exhilarating. Still, despite the defeat, Marcus had always respected the man—his focus, his dignity and his quiet steel. He considered him the archetypal officer and gentleman. He liked the cut of this man's jib and had decided to call him to discuss his potential new purchase.

When they finally spoke, the conversation was brief and unsentimental, just as Marcus had expected.

"I'm a hands-on trainer, Marcus," Taylor had said in his clipped, military tone, "and don't like my owners calling me up all the time, not even old colleagues. You'll get one call per week, at a pre-designated time on a Sunday morning, lasting no more than five minutes, and I'll expect you to answer. You'll be sent one letter each week outlining your horse's progress. Other than that, the only contact we'll have will be at the races or when we meet socially during the summer season."

Marcus admired the trainer's authority and self-confidence. It was rare to encounter someone so unbending in their standards, and he liked it. That night, he told Diana that he had agreed to have his first racehorse with Captain Neville Taylor at his Heath Farm Stables in Lambourn, nestled in the heart of racing country.

Captain Taylor, having asked Marcus how much he was looking to pay for the acquisition, subsequently travelled to a sale in Ireland, armed with the knowledge that he could go to thirty thousand guineas. He knew that amount wouldn't get them a ready-made champion, but it could certainly buy a horse with good breeding, raw talent and the potential to be moulded into a festival contender. His aim was simple: to secure a horse with the credentials and scope to win a race at the prestigious Cheltenham Festival—the mecca for all fans of jump racing and the pinnacle of the National Hunt year.

It was the kind of dream that, once planted, could not be easily dislodged. For Marcus and Diana, the journey had begun. And though they didn't yet know it, that single decision would go on to consume their weekends, dominate their conversations and eventually change their lives in ways they never could have imagined.

Captain Taylor returned with a handsome four-year-old bay gelding by the name of Beacon Boy. With a glossy coat that gleamed like polished mahogany under the stable lights and a proud, alert stance that radiated potential, Beacon Boy immediately caught the eye. His dark, intelligent eyes held a flicker of quiet confidence, and even the stable lads remarked on his calm temperament, unusual for a horse still so young. Beacon Boy had run in two bumpers in Ireland. These races, typically used to assess a young horse's raw potential before being introduced to hurdles or fences, offered a unique testing ground. Bumpers are flat races run under National Hunt (jumps) rules but are only open to horses that have not run previously under normal flat racing rules. The distinction often confused casual fans, but within the training circles, a bumper win was a badge of future promise.

He had run with credit in both the Irish races, shaping with promise behind subsequent winners. His finishes, though not victorious, had shown a turn of foot and a resolute attitude when placed under pressure, qualities that often separated the ordinary from the exceptional in this demanding sport. Captain Taylor, having attended the races personally, had seen more in the horse's mannerisms and breathing pattern than the average observer ever would. With over thirty years' experience as a racehorse trainer, years filled with long hours, bitter winters, triumphs and heartbreaks, Captain Taylor felt that Beacon Boy would prove to be a better hurdler and an even better steeplechaser. His instincts, honed by decades of trial and error, rarely led him astray.

He secured lot forty-two for a sum of twenty-eight thousand five hundred guineas at auction. The bidding had been competitive, with several seasoned buyers showing interest, but it was Taylor's unwavering confidence and final raised paddle that sealed the deal. His judgement had been sound, as under his care and with new owners, Beacon Boy's progress had been remarkable. The gelding settled quickly into the Heath Farm Stables, adapting to the routines with a maturity that surprised even the most seasoned grooms. Morning gallops revealed an impressive engine, and as Taylor had suspected, Beacon Boy began to thrive with obstacles in his path.

Marcus and Diana had enjoyed a thrilling January day at Plumpton, a racecourse situated under the Sussex Downs, when Beacon Boy won his British debut effortlessly, making all the running to win in a two-mile novice hurdle. The chilly wind couldn't dampen their spirits that afternoon. Diana, in a smart navy coat and matching gloves, clutched her racecard with growing excitement as Beacon Boy jumped fluently from hurdle to hurdle, never giving a rival a chance. The race had been barely halfway through when Marcus, binoculars pressed to his eyes, whispered, "He's going to win this. Easily." This feat was quickly surpassed when he won the feature handicap hurdle at Sandown just three weeks later. That day, the cheers from the crowd had been deafening as Beacon Boy surged clear up the famous hill, and the sense of pride the couple felt was unparalleled. This was no longer just a hobby; it was a passion ignited.

As Sir Marcus, Lady Diana, and Captain Taylor stood in the Sandown winners' enclosure, surrounded by photographers, reporters, and fellow owners, a journalist thrust a microphone into the trainer's face. The flashing of cameras was relentless, a storm of shutter clicks capturing the moment.

"That was a brilliant performance from a very promising horse, Captain Taylor. Where do you go next?" The journalists all knew better than to address him as Neville. In racing circles, protocol mattered. Titles earned over years in the saddle or service carried weight, and Captain Taylor was not a man who tolerated informality.

"What do you think, young man?" replied a brusque Captain Taylor, not the easiest of interviewees, before answering his own question. His tone held the usual crispness of someone who didn't entertain idle speculation.

"All roads lead to Cheltenham now."

The big day finally came: Cheltenham of 1987, the National Hunt Festival. The atmosphere around the stables in the week leading up to it had been electric. Marcus had been counting down the days after the Sandown race, unable to focus on business meetings, his thoughts constantly drifting to grassy gallops and the sound of thundering hooves. But the opening Tuesday was now upon them. He and Diana had driven to the course from London, leaving early to avoid the inevitable traffic congestion. They'd risen before dawn, the city still quiet, a thermos of coffee between them, filled with nervous energy and hope. They parked the Bentley in the owners' and trainers' car park before walking the few minutes that led to the great amphitheatre. The car park, already half full, buzzed with anticipation. People spoke in hushed tones about their tips for the day, flipping through racecards and sipping from flasks.

They were early, still over three hours until the first race and five hours until the reappearance of Beacon Boy. They had been invited to their trainer's box, but being their first time at Cheltenham, they decided to walk around the different enclosures first, taking in the atmosphere. They wandered past stands and betting kiosks, through the Guinness Village, and along the rails where eager punters were already picking their vantage points. It seemed that most racegoers, on that chilly March day, had also decided to get there early, as there appeared to be thousands already in attendance. The stands, a sea of tweeds, trilbies, and winter coats, buzzed with excitement.

They recognised those now familiar racecourse smells of crushed grass and beer, cigar and cigarette smoke. The olfactory mix was pungent, nostalgic, and strangely comforting. The smell of fast food wafted through the air—burgers, hot dogs, pork roasting on spits, the smells of a giant barbecue. Vendors called out their specials, and queues began forming already. They saw jockeys coming into the racecourse, wearing suits and carrying their bags on their way to the weighing room. Their movements were brisk, focused, like soldiers reporting for duty. Punters called out to them things like, "Good luck today, Jonjo!" or "I fancy yours in the first, Stevie." It was the sort of camaraderie and spectacle that could only belong to Cheltenham, and for Marcus and Diana, it already felt like the beginning of something unforgettable.

Their own jockey, a semi-toothless young man in his late twenties, was called Jamie Davies. Davies, due to ride Beacon Boy later, was 'retained' by Captain Taylor, which meant that the Captain had priority over any other trainers when claiming his jockey to ride. Captain Taylor always insisted that his jockeys appeared in his box precisely forty-five minutes before lunch was served, wearing suits and ties, to meet his friends and owners and answer their questions. The jockeys all knew that they would be on the wrong end of a bollocking should they not leave the box within five minutes of the guests sitting down for lunch.

Marcus and Diana walked across the lawn, with the impressive stands to their left and the glorious sight of the Cotswolds, a light covering of snow illuminating them on an overcast day, like a scene on a Christmas card. Bookmakers were already taking bets. Sir Marcus noticed two rather gauche types shouting out odds. One, wearing long blonde hair, was dressed in a white suit and sheepskin coat and smoked a large Cuban cigar. Marcus recognised him from Sandown Park, where he'd relieved him and his brother of a thousand pounds when Beacon Boy had been the subject of his one hundred and twenty-five-pound winning bet at eight to one. He also recognised the slogan:

'YOU PLAY; ARCHER BROTHERS PAY.'

Then, somewhat to his consternation, he heard one of the long-haired men, adorned with plenty of bling, cry out, "Oi, Guv'nor!"

Marcus made the mistake of looking around and found himself looking squarely at Joss Archer. "Your 'orse gonna win today, Guv'nor?" Marcus wasn't often embarrassed but felt himself redden, having attracted the attention of several punters around the Archer Brothers' pitch. "I certainly hope so," spluttered Marcus. "Perhaps I'll come down later to have another bet with you," he said, immediately taking Diana's hand and leading her away.

"Fucking toffs," Joss muttered under his breath, smiling to his brother, Wayne.

Dan Perry and Mark O'Brien had taken the day off and travelled up to Cheltenham from Paddington on the train. Dan had asked Ciara to join them, but slightly to his annoyance, she'd declined his offer. He'd asked her one evening the previous week in a smart London restaurant while they were being entertained by brokers hungry to get Sinclair Bank's business. Dan and Ciara had been an item ever since the evening after the ill-fated Christmas party. Some nights would be spent at Dan's flat, and others at hers, but some apart too. She had insisted to Dan that their relationship should be kept strictly secret; they hardly wanted everyone in the office, let alone the Stock Exchange floor, gossiping about them. Anyway, their whirlwind romance had not featured any arguments until they'd got home to Dan's flat that night.

"For the life of me, I don't understand why you won't come to the races with me and Mark next week. What the fuck is it with you two? I'll bet you'd come if he wasn't going."

"You stupid bastard," Ciara raged in reply. "How fucking dare you still be intimating that there's something between us, you jealous prick. How many times have I told you that we just knew each other as kids back in Ireland?"

She stormed off then, to return to her own flat, even having considered giving Dan back the extra set of keys he had made for her. The following day, however, they quickly made things up, with Dan venturing a grovelling apology and presenting her with a large bunch of flowers when he arrived at her flat that evening.

As Dan and Mark had not been invited to any corporate entertainment that March Tuesday at Cheltenham, they decided to make The Arkle Bar their base and try to scrounge whatever invitations they could for more luxurious and less crowded surroundings, should the chance present itself later in the day. Near the front of the crowded bar, Dan thought about Ciara. She would be trading on the floor right now, missing the fun and excitement of all this. Obviously, she had been right; there could not be any connection with Mark, could there? After all, Mark had become one of his mates ever since the killing in the shares they had made last year. They often drank together. No, he would not lie to me, mused Dan. He thought that maybe she cared for him so much that she did not want to encourage him to gamble by going to Cheltenham. His debts had started racking up again, and she had recently noticed the Archer Brothers statement lying open on a table in his flat. That bill for seven thousand five hundred pounds had taken some explaining.

Mark and Dan, having drunk a few on the train earlier and another couple of pints at the pub outside Cheltenham Station, were now set for a full-on afternoon of tumultuous inebriation and, in Dan's case, heavy gambling. With no box to go to, The Arkle Bar seemed the next best option. It was situated at the bottom of the viewing lawn, underneath the luxury boxes. Dan knew that Beacon Boy was running in the Novices' Handicap Hurdle later and had been told by his father the previous day that Sir Marcus and Diana were going to be at the races, entertained by their trainer, Captain Neville Taylor. He harboured hopes that they would bump into Marcus and receive an invitation. Still, The Arkle Bar would do for now. It was like a high-ceilinged farmyard barn inside, sparsely furnished with framed pictures of newspaper clippings celebrating past heroes of Cheltenham's glorious history. Legends of the turf, both equine and human, looked down on the huge throng of punters within. Paraffin-burning stoves were strategically placed around the floor, keeping out the frosty weather outside, and long wooden ledges surrounded the walls and pillars as a resting place for scarves, papers and drinks. Any amount of champagne, gin, vodka, whisky and sloe gin would be consumed that week, but the bestseller by a distance was Guinness, the favoured tipple of the Irish. With two hours to go before the first race, the bar was packed and rocking with English and Irish punters, both young and old, affluent and poor, with loud laughter ringing out as they all drank in the atmosphere of Cheltenham's magic and the anticipation of the high-quality sport to come.

Captain Neville Taylor's box was high up in the main stand, with a breathtaking view from the balcony. His guests were a mix of old friends built up over a lifetime and a few select owners. They would enjoy smoked salmon and prawns, followed by medallions of beef and new potatoes, all washed down with copious amounts of Chablis and Châteauneuf-du-Pape. Various racing celebrities, including a few other trainers, would be asked to join the guests after lunch for a drink or two in passing.

"Hand me that bottle, young man," Captain Taylor said to the waiter as he took the open bottle of champagne from the waiter's hand and started pouring the bubbles into two flutes before handing them to Sir Marcus and Diana.

"Not bad to have a runner at Cheltenham in your first season as an owner, old boy. And a fancied one at that. I hope you're going to have a decent bet. I saw Beacon Boy was about 4/1 earlier."

"Our horse, Neville, and as yet I haven't had a bet," replied Marcus, winking at his trainer. Diana smiled gracefully in approval, as Beacon Boy was in both their names as owners.

"Damned rude of me. Forgive your trainer's rude oversight, please, Diana," ventured the trainer before continuing, "Now, about that bet. Do you have an account with anyone down there?" he asked, pointing in the direction of the betting ring.

Marcus replied, "I don't actually, but when we won at Sandown, I did back him with that loud, long-haired fellow on the rails."

"Ha! The one with the long blonde hair, white suit and enough gold to sink a battleship?" ventured Captain Taylor. Marcus smiled and nodded. The Captain continued, "Joss Archer and his brother Wayne. They're the biggest bookmakers on the rails in the South of England, dogs and horses. And they usually offer the best prices. They may be wide boys, but they're OK. In fact, I like them enough to have an account with them. I may ask you to do something for me with them after lunch. I'll give you my account number. They're used to my envoys placing bets on my behalf. I can't be seen betting on the rails. Bad for the image, you know. Besides, I'll be saddling up Beacon Boy and giving that Davies lad tactical instructions so that we have the best chance possible of landing you your first Festival winner and taking those Archer boys to the cleaners in the meantime! Talk of the devil, here's our jockey now."

James Davies approached his boss and the owners of his sole ride of the day. He had already had a surreptitious word with the waiter on the door of the box to ask how long was left until lunch was served. It wouldn't do to outstay his welcome.

Back in The Arkle Bar, Dan and Mark had enjoyed three pints of Guinness each and a bottle of champagne. The first race was only half an hour away. Dan was both tense and excited. If there was ever a place to win money, it had to be Cheltenham or Royal Ascot, he thought. He had a large ante-post bet on the first race, the Supreme Novices' Hurdle. Mark had received information from his father in Ireland, a passionate racing fan, that Kissane, the 4/1 favourite, had been working brilliantly at home and was very strongly fancied. Dan had called the Archer Brothers Racing Office in Walthamstow the week before and had placed three thousand to win at 4/1, which included fifty pounds for Mark.

Ante-post bets are wagers placed before the final declarations of any given big race are made. Betting ante-post can provide value for money, as the odds are likely to become shorter after the declarations are made, with some fancied horses likely to have been withdrawn. Conversely, the risk of betting ante-post is that the punter loses his money if his selection is not entered at the final declaration stage. Dan had no worries on that score at least, as Kissane was not only a definite starter, but he had also been further backed into clear 3/1 favouritism. They drained the remains of the Black Velvet and headed out of the packed Arkle Bar towards the betting ring.

"Time for a little top-up, mate," Dan said to Mark as they stood in front of the Archers' pitch. "Those idiots are laying Kissane at seven to two."

The Archers were indeed showing a standout price of seven to two, while most of their rivals were offering a slightly skinnier 3/1.

"Don't you think you've done enough already, Danny boy?" Mark suggested, turning to Dan. His words, however, fell on deaf ears. Dan had vanished.

Already standing at the Archers' pitch, Mark spotted his colleague in discussion with Joss Archer, who took a drag of his cigar and shouted out, "TWENTY-EIGHT HUNDRED TO EIGHT HUNDRED, KISSANE, DOWN TO BOY." Mark grimaced.

Dan reached for the diary in his right-hand pocket, the same diary in which he kept a record of all his bets and a note of how much he was owed, or, more commonly, how much he owed the Archer Brothers. His latest investment of eight hundred pounds stood to net him a profit of two thousand eight hundred pounds. This was on top of the three grand he had placed last week, ante-post at 4/1. Yes, this is going to be my day, he thought. Fourteen thousand eight hundred pounds. Enough to shut that lairy bookmaker up.

The day was cold and sunny. Dan, surveying the blue sky above, felt contented, very excited and in a fine mood at what might lie ahead that afternoon. The typical optimism of a gambler, blissfully ignorant of the lurking horror ahead.

CHAPTER 10

They squeezed their way through the hordes of punters in the betting ring and into the members' enclosure. The noise was deafening, a mixture of chatter, laughter, and the ever-present shouting of bookmakers. The thick scent of beer, cigarettes, and damp turf hung in the air, mingling with the faint sweetness of cigar smoke. From his vantage point on the lawn, Dan could see Kissane parading up the track to his right. A big, rangy gelding, he had the physical attributes of a boxer. He looked imposing, almost arrogant.

Dan stared at him with a mix of admiration and desperation, his heart thudding against his ribcage like a caged bird. There was something about Kissane's gait that filled him with dread and anticipation in equal measure, a living metaphor for the gamble he was about to take.

Dan looked at his *Racing Post* to see who owned the beast and saw that Kissane was the property of a Miss Aisling O'Connell. The name meant nothing to him, yet it prompted his mind to wander. He wondered if she was as nervous right now as he felt. He doubted if her heart was pumping as fast as his. She probably didn't owe two hard-nut East End bookmakers seven and a half grand, not to mention the looming potential liabilities. The prospect of the debt rising to over eleven thousand pounds made him feel sick.

His stomach twisted like a wrung-out cloth. This wasn't the first time he'd found himself backed into a corner, praying for a long shot to come through. He remembered the last time he'd been in this kind of trouble and how he'd recovered the situation by committing a criminal offence. A sharp pang of guilt bit into his thoughts. There would be no more insider dealing now, not since his bollocking from Sir Marcus. That moment had sealed the lid on any future attempts at clever little shortcuts. He was a marked man.

He needed winners today. Desperately. No ifs, no buts. Just winners. And preferably a miracle.

He tried to brace himself for whatever outcome there might be. At school, he'd read Rudyard Kipling's poem *If*. It was one of the few things from English class that had stuck with him. Dan remembered the famous words about triumph and disaster and treating 'those impostors just the same'. Powerful stuff, but difficult to live by. He wasn't sure that, in his gambling, he could treat the two impostors equally. The truth was, triumph intoxicated him. Disaster destroyed him.

There were people among the scrum on the lawn that he recognised—former colleagues, racing acquaintances, even a few clients—but the last thing he felt like at one fifty-five that afternoon was socialising with any of them. Mark guessed how Dan was feeling and decided to keep his own counsel, at least until after the race. The silence between them was comfortable. Mark always knew when to speak and when not to.

"Hey Dan m'boy. I thought I'd see you here."

Dan heard the voice of Sir Marcus Holderness directly behind him, that unmistakable blend of clipped formality and casual charm. He turned around to see a jovial-looking Sir Marcus and Diana beaming at him. Dan felt the awkwardness crawl across his face. He inwardly grimaced but didn't show it, faking a smile as he shook Marcus's hand and kissed Diana on both cheeks. He prayed they'd go away.

"We're watching down there," said Marcus, vaguely pointing to a spot beyond. "Must rush, as they're nearly off, but why don't you and your friend join us in Box 147, Captain Neville Taylor's, after the race," he continued, before glancing at Mark. "We can do the introductions later, but he told me that if I found any waifs and strays, I could ask them to come up after lunch. Your dad won't thank me for saying this, but I may as well tell you that the good Captain has advised me to have two decent bets on our horse, one for himself and the other for me."

Dan's ears perked up. Beacon Boy. The name rang in his mind like a bell. Whilst relieved they'd gone, Dan was pleased to have got the invitation to the box and absolutely delighted about the Beacon Boy tip. He'd thought about backing it earlier, but now, armed with that information, he'd have to go in large. The tip wasn't just casual pub talk, it was a gold-plated nod from one of the most discreet old-school operators in the game.

He looked at Mark and managed a wry smile.

"Can't ignore info like that, mate. It's from the horse's mouth!"

Mark raised his eyebrows and shook his head.

"You must have a death wish," said Mark.

Dan gave a short, nervous laugh. He knew Mark wasn't joking. The starter called the jockeys to line up. The butterflies and apprehension that Dan had been briefly relieved of, thanks to the intervention of Sir Marcus and Diana, returned in force. He could feel the sweat prickling beneath his collar, his tie suddenly suffocating.

"They're off." The tapes rose and a massive roar went up from the crowd, thousands of English and Irish punters full of hope and expectations. Triumph or disaster. The emotional weight of that binary choice pressed hard against Dan's chest.

Kissane got away well and was in fourth place as the twenty runners jumped the second flight of hurdles. Dan felt content. He was sure the horse would stay the trip easily.

He clenched his fists tightly, barely breathing, willing every stride forward. For a moment, time seemed to slow—the beat of hooves like thunder in his ears, the crowd a distant murmur, and his future balancing on the haunches of a horse named Kissane.

"Keep her up there," he murmured. He didn't want to see Kissane get boxed in behind the pack. So far, so good. The pace was strong and Kissane had a high cruising speed. They were over the fourth from home. The pressure was on. Running down the far side of the course, Dan's hopes were rising. The runners reached the top of the hill and swung left-handed into a dip before getting to the straight and then the exhausting climb up the hill to the winning line. They were over the third last. Second now and challenging for the lead. Still travelling powerfully. The Irish began to roar their favourite home. They were into the home straight. Kissane took up the running.

"Come on, Kissane, no danger!" screamed Dan. The noise level would have surpassed that of any Cup Final. Kissane was joined between the final two hurdles by three challengers.

"Fight back, you bastard!"

"They're turning on the tap!" roared the commentator. "Kissane being attacked on all sides. Tartan Tailor cruises to the lead. Kissane dropping away!"

Tartan Tailor, a 14/1 chance, was the winner. Kissane did indeed drop away, rather badly beaten, sixteen lengths.

"Disaster," murmured Dan. He felt like he was going to crumble in disappointment. All the fun of the day dissipated instantly. Mark tried to console him.

"Mate, there's still Beacon Boy to come. As your man told us, it's straight from the horse's mouth, and in this case, 'the horse's mouth' is one of the top trainers in the country. At least back it to win your stake back on Kissane."

After a few more minutes, Mark and Dan walked off in different directions, having agreed to meet back in Box 147. Mark said he'd follow him up there after joining the long queue for the gents.

Over an hour later, there was still no sign of Mark. Dan felt embarrassed when asked by Sir Marcus who his friend was, and more importantly, where he was. Dan put the thought out of his mind as he mulled over his life. He should be having fun. It certainly looked like everyone else was. He thought about his life, his job. About Ciara.

About his gambling. Was he out of control? He'd recently been taking it more seriously than his career. In the box, he'd heard Captain Neville Taylor ask Sir Marcus to place a wager of five hundred pounds to win on Beacon Boy. The Captain had written his account number on a piece of paper and handed it to Sir Marcus, asking him to place the bet with the Archer brothers and to invite them up for a brandy and a cigar whenever they pleased that afternoon. It wasn't lost on Dan that it was hardly ideal that his father's old friend was getting closer and closer to the Archers. He knew he wouldn't be able to pay if Beacon Boy failed to do the business.

What would the Archers do then? They'd soon find out, probably that afternoon, that Sir Marcus Holderness and his dad were old friends. They'd no doubt mention any unpaid debts to Marcus before any 'alternative' action was taken. Gambling debts were not enforceable by law. Dan wondered what the alternative might be. Probably a couple of broken kneecaps, he thought sadly.

When Sir Marcus had returned to the box, having duly placed the wagers, Dan made his excuses and left the room. He walked down the stairs and outside, then back up to the rails, where Joss Archer was in full flight.

"SEVEN TO TWO BEACON BOY, SEVEN TO TWO I'LL LAY," shouted Joss Archer. Dan pushed his way through the crowd to the front of the queue.

"Hello, son. What can I do for you?" said Archer, with just a hint of disapproval about him, Dan thought, thinking of the ever-burgeoning debt.

"Any chance of a bit of four to one Beacon Boy?" said Dan, just as another punter thrust six hundred pounds in cash into Joss's hand, saying,

"Six hundred Beacon Boy at seven to two."

"SIX HUNDRED AT SEVEN TO TWO, BEACON BOY, TICKET EIGHT ONE TWO," shouted Archer back to his brother Wayne, handing the punter a ticket and adding, "Three to one now, bruv."

Dan cursed. He remembered briefly backing a dog under not dissimilar circumstances at Walthamstow one night. Archer had helped him out there with the price. The result hadn't helped, though.

"Joss, please mate, give me seven to two," begged Dan.

"How much?" came the reply from the flamboyant bookmaker.

"Four thousand at seven to two."

Joss paused in his stride.

"Are you sure, son? Your account is racking up a bit," asked Archer, but without waiting for Dan to reply, Joss shouted out to his brother,

"FOURTEEN THOUSAND TO FOUR THOUSAND POUNDS, BEACON BOY, DOWN TO MR PERRY."

"Thanks, Joss, appreciate it," said Dan.

"That's alright, son. I know you're good for it. You can pay me in the box later if by any chance it loses." Joss winked at him.

It was nearly four o'clock on the Tuesday of Cheltenham. The fourth race of the day, a two-mile competitive handicap hurdle. Overcast, with a strong wind. A few specks of rain in the air. He hadn't returned to the box. Dan couldn't bear the thought of confronting either of the Archers should the horse be defeated. He'd owe fifteen thousand three hundred pounds. What on earth would he do? He stuck his hands in his coat pockets and walked out of sight of the bookmakers to find a suitable position. He needed to watch this alone. He vaguely wondered where Mark had got to. He wasn't sure whether he was pleased or not that he'd disappeared.

Beacon Boy had looked good running down to the start. Unflappable, on his toes, his chestnut quarters gleaming. He looked ripe and trained to the minute. Jamie Davies, the jockey, sported the blue and white hoops colours of Sir Marcus and Lady Diana.

Dan felt his heart beating fast, trying to steel himself for what was to follow. Triumph or disaster. He couldn't deal with any more of the latter. Down at the start, the runners circled each other warily. He wondered what instructions the Captain had given Davies. The starter called them in.

"They're lining up," called out the commentator. "They're off."

Dan looked away from the runners initially, unable to stand the tension. He looked up from the proceedings towards the top of the hills in the distance. Suddenly, he didn't want to be there. He just wanted a happy life, away from this, maybe with Ciara. No more stress. No more gambling. Focus on his job instead. No more worrying about this stupid sport, or the Archer brothers, or debts, or the consequences of not paying them.

Scaramanga, a natural front-runner, was the first to lead, with Beacon Boy right there on his outside. James Davies had been told by Captain Taylor to ride his horse up with the pace and not to get left behind early. The ground was still officially good, despite the drizzle that had been falling for the last hour or so. Beacon Boy was not as experienced as some of his fourteen rivals, and Davies kept him up with the pace to give him a clear view of the hurdles and to reduce the risk of him falling in front of a stumbling competitor. Dan was no longer watching. He knew that he'd leave straight away if the horse was beaten. He'd return to the town early and catch the train back from Cheltenham to Paddington. Fuck Mark, he thought.

He listened to the commentary as he slowly edged his way towards the exit of the members' enclosure. Beacon Boy's jumping of hurdles was "smooth," he heard the commentator say. Still up there. Not much further. The hairs were standing up on the back of his neck.

"Please, God." Dan closed his eyes.

Beacon Boy made his first mistake at the second last when challenging for the lead. In horror, Dan turned to watch, but Davies had got the horse balanced again and was challenging strongly as the last flight approached. Scaramanga and Beacon Boy had pulverised their rivals and had pulled ten lengths clear of the chasing pack. Captain Taylor's orders had been proven right. The crowd were in full cry. Half a length down coming to the last, Davies knew he had to go for a big one. He had the inside rail, the shortest but most perilous route, but victory was in sight.

And then it happened. Scaramanga jumped the last in front, but Beacon Boy took off too soon and fell heavily, breaking his neck. He died instantly. James Davies got quickly to his feet and under the rail as the chasing pack thundered home, before hurling his whip to the ground.

Dan stood there, wanting the ground to swallow him up. At that point, he felt so miserable he'd have almost chosen to give up his own life. He felt the panic begin like an engine revving up from his abdomen. Tension grew in his face and limbs, his mind replaying the horror of what he'd just witnessed. He became short of breath and nauseous. In these moments after his personal hurricane, he understood his gambling addiction... but with hands trembling, he still reopened the *Sporting Life* to look for any last-chance saloon bets, anything to satisfy the primal urge to get him out of this hellhole on the hills and to safety.

His heart was racing even faster now. Dan's eyes scanned the *Sporting Life*, the panic still welling up inside. He found a bench, unattended on the lawn, and lit a cigarette to try and calm himself. Within seconds of searching for one last 'getting out of jail' bet, he flung the newspaper onto the grass, his only movement now the trembling of his limbs and salty tears darkening his sleeves. He remained there, eyes closed, unaware of the passing afternoon.

"And the runners are going down to the start for our next race..."

The commentator's words regained him his composure. Opening his eyes to the descending remnants of sun, he looked up at the sky, brilliant white against the blue. He could still feel himself trembling, but he knew at that point he was not going to bet again that day, nor that week. Who knew how long? Maybe this was the beginning of the rest of his life. Or maybe it was the end of his life too.

He took a very deep breath of the cold Cotswolds air, cursed out loud to the disapproving looks of a couple of elderly, tweeded-up lady racegoers, and stood up.

He took another deep breath and started walking, briskly at first, off the lawn, out of the enclosure, then left onto the tarmac and up the hill, quickening his pace to a jog as he went. He wanted to be out of this racecourse and out of this game right now. He left the exit behind him and took a cab from the rank up by the horseboxes opposite the racecourse. He told the driver to take him to Cheltenham station, but once on their way, he had a change of plan. Despite leaving before the last race, he knew he'd still have a long and boring wait at Cheltenham station before the next train arrived. He could stop off at a pub for forty-five minutes. He needed a drink.

He asked the driver to recommend a boozer.

The pub was huge and very crowded. There seemed to be so many televisions it reminded him of a trading floor, only with alcohol allowed. There were plenty of punters who'd left the track early, reading the *Sporting Life* and the *Racing Post*, hoping to back the winner of the next race. And there were the locals, mostly elderly, who used the betting shop in nearby Winchcombe Street. Same routine: pub, betting shop, pub, betting shop.

He ordered a large brandy and turned to look at one of the screens. An advert for Yellow Pages, then another, this time the Government promoting a public offering of shares. British Petroleum shares were going to be offered to the public in October. Dan wondered where he'd be by then. He certainly wouldn't be in a position to buy any shares for a long while.

Before the racing resumed, a final advert caught his eye. There were images of a couple beaming with excitement at the news they were being given a loan. "GET A LOAN WITH THE HALIFAX, WITH THE HALIFAX," a pretty young thing in a suit was singing.

He ordered another brandy. He could sleep on the train. He lit a cigarette before noticing two men in deep conversation at a table on the other side of the pub. A man, possibly in his sixties, with long dark hair and wearing a suit, was talking to another man, back turned to Dan, at least thirty years his junior. They were getting rather animated, enough that he could make out their Irish accents. The older man was shaking his head. The younger picked up two empty pint glasses and headed to the bar to order more Guinness.

As he did so, Dan's jaw dropped. The younger of the men was Mark O'Brien.

"You might have told me you were going to fuck off and leave me in the lurch," Dan said to his colleague.

"Mate, I'm so sorry," said Mark, turning a deep shade of red. "The trouble is, after I left you in the Arkle Bar, I bumped into my dad," said Mark, gesturing in the direction of the long-haired man in the suit. "I'll get these. Come and meet him."

"I've heard so much about yer," said Kelvin O'Brien. Dan already thoroughly disliked the man now sitting in front of him. The expensive suit didn't go with the long black mane of hair, nor the brown boots, nor the tattoos on his neck that he sported.

"I had no idea he was coming over," said Mark.

"Dat's roight," said his father in a broad Ulster accent. "I tort I'd come over since some of me pals were commin' over loike, and oi needed to com anyway what with som' business matters in London dat need attending to."

Dan asked what business he was in. Kelvin O'Brien stared directly at Dan for a few seconds without answering. He didn't like Dan either. Eventually, he replied, "Oi'm a businessman, son. Leave it at dat, I say."

Another man interrupted them, another Irish accent.

"Hi Mark," said the younger man before addressing Mark's father. "I've got the car outside, Mr O'Brien." The young man was about the same age as Mark.

"Oil be outside in a couple of minutes, Seamus," said Kelvin O'Brien as he got to his feet. He took two ten-pound notes from his pocket and gave them to Mark.

"You boys have a few drinks on me on the way back. Oi'd offer you a lift but the car's full, isn't that roight, Seamus?"

"Yes, Mr O'Brien," replied his driver.

Kelvin O'Brien turned back to the boys and shook their hands, not looking Dan in the eye, before saying to Mark, "We'll talk in the week, roight, son?"

"So we will, Daddy," replied his son.

They said little on the train returning to Paddington, partly because both had had a lot to drink and were content to sleep through most of the journey. Dan was furious with Mark anyway, for both the ludicrous tip he'd passed on from that turd of a father of his, causing him to risk much more than he normally would on the ill-fated Beacon Boy, and for disappearing all afternoon and leaving him to make small talk with bloody Marcus and Diana.

He downed the remainder of the brandy he'd bought from a man with a trolley, replete with drinks, crisps and sandwiches, and felt his heavy eyelids gradually unable to stay open. By the time the train reached Swindon, both he and Mark were snoring.

At Paddington, after agreeing they'd talk at work the following day, Dan hailed a cab.

The cab arrived outside Ciara's flat at eight o'clock. He thought it best to ring the buzzer to alert her that he was back, rather than just letting himself in. He wanted so badly to talk to her about the day he'd had, the Archers, the O'Briens, the debt, and his plans to abandon betting. She'd help him give it up. They'd do it together.

No reply. Dan cursed as he let himself in. Where was she? He watched the news. Surely she'd have told him if she was going out. She knew he'd be back that evening. At ten o'clock, he ordered himself a pizza. He watched a political documentary about the privatisation of national industries such as Cable and Wireless, British Telecom, British Petroleum and British Gas. Eleven o'clock. Still no sign.

Shortly after midnight he heard a key in the latch. She was back. He wondered whether this was the right time to have a serious conversation with her, but opted to wait for another day. She was hardly in a chatty mood anyway. When she explained, rather impatiently, that she'd been out to dinner with her father, who was over from Ireland, Dan's temper began to boil over.

Out with her father, over from Ireland. Funny coincidence, that. She and Mark must think I'm fucking stupid, he thought. Mark's father over? Her father over?

He remembered the times he'd tried calling them at work, only to be told that neither was there. There was also the time they'd disappeared all afternoon, the day he'd first taken Ciara down to the floor for her interview. Mark had said he'd introduced her to the other traders and let her go home, before sustaining a migraine and going home himself. Dan hadn't believed him at the time. He hadn't directly asked Ciara about it since they'd started dating, as it seemed to hit a raw nerve in her every time he referred to the nature of her relationship with Mark. And there was the night of the office party. Funny that the only two people in the department who hadn't made it to the event until after the explosion were Mark and Ciara.

She climbed into bed beside him.

"Jesus, you stink," she said coldly, referring more to the stench of alcohol than Dan's hygiene.

Dan leaned to his side and switched on his bedside lamp.

"I don't know what to think any more, Ciara," he continued. "Mark left me on my own after the first race, and didn't come to the box we were both invited to. I found him hours later in a pub in Cheltenham, talking to an Irish guy who he claims is his father. Now you're coming up with the same type of bullshit. You're shagging that Irish bastard too, aren't you?" He paused before continuing.

"Well fuck me, you've ballsed up your excuse this time. Where did Mark go to meet you after I left him at Paddington? You saw him, didn't you? He introduces me to his arsehole of a father, shit, they even look the same, then you come up with this fucking lie about going for dinner with your old man, who by an amazing coincidence is also over from Ireland. And you conveniently forget to tell me this until now because, in reality, you've been double-dating that Irish wanker behind my back for ages. Now why don't you start telling me the fucking truth for once? Oh, and just for good measure, I've absolutely done my bollocks thanks to that Irish prick father's duff information."

Ciara's bottom lip was trembling. Dan had been prepared for her to try and hit him, and intercepted her punch when it came, despite his inebriation.

"I hate you, Dan. Fuck off out of my flat or I'll call the police, you bastard."

Dan needed no more asking. He pulled on his clothes and stumbled out of her flat into the cold night air.

CHAPTER 11

They ask you twenty questions. Dan had undergone the questionnaire back in March, when he'd rung the Gamblers Anonymous 24-hour emergency helpline, shortly after breaking up with Ciara. That particular night had been one of the lowest points in his life—a blur of tears, regret, and overwhelming loneliness. The pain had become unbearable, and in a moment of weakness, he had almost picked up the phone to call his bookie. But instead, his trembling fingers dialled a different number. The lady who picked up had been understanding, comforting even. She spoke with a warmth that wrapped around him like a blanket. She'd listened to him as she had listened to so many hundreds before. Her tone never wavered, calm and steady, allowing him to breathe through the pain. She was trained to let the caller spill out as much about his life as possible, and how it was affected by gambling—and Dan had spilled everything. His voice cracked under the weight of months of guilt, his confession tumbling out in fragments: the lies, the losses, the loneliness, the debt, and the damage he'd done to those who had trusted him.

After a while, once the silence had begun to grow long and heavy between them, she gently asked him if he felt up to answering the questions. He hesitated. Part of him didn't want to hear what he already knew.

"Do you, or did you, lose time from work or school due to gambling?"

"Yes, both," he replied quietly. He thought back to the countless mornings he'd missed meetings, to the work he'd skipped at school, to the excuses he'd made—stomach bugs, phantom headaches, imaginary emergencies.

"Does gambling affect your reputation?"

"Yes. Everyone in the stock market, and all my friends and family, know I gamble." He hated admitting that. Hated how it felt like wearing a badge that screamed irresponsible.

"Do you ever gamble to get money with which to pay debts or otherwise solve financial difficulties?"

"Yes. I always try and gamble myself out of trouble." He could see it all: the overdrafts, the final warnings, the credit card limits exceeded. All the times he'd doubled down, hoping this would be the one bet that saved him.

"After losing, do you ever feel that you must return as soon as possible to win back your losses?"

"Yes, always." That one stung. It reminded him of nights where he couldn't sleep unless he checked the late-night race results. When hope became obsession.

"Have you ever committed an illegal act with which to finance your gambling?"

"Yes. Rather not say what though, if that's OK?"

He wasn't going to risk telling a complete stranger about the Geneva Electric/Standard Telecom coup. That secret was one he intended to take to the grave—a ghost lurking in the shadows of his success.

The questions continued. They came like waves, some gentle, others crashing into him with a force that almost took his breath away. There were a few "no's" along the way, but the majority of answers were in the affirmative. With every "yes", the weight on his chest grew heavier. He already knew she was going to tell him that he was a head case, that he had a problem. But it was the final question that silenced him, that cut through all his defences like a razor through paper.

"Have you ever considered self-destruction or suicide as a result of your gambling?"

Tears began welling in his eyes. The question hung in the air like smoke, choking him. He couldn't bring himself to answer. His throat constricted. All he could do was breathe—shallow, gasping breaths. There was a pause.

"Hello, are you still there?"

Another pause. She'd expected it from this lad. Those gamblers who were only borderline cases always automatically replied "no" to question twenty. She'd suspected this one was worse than her usual type—the kind who walked the razor's edge, pretending everything was fine while the ground crumbled beneath them.

"Y, yes, I'm still here," he croaked, voice raw.

She didn't need to hear his answer to the final question—the final release. She already knew. The silence had spoken for him.

The evening following his conversation with the kind lady at Gamblers Anonymous, Dan found himself walking down the steps of an old building near Westminster. The city felt distant and strange that night, like it didn't belong to him anymore. His expensive suit felt too tight, his polished shoes too heavy. He half expected someone to see him and call him a fraud. It was quite clearly a school, probably a nursery school, he thought, as he walked down the corridor. Children's paintings adorned the walls—scribbles of rainbows, animals, stick figures with smiling faces. The contrast was jarring. He was looking for the Assembly Room.

"Are you here for tonight's meeting?" asked a friendly face, holding a clipboard. Dan replied that he was, his voice a little shaky but grateful.

"May I start by taking your name?" The man's tone was welcoming, almost cheerful. It was like Dan had walked into a gathering of old friends rather than a room full of broken souls.

Dan smiled for the first time in what seemed like an age and replied, "Er, this is the Gamblers Anonymous meeting, isn't it?"

"Yes, my friend, it is. Forgive me, I only meant your Christian name," the friendly face chuckled. "I'm Gerry."

There was a warmth in Gerry's eyes, a kind of weathered understanding, like he'd seen it all and survived it. "Tea and biscuits over there, donations box next to them. That's Lenny with the box. He's only there to make sure none of us are tempted to put the tea and biscuit money in the fruit machine at the pub later. You're welcome to join us for a drink after the meeting. After all, we're allowed to do that, eh, my friend?"

Dan smiled. His mates would be at Walthamstow dogs now, shouting at race cards and spilling beer on their ties. He looked around at the simple room, the plastic chairs, the flickering overhead light, and for the first time, he felt safe.

"Yes, I dare say we probably are, Gerry."

The meeting started. Gerry was standing at the podium with a microphone. He had a presence about him—not loud, not flashy, just firm. Solid. He requested the audience to stand, and that they read aloud the Serenity Prayer used in Alcoholics and Gamblers Anonymous meetings throughout the world. For Dan, this was the beginning of something new-not redemption just yet, but the first steps toward it.

God, grant me the serenity to accept the things I cannot change,

Courage to change the things I can,

And wisdom to know the difference.

Amen.

The audience sat. Gerry continued:

"Welcome to all of you. We have most of our usual faces here tonight, but I'm delighted to say a couple of new ones too, so could you please give a welcoming hand to Maria and Dan."

The audience clapped. Dan smiled. Maria blushed.

"Now, I'm delighted to ask Robin to come forward and collect his two-year pin."

Robin collected his award for abstaining from gambling for two whole years. More clapping.

"And this is a very special evening because I want you to give a really big round of applause to Gary, who has earned his ten-year pin!"

Thunderous clapping and cheers went up from the twenty or so strong contingent. Dan wondered what it would be like never to gamble again. When he'd had those dark thoughts on the lawn during that disastrous day at Cheltenham, he'd vowed never to bet again, yet even before he'd arrived home, he'd harboured strong desires to gamble—just hours after sustaining the worst losses of his life. He'd related this to the lady on the Gamblers Anonymous helpline, who had assured him that this was very common. She'd recommended that he try going to a meeting, and to see if, by sharing his experiences with others in a similar position, the temptation to return to gambling could be resisted.

"Great stuff, thank you," Gerry announced. "Now, for the benefit of our new members, Maria and Dan, it's a tradition at these meetings that we offer new members the opportunity to say a few words about themselves first.

"You can be as long or short as you like. Don't forget, friends, that you've already made the first brave step to your recovery merely by being here. I know it can be intimidating, talking to complete strangers about experiences that you've suffered through your gambling, but by sharing our experiences together, we can find that inner strength to rebuild our lives.

"So, Maria, without any further ado, would you care to come up to the podium and tell us a few words about your situation, please, my luv?"

More applause. Everyone in the room turned to look at Maria, the only lady there. She was a Middle Eastern woman in her late thirties, expensively dressed and extremely beautiful, thought Dan. He recalled having recently read in the newspapers about an Arabian princess who had blown millions in the elite London casinos – Aspinall's, the Clermont Club and Crockfords. Was it her? he wondered.

Suddenly, an air of expectancy had fallen over the assembly as they waited for Maria.

"No, no, plees, I so sorry. Not ready speek. Prefer to jus leesen."

Gerry quickly intervened.

"Well, Maria, that's absolutely no problem whatsoever, my luv," then correcting himself, "I mean, my friend. You can take things entirely in your own time. There's no obligation here."

He looked towards Dan.

"Perhaps, Dan, you may like to say a few words?"

Now they all looked at Dan. Would this one get up?

Dan got to his feet and walked up to the podium. Lots of clapping followed.

"Go on, Dan," beckoned a stranger's voice from the crowd.

Gerry again:

"Well done, Dan. Now, before you commence with what you wish to share with us this evening, please could you both start and finish by telling us your name, followed by the words: 'I am a compulsive gambler'."

Rather like the reading of the Serenity Prayer, Dan could not help feeling that this was a little silly. He wasn't even vaguely religious, and poor Maria had been made to recite the words of a Christian prayer when she was most probably a Muslim. Furthermore, Gerry had announced their names to the audience several times already, and they were obviously all compulsive gamblers – that was the whole point of this exercise, surely?

He saw Gerry as something of a cross between Arthur Daley and Bruce Forsyth, one a comical actor, the other a game show presenter of the time. Still, he complied.

"My name is Dan; I am a compulsive gambler."

Lots of clapping.

Dan looked at his audience. People from different backgrounds, different creeds. Different classes. All with one thing in common.

"It started when I was at boarding school. My parents had coughed up for me to go on a school trip to the opera in Covent Garden. A few of us saw this as an opportunity to abscond and spend a few hours drinking in London. One of my pals knew a seedy casino in Soho – I think it was illegal, as we had no trouble getting in, and you needed twenty-four hours' notice to become a member at anywhere decent.

"Anyway, we blagged our way in, had a few drinks and played roulette. I only had twenty-five pounds on me, but despite buying some drinks I remember having over a hundred and fifty quid by the time we got back on the coach. Needless to say, we got caught and sent to the Head. We were told that we'd only avoid expulsion if we were honest about where we'd been. We got sent home for a week during the term as punishment.

"During the following school holidays – it was Easter – my friends from the casino met up at the races. We were all with our parents, as Easter Saturday at Plumpton Races is a big social occasion in Sussex. I remember each of the six favourites won, and I backed all of them. On the Bank

Holiday Monday I returned, this time on my own, and again returned home with my pockets bulging.

"I was truly bitten by now and spent the rest of my schooldays buried in the Sporting Life, which a day boy brought in for me each day. I spent every Tuesday, Thursday and Saturday afternoon in a dingy betting shop, whilst my peers would either be playing sport or revising for exams.

"At first, some of us would venture off to race meetings such as Brighton, Fontwell or Goodwood, but the others didn't have the bug as bad as I had, and eventually, I just went on my own.

"School finished, I failed all my A Levels and didn't get a place at university or college. Not that I cared. All I wanted was a job which would pay me money that I could use for gambling. I got fired from my first job in the City due to gambling.

"It was Royal Ascot week and I'd pretended to be ill. Needless to say, I was spotted at the racecourse by one of my bosses, who was there legitimately. I got a new job as a junior in the stock market, a 'bluc button'. I was good at it too, and quickly promoted. Trouble is, the more I got paid, the more I gambled."

Dan told his audience about getting into debt, trying to gamble his way out of it, about the Archer brothers, the dogs. He felt comfortable here and in full swing, and even dared mention that he'd done "something illegal" to fund his gambling. He told of his break-up with Ciara, and the nightmare at Cheltenham, and the depression and despair that followed.

He knew that he'd be back here next week, and the week after. He was determined to sort his life out without gambling.

"My name is Dan. I'm a compulsive gambler," he finished.

Gerry, the leader of the meeting, watched Dan as he sat back down in his seat. The longer he'd attended these meetings, the better his perception had become as regards new members' chances of remaining clean. It never got any easier not to feel sorry for them, though, whoever they were, because it always reminded him of his own self-destruction many years earlier.

It made no difference if they were cleaners, rich Muslim women or posh public schoolboys from the City. All had the same problem. He had an inclination that Dan might make it.

"Well done, Dan, you did yourself proud," said Gerry.

Dan had to force himself not to break down in tears. Nobody had paid him a compliment in a while.

"Thanks, Gerry, I'll see you next week," he replied.

CHAPTER 12

— April 1987/ October 1987

The letter had come towards the end of April, preceded by two statements requesting that payment of £15,300 be remitted forthwith by cheque to Archer Bros Ltd, Walthamstow. The letter had stated in a sinister tone that:

'THIS PAYMENT IS OVERDUE AND UNLESS YOUR REMITTANCE IS RECEIVED IN FULL, WITHIN 7 DAYS, FURTHER ACTION WILL BE TAKEN TO RECOVER FUNDS.'

It was signed not by Joss or Wayne Archer but by an anonymous squiggle, underneath which it said 'Accounts Manager'. The squiggle, indecipherable and impersonal, made the letter feel even more menacing. Dan had ignored the previous statements, subconsciously hoping that some miracle might suddenly befall him, but he knew that it was now time to confront the situation. It had gone too far. His heart sank every time he looked at the mounting stack of unopened envelopes, shoved haphazardly into a drawer in his kitchen, each one a silent reminder of the life he was trying to forget.

He'd been to the Gamblers Anonymous sessions each week since his first visit, sometimes twice if he'd been tempted to relapse, and had mentioned his debt to Gerry one evening over a drink. Gerry, one of the few people who truly understood the storm Dan was navigating, had suggested that he try to go and see the Archers in person, however scary it might seem. "You can't outrun it forever, mate," Gerry had said, patting his shoulder in that reassuring way he had. "Best to face it head-on. That's the only way you'll beat it." Dan knew he was right. Hiding had never made the problem go away.

To Dan's immense relief, Joss Archer could not have been more jovial on the phone when he'd made the call. The man's tone was strangely upbeat, his laughter a bit too hearty, his friendliness unnerving. Dan told him that he had no money to pay him but promised to repay the money on a monthly basis. He asked Joss if they could meet for lunch one day to discuss terms, as Walthamstow wasn't too far from the City. It would be public, neutral ground, or at least that's what Dan hoped. Joss didn't even hesitate. Dan wasn't sure how serious Joss was being when he'd replied:

"All right, son, we'll work something out without me employing our 'traditional' methods of recovery, but I want to go to that City Circle place in the City where all them birds wear stockings and suspenders… and you're going to foot the bill, skint or not."

He chuckled at his own joke, but Dan heard the edge beneath the humour. There was always an edge.

The City Circle was a thriving restaurant near the Bank of England, where the most scantily dressed young waitresses served City gents long and boozy afternoon lunches. It wasn't Dan's kind of place, but he knew of it. Everyone in the City did. To take Joss Archer there was going to be expensive, thought Dan, but he quickly understood that if they could come to an amicable agreement, it would be infinitely preferable to waking up on a Saturday morning at home to see his car burnt out, or to be confronted by heavies at any given time, employed to use the 'traditional' methods of debt collection. A few hundred pounds for a slap-up lunch was a small price to pay for peace of mind, even if it left him eating beans on toast for the rest of the week.

Dan booked for 12.45 and arrived at 12.30. He did not think it would be smart to risk leaving Joss Archer waiting. Not only would that have been impolite, but he also feared it might provoke the wrong kind of reaction. The restaurant was already full of male bankers and stockbrokers, in exuberant spirits that Friday afternoon. The clinking of glasses, the loud guffaws, and the low hum of celebratory chatter filled the air. The only women present were the waitresses, exuding an air of sexuality as they hovered around tables like bunny girls in a strip joint. It all felt a little surreal. Dan adjusted his tie, suddenly conscious of how tight it felt around his neck.

He ordered a beer and looked about him, noticing that, without exception, all his fellow lunchers were dressed just like him, in sober suits and ties. Uniforms of success. He silently prayed that Joss would be similarly dressed, so as not to show him up, but somehow considered that unlikely. Joss had never been one for understatement. Brash, loud, gaudy, Joss Archer. Dan could practically hear his voice before he even arrived. How could I have got myself into this situation?

he thought. This wasn't supposed to be his life. He reflected that at least he'd started on the road to recovery.

It had been barely over a month since Cheltenham. That week had changed everything. He'd coped up until then, scraped by emotionally and financially. Now he was flat broke. Everything was crashing down around him. At least he hadn't had a bet since. That was something. That was progress. He wondered if he'd hit the 'rock bottom' that he'd heard his fellow sufferers refer to at Gamblers Anonymous. Maybe this was it. The final reckoning. The moment when everything you've buried claws its way back to the surface and demands to be paid in full. He wondered how Joss would be here, outside his comfort zone. This place could hardly be more different from any racecourse restaurant, let alone the bar at Walthamstow dogs. There were no dogs barking here, no frantic shouts at the finish line, just polished cutlery, gleaming wine glasses, and suits with cufflinks.

As all these thoughts flew through his mind, he suddenly heard the noise level in the restaurant descend into an eerie silence. It was like someone had turned down the volume knob on the world. A hush fell over the diners like a cold breeze. Heads turned. Glasses paused mid-air. And Dan, heart thudding like a drum in his chest, knew before he even looked up that Joss Archer had arrived.

There were large marble steps that led from the entrance and reception of the City Circle at street level down to the restaurant below. Standing halfway down the marble steps was a man in his mid-forties, sporting long blond hair, an open-necked shirt, and a large gold medallion. He was wearing a white suit and shirt, and grey cowboy boots. He puffed on a large cigar as he surveyed the looks of the astonished lunchers beneath him before he spotted Dan. He broke into a broad grin.

"'ALLO SON," he boomed.

A ripple of nervous laughter emanated from the throng as Joss Archer joined Dan at the table before the noise level returned to its previous volume.

The lunch went rather better than Dan had anticipated. Joss was clearly in his element and enjoying himself. Most importantly, he was conciliatory, and they came to an agreement that Dan's account with Archer Brothers would be closed, and that Dan should pay off a minimum of five hundred pounds per month until the debt was repaid.

Dan was overcome with relief. There was no need to take out another loan; he had enough of those already, and he'd quite comfortably be able to make the monthly repayments. He promised Joss that any bonus he received before the termination of the debt would be paid straight to Archer Brothers.

Dan was very confident that the debt could be repaid by the end of the year, as he was contemplating taking on a trading position in the stock market that would make Sinclair

Bank an absolute fortune and ultimately him, a huge bonus. And this time it would be entirely legitimate.

The summer rolled on by. Dan remained committed both to his five-hundred-pound monthly repayments and to attending regular meetings of Gamblers Anonymous. He threw himself into his work, always the first to get in each morning and the last to leave at night.

His team were making big money as the stock market continuously hit new highs. His reputation in the Bank soared as prices surged higher. The bull market had started in the summer of 1982, fuelled by lower interest rates, hostile takeover bids, leveraged buyouts and a raft of corporate mergers, leading to companies raising huge amounts of capital to finance such deals.

A leveraged buyout involves a company raising capital by selling bonds to the public. They paid high interest rates as they were not guaranteed by the government and therefore carried a reasonable degree of risk. These were known as 'junk bonds'. IPOs were another feature of this bull market, with companies offering shares to the public for the first time at a discounted price. This was also the very beginning of what was to become the technology boom.

Investors had caught on to the idea that computers and technology would spur a feast of new business opportunities.

By the end of September that year, Dan noticed that both the analysts at Sinclair Bank, for whom he had little time, and also the Bank's equity traders had become almost blasé in their attitude to the direction of the stock market, talking as if it would never fall again.

It was usually the case that even in a bull market, prices would correct themselves when traders, analysts, the media and the general public were all of the same opinion. He knew that it wouldn't take much bad news to cause such a 'correction'.

With this in mind, Dan called a meeting of the Bank's risk committee. He pointed out at the meeting that all the Bank's equity books were heavily long of stock. Even his own option traders had very few short positions, although they had bought plenty of puts, downward 'bets', back in June when there had been a general election. A Labour win back then could have fuelled a major downturn, but the Conservatives prevailed, and the prices of those puts had largely evaporated.

Dan had an overpowering feeling that a wind of change was forthcoming. He told the risk committee that he wanted permission for his team to build substantial bear positions, at the very least enough to protect the Bank in the event of a market downturn. He'd heard an old saying: "When the dentists are buying, it's time to get out." Most of the great crashes in history occurred when the investing public were caught in the same bubble. This time it wasn't just the public but market professionals too. All of the same opinion. Bubbles burst. Markets crash. The risk committee had taken very little time to approve Dan's strategy.

The two weeks leading up to Monday 19 October 1987 had not been particularly profitable for Sinclair Bank in general, but due to Dan's strategy, at least the traded options department had outperformed and severely limited losses sustained by other trading departments within the Bank. Sentiment in the markets seemed to have changed, although most investors considered that the turnaround in prices was merely a short-term correction. Not Dan.

Ray Plewcinczky, an American director at Sinclair Bank, was head of the Global Risk Committee. Recently, he'd transferred back to the New York office from London, although he practically commuted between the two, usually visiting London for three days each month.

During these brief visits, the traders would tease him about his choice of coloured designer jackets and his propensity to wear sunglasses, both in and out of the office. And brown shoes. Nobody else wore brown shoes. Ray was in his mid-forties, with fading wisps of blonde hair and a slight paunch gleaned from too many client lunches. He had the demeanour of an American through and through, and whilst standing out among his more soberly dressed English colleagues, he was universally respected and popular.

Ray had enjoyed a highly successful career as a trader at other banks before joining Sinclair, initially in New York and then London, after Sinclair had made him an offer he felt he could not refuse. He was Dan's predecessor on the proprietary trading and derivatives desk and had personally hand-picked Dan as his successor.

They had initially met several years earlier when Ray had just started at the Bank as a senior trader on the Wall Street Exchange. Dan and two other colleagues, all relatively junior at that time, had been sent to Manhattan for a week to see how things worked on 'the other side of the pond'. Ray liked Dan from the start. During that week on the trading floor, Ray had been impressed by the speed at which Dan evaluated changes coming in the direction of the markets.

"It's like he can smell it. He knows where the money is going. It's just uncanny," he reported back to Dan's boss in London.

He called Dan from his New York apartment on the morning of 18 October.

"Hey, buddy, sorry to call you on a Sunday morning but have you seen what the Dow did on Friday night?" He guessed that Dan would most certainly have known. A sharp fall on Wall Street had led to frenzied commentary in the weekend newspapers that something more sinister lay ahead.

"The Treasury has threatened to devalue the dollar in order to narrow the US's ever-expanding trade deficit. Looks like we may be in for a bloodbath tomorrow, Dan. You guys still short?"

"There was a full-on hurricane over here last Thursday night, Ray," said Dan, referring to the huge storm that had hit the UK three nights earlier.

"All the electrics went down and the market over here was closed as a consequence all Friday, unable to react to the weak performance on Wall Street. That's going to cause extra panic. I think the strong current is going to precede a financial tsunami, Ray," Dan ventured, before explaining that his team were perfectly poised for any potential collapse in prices. Indeed, they were, as he'd instructed all of his traders to build large long put positions (down bets) straight after he'd got the risk committee's approval. Every stock that they covered in the traded options market, from oils and electricals to retailers, miners and all industrials, Sinclair Bank's option dealers were short, with their burgeoning put positions created over the course of the last three weeks, poised to explode in the case of a further, sharper downturn.

Dan rose before 5.00 am the following morning. He'd hardly slept due to the adrenaline coursing through him. The market hurricane, as opposed to the recent storms, was now due. Even before the UK market had opened for trading that Monday morning, stock markets in and around Asia plunged. Investors moved to liquidate positions, creating a cascade of panic. The most severe case was New Zealand, down a horrifying 60%. A veritable tempest of a crash was now underway.

He was at his desk by 6.00 am. For once, he wasn't the first in, as most of the equity traders and analysts were aware of the weekend's events and had felt the need to be completely on top of their positions that Monday morning. The mood was tense among the equity traders, all of whom were heavily loaded up with stock, already battered over the previous few trading days and sure to get decimated when the market officially opened, now at 8.30 am rather than 9.30. After an earlier-than-usual morning meeting with heads of each relevant desk, Dan decided to walk down to the floor for the opening, as he felt he'd be better employed keeping watch over his own traders there. He also wanted to watch history in the making.

Dan had never seen anything like it before. The atmosphere was electric, not like Cheltenham; this was different. Traders and brokers with real fear etched on their faces. The bell rang, and all hell let loose. Back up in the offices, not just at Sinclair but at all the other banks, many traders were refusing to take incoming calls to avoid taking on more stock from panicked shareholders. Nobody knew the right price of anything. The normally orderly market had been thrown into total confusion and chaos, with wild fluctuations in prices. The panic ensued in the Traded Options market.

Dan moved from sector to sector, telling his traders to keep calm amidst the furore and not to deal in large size. He was aware that his team were making a fortune and that it would be easy to buy all the positions back quickly as an ocean of sell orders hit the market, but this was history in the making, and panic and fear were the order of the day. They would buy stock back at heavily discounted levels, only buying in decent size when orders to sell considerably below the market price came in. There were periods during the course of the day when share prices rallied as investors considered the market oversold, but these rallies were short-lived, and prices soon dipped lower again as waves of red covered the trading screens. By the close of play that day, over three hundred billion pounds had been wiped off the value of the FTSE 100 constituents, rendering the FTSE over three hundred points lower, a 24.4% loss that exceeded, in percentage terms, even that of the great crash of 1929.

The closing bell at 3.30 marked the close of the options session that day. The floor resembled the aftermath of a great battle: some wounded, some dead, some triumphant. All moved by the experience. It had indeed been history in the making. Dan knew that his own personal financial problems were likely to be over. He could hardly wait to see how much his lads had made on his strategy. A lot of the positions, the majority of them, had been unwound throughout the course of that manic day, leaving the department's exposure to whatever the market held in store over the next few days relatively small. When the profits and losses were totted up collectively, the Options team, including Dan's own positions, which he took on a proprietary basis, amounted to just short of one million two hundred thousand pounds. The equity traders had lost just short of a million. Dan's strategy had effectively saved the day.

The press described that memorable day as "Black Monday." Two weeks later, Dan was called into a meeting by Ray Plewcinski.

"Hey, buddy, how do you fancy becoming a director of this place? And don't make it difficult for me, but from the size of the bonus you're due, it would be kinda rude to pay so much money to someone who's not a director."

Dan was paid a bonus of one hundred thousand pounds on 1st December. Having banked the cheque, he called Joss Archer and invited him to lunch again at the City Circle. He explained that he had good news. Joss appeared more formally attired the second time. Dan grinned as he handed him an envelope with a cheque inside, exactly covering the remaining balance of his debt. Joss took a swig from his gin and tonic and dragged on his cigar before opening the envelope.

"I figured it might be this," said Joss, clearly impressed. "Just didn't expect it so soon. Told you I always get my money in the end, eh?" Dan smiled, somewhat nervously. Joss continued,

"Now that you're back in the land of the living, son, I'm not going to recommend that you reopen your account, although I won't stop you if that's what you really want. I think you should stay away from gambling for a while."

"I'm not coming back, Joss," said Dan earnestly.

"Pleased to hear it, son. Now listen up, Wayne and I are giving a dinner, a Christmas dinner if you like, for all our best clients later in the month. Alright, it's not exactly 'our' party, but the tickets were difficult to come by. I got them off another punter in my debt, a member of the Jockey Club, no doubt terrified that a scandal would break if it got out that he had acquired huge gambling debts. And this buys my silence until he's come to an arrangement, like you did. It's going to be well posh, black tie, and held in The Grosvenor House Hotel in Mayfair. The whole of racing's glitterati will be there, including that Captain Taylor. Your mate Sir Marcus and his wife have accepted. I'd like you to come as a mark of how grateful I am to you for coughing up this fast. Wayne and I would love to see you there."

"Wow, sounds great," said Dan.

"And you need to bring a bird," said Joss.

Dan thought before replying.

"I have someone in mind already. Someone at work that I used to go out with, but I'm not sure if she's in a relationship or not at the moment." Dan thought momentarily of Mark O'Brien.

The niceties over, they got down to the serious business of studying the waitresses and devouring more bottles of wine than Dan cared to remember when waking up the following day. Joss asked about Dan's life and his work, and his sex life.

Dan replied that he hadn't had much on that front since he parted with Ciara but pointed out that he still saw her each day in a work capacity. Joss suggested that he bring her to the party at the Grosvenor, and Dan replied that he'd thought just the same. Dan was fascinated to hear about Joss's life, and more about the bookmaking business. They talked for hours; Joss had told Dan about the robbery at White City all those years ago. Suddenly, something that Joss said made Dan sit upright.

"What did you say they were wearing when they attacked you? Did you say Mrs Thatcher masks? The two people the police are looking for from last year's attack on our party at Tower Bridge were spotted wearing the same, whilst they were running from the scene."

"She's a popular lady with some, that Mrs Thatcher," said Joss.

Dan felt uneasy about the coincidence. Not every violent crime was committed by offenders wearing Mrs Thatcher masks. He passed off the thought.

Chapter 13

— *Early December 1987*

Dan was a reformed man. He often reflected on how different his life had become since he quit gambling. He remembered those Saturday mornings that bled into the late evening at betting shops, the deafening roar of race crowds, and the bittersweet taste of both victory and loss. In those days, his self-worth hinged on numbers and luck. But that was then. Now, here he was, affluent and the youngest-ever director of Sinclair Bank, with a spectacular career ahead of him. His crisp suits, corner office, and the steady hum of the trading floor were far cries from the murky corners of betting shops and dog tracks.

Part of him still missed the thrill of betting, particularly the trips to Walthamstow or the racecourse. There was something primal about it, being surrounded by shouting men, flashing odds, and the thunder of hooves on turf. It gave him an adrenaline rush that the stock market never quite managed to replicate. But whenever he experienced serious cravings, he returned to Gamblers Anonymous as soon as possible. Though he now attended only once a week, those meetings remained his anchor. Listening to others' stories reminded him how easily he could fall again.

He felt a twinge of regret over the insider-dealing incident he had been persuaded to partake in by Mark O'Brien. It had been a lapse in judgement, fuelled by desperation, greed, and misplaced trust. The time had passed quickly since that dark chapter in his life, and while he had moved on, it still hovered at the edges of his conscience like a stain that wouldn't wash out. He had read in the *Financial Times* that an investigation had taken place, but the Securities and Futures Association found no hard evidence of insider dealing and subsequently closed the case. He had sighed in relief when the article had concluded with those words.

At the time, he had been desperate, and fortunately, nothing came of it. No scandal. No disgrace. But he knew how narrowly he had escaped the jaws of ruin. He was immensely grateful that Sir Marcus had intervened; otherwise, it might have become a habit. Sir Marcus had always seen potential in Dan, and that intervention had possibly saved not only his job but his future.

His relationship with Mark O'Brien had cooled, and they no longer socialised over drinks, but they maintained a strictly professional rapport. It was civil, but distant. Mark's performance as an options trader had been highly satisfactory, impressive even. The numbers spoke for themselves, and Dan had to admit he was good at what he did. Still, part of Dan wished for Mark to underperform. He had never forgiven him for sleeping with Ciara and still felt betrayed by the lies they had concocted behind his back. That betrayal stung in a quiet, persistent way.

How convenient it would have been to have 'let him go', the euphemism for firing someone. The decision would have raised eyebrows, but he could have justified it with numbers and subtle performance critiques. He truly disliked Mark and most definitely did not trust him. There was something in his eyes, calculating, secretive, that Dan had never been able to ignore. He was not at all surprised that his father was so revolting, a hard, unpleasant Irish thug who could in no way have been Ciara's dad. Dan recalled the man's sneer, his rough tone, and the faint odour of stale beer.

He wasn't even entirely sure that he was Mark's father, although they did bear a resemblance. There was a shared coldness in their eyes. He couldn't fathom why Ciara had so blatantly lied to him about having dinner with her father that dreadful night after Cheltenham, unless, as he suspected, she had actually been with Mark instead. The thought made his stomach churn even now.

He had discreetly asked others on the trading floor if Mark and Ciara were an item, but no one seemed to know for certain. They had perfected the art of concealment. If they were, they were clearly covering it up, and that secrecy only deepened Dan's mistrust. The one thing missing from Dan's life was a girlfriend, and at that particular moment, he inwardly acknowledged that the only girlfriend he wanted was Ciara.

Ciara had also performed well and was no longer a junior trader. Her rise had been steady and well-deserved, though some might whisper that Dan had helped her along. Dan had been quick to promote her shortly after their breakup, perhaps too quickly, as the promotion had not been entirely due to her progress as a trader. It had been a strategic move, driven as much by emotion as by logic. Not only did Dan believe she would be grateful for this advancement, but it also provided him with the opportunity to move her to a different sector, as far away as possible from the electricals crowd and Mark O'Brien.

Now that she managed her own book in the stores sector, right across the floor from electricals, it would ensure she spent less time in Mark's company. He monitored that floor plan like a battlefield map, carefully observing interactions, proximity, and movements. It was exhausting, but necessary. He still cared too much.

As confident as Dan was in trading the markets, he was anything but confident about winning Ciara back. Her presence still unsettled him. She had that same sharp wit, the same magnetic charm. He was also more than a little apprehensive about asking her to the Archer's bash at the Grosvenor House Hotel. What if she said no? That single rejection could be a dangerous trigger for the addiction he held within.

One weekend, he visited his parents in the countryside, and over a Sunday lunch pint in the local pub, he confided in his father about his dilemma. The pub had the smell of oak and old beer, and it always felt like stepping into a simpler world. Brian Perry listened intently to his son's predicament but had no doubt about the advice he would give.

"Have some guts, m'lad. You won't lose anything if she says no, and if she does, you'll know where you stand. If she makes an excuse, at least she'll know you're interested, and then it's up to her to give you the right signals. Either way, you'll go mad wondering what might have happened if you don't ask. You ask your mother. We went through the same rigmarole when we were courting. The best thing I ever did was ask her out for tea. And I mean tea, not dinner. It was during the Blitz. I asked her in The Strand tube station one night when the Luftwaffe were giving us another pounding. You've got it easy, sunshine!"

His father's words echoed with warmth and conviction. Dan had always admired his parents' love story, one forged in fire and war, resilient and timeless.

Armed with his father's advice, Dan's mind was made up. That Sunday night, he called Ciara and felt a mix of relief and nerves when she answered the phone. The moment her voice reached his ears, a rush of memories came flooding back—laughter in bed, debates over wine, quiet walks through Hyde Park.

"Hey, Ciara, how's it going?"

"Dan?"

"How do you know it's me?" Dan replied, somewhat timidly.

"I'd recognise that star trader's accent anywhere. Am I in trouble or something?"

"Er, actually, I wanted to extend an invitation. To a party."

They spent nearly an hour on the phone, catching up on each other's lives outside work since the day she had sent him packing from her flat. Their conversation flowed freely and with good humour. Ciara had already heard through the grapevine that Dan had stopped gambling. He had even made a jovial reference to his Gamblers Anonymous meetings one day while reviewing her trading positions in the stores sector. He explained about the recent lunch at The City Circle with Joss Archer and the reasons for his invitation, but he carefully refrained from asking her if she was in a relationship, let alone mentioning Mark O'Brien.

"So, will you come? As my guest?" Dan asked, eager to ensure she understood his intentions.

He definitely noticed a moment's hesitation, a tad too long for his liking, before she accepted.

The 1987 Jockey Club dinner was scheduled for the Friday before Christmas at the magnificent Grosvenor House Hotel in Mayfair. On the Thursday morning, the day before the dinner, the stock market was already in Christmas holiday mode, and trading was extremely light, with many City employees having been out the previous night. Dan sat with his feet up on the desk, reading a copy of *Mayfair*, a semi-pornographic glossy magazine, while occasionally glancing at his screens. He finished his coffee, tossed *Mayfair* aside, and put on his shoes and suit jacket before walking down to the Stock Exchange.

The London Options Clearing House was an office located on Throgmorton Street, staffed by a clerical team of about ten employees. They provided detailed computer printouts showing the positions each bank or trading house held in every option on a daily basis. It was the onerous task of a Blue Button to ensure he arrived at LOCH by 7:00 am each day to hand-deliver these printouts first to the Sinclair Bank dealers on the trading floor and then to Dan back at the head office in Broadgate. Each time Dan visited the floor, he had already spent some time examining his traders' positions through these printouts, making notes indicating where, in his opinion, a position was too large, too small, or needed to be closed down.

That Thursday morning, he followed his usual routine, armed with the documentation, and spent a few minutes chatting with each of the traders. He had decided to leave the stores positions until last so he could speak with Ciara about where to meet the following night. However, as he walked over to her pitch, he was slightly surprised not to see her trading or at least studying her positions. A trader from another bank said to him, "If you're looking for Ciara, mate, don't bother; she's gone home sick."

"Nice of her to tell me, but thanks," Dan replied, his heart sinking. He would look rather foolish if he turned up at the Grosvenor House the following night alone, and Joss would surely poke fun at him. Optimistically, he considered it better that she had chosen to be ill today rather than tomorrow. He wondered if she simply had a hangover. Deciding to call her, he made the short walk out of the exchange and across the road to the Sinclair Bank 'box', a room where the options traders resided outside trading hours during the day. He placed his LOCH printouts on a desk and dialled her number.

"You have reached Ciara Rogers. I'm not here at the moment, but please leave your message and the time of your call after the tone. Thank you." Irritated, Dan hung up the phone and returned to the office. He would try again later. By 6:00 pm, he had called her a further ten times, but to no avail. Ciara certainly had her moments, but she was not unprofessional, he thought, growing increasingly frustrated. His irritation only intensified when he suddenly realised he had left his LOCH printouts and notes back in the traders' box. He swore under his breath. Now he would have to go all the way back to retrieve them. He knew that the traders would all be either in the pub or on their way home by this stage, so he decided to return to Throgmorton Avenue and collect the printouts. He hoped that one of the traders had noticed he'd left them and locked them away for safekeeping, but it was a chance he could not take. He would not risk leaving them unattended.

As he had expected, there was nobody in the box when he arrived at 6:30 pm. There was no sign of the printouts either. He decided to check the traders' drawers, feeling slightly guilty about doing so. He resolved to turn a blind eye to anything inappropriate he might find. Nothing in Kevin's drawer, nothing in Dave's. When he opened Clive's drawer, he found nothing but dirty socks, boxer shorts, and a soiled shirt. He winced at the smell. Dirty stop-out. He continued his search. Nothing, nothing, nothing. When he reached Mark O'Brien's desk, he noted that it was the only drawer so far to be locked. They must surely be in there, he thought. He would have to leave it until morning and come back for them then.

He sat down in Mark's chair and turned on a screen to check the latest movements on Wall Street. He began jabbing at the keyboard, scrolling through various share prices that had a bearing on Sinclair's own positions. One of them was moving slightly against them. He hit his fist on the desk in frustration, partly due to the price but also out of annoyance that he couldn't find his notes, which were written on the missing LOCH sheets. And then there was this Ciara situation. As he leaned over to turn off the screen, he noticed that in hitting the desk, he had somehow knocked the keyboard askew, dislodging a small key. The same key to Mark's drawer. Relieved, he took the key and unlocked the drawer. As he pulled it open, he gasped at what lay before him. Inside was an unopened white shirt, still in its packet, and a black bow tie. A pair of polished black lace-up shoes lay next to them, but there was more. Behind the shoes, at the back of the drawer, Dan found himself staring at four sinister-looking revolvers. He instantly recognised their makes, recalling from his history lessons at Lancing the choice of arms used by the IRA in the 1970s. Two were C96 Mausers, and the others were Colt .45 automatics. Trembling, he opened the smaller drawer above the large one, where traders usually kept pencils and stationery. The pencils and stationery were neatly arranged at the top of the compartment, but underneath, the drawer was lined with live bullets.

He lit a cigarette and rapidly considered his options. He had to talk to Ciara. Or should he go straight to the police station in Bishopsgate? He certainly didn't want to linger here. What if Mark returned? He quickly shut the drawers, relocked them, and replaced the key back underneath the keyboard. Ciara's desk was by the door of the box, the only one he hadn't opened. It was unlocked. He decided to take a peek. Nothing in the top compartment except lipstick, pencils, mints, and stationery. He swung open the bottom compartment. What he saw left him shaking with concern. If he had been shocked to discover the pistols and ammunition in Mark's drawer, what lay in Ciara's disturbed him just as deeply. No guns, no bullets, just a bunch of ten masks, all bearing the face of Mrs Margaret Thatcher, grinning up at him, lying on his LOCH computer printouts.

There was a bank of public payphones around the corner from the Stock Exchange. Dan ran the short distance and dialled Ciara, only to reach her answer machine yet again. He breathlessly left a message. "Ciara, it's me. We must talk. Please call me urgently at home." He deliberately didn't specify what was so urgent, as he wasn't sure about the relevance of the masks. He wanted to see her reaction when he asked her why she had them. He felt distinctly uneasy. He recalled Joss Archer describing the time he and his brother were attacked by Irishmen in Mrs Thatcher masks. And then there was the police report after the Tower Hill bombing, which indicated witnesses had seen two men in the same masks fleeing the scene of the crime. Now certain that Mark O'Brien was up to no good, he wanted to find out for sure what was happening. He changed his mind about going home and waiting for her call, better to go straight to her flat and catch her off guard.

All these thoughts raced through his mind as he caught a taxi. He dreaded the thought of arriving at her flat and finding O'Brien there, but he decided that he could always run, he'd go directly to the police in that scenario. At least he knew that Mark's guns were secure in his desk. He also knew that neither Ciara nor Mark would have any idea what he had found in the box earlier, and would therefore be unaware of his suspicions.

Ciara's flat was now in Fulham, having recently moved from her pad in Notting Hill. The black cab slowly trundled through the London evening traffic, Blackfriars, Embankment, Westminster, Victoria, Sloane Square, before finally turning onto Fulham Road, passing his own flat, then Stamford Bridge and Fulham Broadway. They were very close now. Dan felt a wave of fear wash over him; he hadn't felt like this since Cheltenham back in March. As the cab entered Ciara's road, he asked the driver to stop thirty yards from her flat.

Ciara's flat was on the ground floor of a Victorian mansion block. He noticed that the lights were on. This is it, he thought, as he firmly pressed the buzzer. No reply. He tried again, but to no avail. Unsure of what to do next, he was relieved to find the front door of the mansion block opened by an elderly lady leaving the premises.

"Excuse me," said Dan. "Do you live here?"

The old lady smiled at him. "Yes, young man. Who are you looking for?"

Dan explained. "I'm looking for Ciara Rogers."

"Yes, I saw Ciara only this morning. Such a lovely young girl. She sometimes comes and has coffee with me on Sunday mornings."

Dan elaborated that he was a friend of hers from work and expressed his concern that she had gone home earlier without any explanation and hadn't answered any of his calls.

"Well, let's have a peek from the outside," said the old lady. She led Dan around to the front window. The window was open a few inches. There was no sign of Ciara, but they could distinctly hear music emanating from the flat.

"Perhaps we should try knocking on her front door?" the old lady suggested, clearly pleased to help. They returned inside the building, and Dan banged heavily on the door, the music growing louder from within. If there was anyone there, they weren't in answering mode. She was probably in her bedroom with that horrible Mark, Dan thought gloomily.

The old lady said, "I think we should speak to the caretaker. He lives in the basement. I know he's in, as I just spoke to him a few minutes ago about people putting their rubbish bags out too early. Such a nuisance. Attracts rats, you know, dear."

Ten minutes later, Dan and the old lady were back inside the building, this time with the caretaker, who had keys to all the flats under his watch.

"I hope you're not making a big mistake, mister," said the caretaker in a broad West Country accent. "Folks get right pissed off if I enter their premises when it's not an emergency."

"You won't need to. I shall go in alone," replied Dan.

"I ain't letting you in alone, mate. You might be one of them burglars. Then I'd be in the shit. I'll come in too, if you don't mind."

The old lady winced at the bad language and smiled at Dan. "I'm going to be late for my bridge night, so I must be off. I hope Ciara's okay," she said as she turned away from the two men and headed back towards the main front door of the block.

The caretaker let himself into the flat, followed by Dan. The music was quite loud. A pair of Ciara's shoes lay haphazardly by one of the sofas in her living room, and a skirt was strewn across the floor. Dan called out to her. Nothing. He looked in the kitchen, definitely signs of recent activity. He saw a half-eaten sandwich in its wrapper and an open bottle of vodka, half-empty. She had certainly been here recently. Dreading the prospect of entering her bedroom, he walked down the passageway to her room, closely followed by the caretaker.

"Here goes," he said, steeling himself. Dan knocked on the door. "Are you in there, Ciara? I've been so worried about you. Are you okay?"

"She ain't here, mate. Best we leave pronto," said the caretaker. Dan turned the door handle and gingerly peered around the door. He took a few seconds to take in the scene. Ciara was in bed, surrounded by hundreds of sleeping pills. Beside the bed lay a C96 Mauser and a Colt .45 automatic.

In a state of total shock, Dan stared helplessly at the corpse. The caretaker realised what had happened immediately. He told Dan to stand aside as he felt for Ciara's pulse.

"She's still alive. Go on, son, call a fucking ambulance."

CHAPTER 14

The medical term used by doctors to describe a stomach pumping is gastric lavage. It's a cold, clinical term for an emergency procedure that has saved countless lives over the decades. The ambulance arrived within minutes from the nearby Charing Cross Hospital, its siren having already sliced through the London air like a warning bell. The paramedic rushed to Ciara's side, examining her eyes, pulse, and chest, while an ambulance technician scooped the loose pills and placed them in a plastic bag. The atmosphere in the flat was heavy, tense, filled with the remnants of despair and the sterile scent of medical supplies. Satisfied that not only was she alive, but that this overdose had likely occurred within the last few hours, the paramedic felt confident that she would be saved.

Gastric lavage rarely fails to work if a patient is treated within four hours of taking an overdose. The human body has a strange resilience, especially when swift action is taken. She was lucky; had she spent the night like this, she would either have died or suffered liver failure. The possibility of such irreversible damage hovered in the minds of the paramedics, who had seen too many similar cases end differently. They delicately rolled Ciara onto her side and gently slid her from the bed onto a stretcher. Even unconscious, she looked fragile, a porcelain figure in a chaotic world.

The paramedic asked if she could hear him.

"Try and open your eyes, Ciara. What made a lovely girl like you do this to yourself?" His tone was gentle, fatherly even, as though speaking to a daughter rather than a stranger. He turned to Dan and asked if he knew of any reason why Ciara would try to take her own life.

Dan didn't know. Not really. Not in a way that made sense. He had certainly never seen Ciara severely depressed. She'd always carried herself with poise, with confidence, even when she was stressed or distracted. All he knew was that she was caught up in something she shouldn't be, and this was the end result. That much was clear now. He wasn't going to explain any of this to the police just yet, let alone the paramedic. Not until he had answers. He wanted to get the truth from Ciara himself. She wouldn't be accompanying him to the Grosvenor House tomorrow, that was for sure. That chapter, whatever it was, would have to be rewritten.

In the ambulance, she opened her eyes and emitted a long groan, a painful, confused sound that sent a ripple of hope through Dan. She was conscious, and that mattered. He reached for her hand, which she gripped fiercely before bursting into choking, almost hysterical tears. It was as though the dam had broken and all the emotion she had buried came flooding out. The ambulance technician took out a small syringe and pricked Ciara's arm to sedate her, while the other staff in the ambulance offered soothing words of comfort and reassurance.

"Okay, Ciara, we're nearly there now."

"Don't worry, love; you're in safe hands."

"Things will get better for you, love."

They all knew that weeks of counselling and therapy lay ahead for Ciara. Possibly months. Would it work, though? So many failed suicide attempts resulted in the patient repeating the process. Sometimes it wasn't just a cry for help, it was a cycle. At Charing Cross Hospital, the paramedic explained to Dan the process involved in gastric lavage and told him that he would be best advised to go home that night, and that Ciara would be better off talking to him the following day. Let her rest, he said. Let her body recover before her mind faces the weight of explanation.

Dan did not manage to get any sleep that night. He lay awake in bed, staring at the ceiling, haunted by images of Ciara lying motionless on the bed, her pale face surrounded by pill bottles and despair. He needed Ciara to talk to him, to tell him the truth. How much clearer would the situation be then? His mind ran through every conversation, every hint, every glance that might have meant something. He didn't have to wait long. He was back at the hospital at 8.00 am the following day and used a telephone box to call the office to explain that he would be late. He didn't mention Ciara. He didn't know how to.

Suicide patients were allowed a single room next to the ward, at least for a day or so after admission. It was hardly luxurious, however. No telephone, no television, nothing with wires. The walls were blank, oppressive in their blandness. There were bars on the window and a cupboard without hangers. Everything potentially dangerous was absent, stripped away by precaution. A nurse would check in every hour. Dan checked with reception to see which ward Ciara was in and was told to take the lift up to Floor 3 and ask for the ward sister.

"She's fine physically; at least she will be sooner rather than later. She's very distressed, however. She's been asking for you," said the ward sister, her voice soft but steady, as if trying to project calm in the midst of so much emotional turbulence. She led Dan into the room.

"Hi, Ciara, sweetie. Here's someone to see you. I'll leave you both alone for now." The sister turned and left them staring silently at each other. The hospital room was quiet, save for the faint sounds of footsteps in the corridor and the occasional beep from a distant machine. Ciara's eyes were red from crying. She looked older, more fragile, like someone who had seen too much in too little time. Dan broke the silence.

"Thank God I found you in time last night." He sat on the chair beside her bed. Ciara started crying again. Then, between sobs, she spoke.

"Hold me, Dan." Dan held her. He felt the tremble in her body, the vulnerability that she rarely allowed anyone to see.

"Dan, I'm so sorry. I've done something terrible. So terrible that I've put both of our lives in danger."

Dan released her from his hold and held her hand as he sat back in the chair. "Your life's not in danger, my love. The sister told me herself," said Dan calmly before venturing, "The reason I came to your flat last night was that I knew something very sinister was happening. Ciara, listen, babe, I know how much you hate me saying this, but if you're involved in anything, anything at all, with Mark O'Brien, it's vital you tell me the truth. You're alive, I'm alive, and we'll stay alive if you explain to me what's going on."

Ciara had stopped crying now and wiped the tears from her face. She looked down at her trembling hands, then back up at Dan. "Okay, Dan, I'm going to tell you everything."

"Take as long as you like, babe," said Dan, still holding her hand. He knew the truth was about to be revealed.

"Oh my God, I don't know how I got in so deep. I told you on that first day when you took me down to the Stock Exchange after my interview that I knew Mark from my days in Ireland as a kid. Well, that was true, and we did have fun together, partying, drinking, enjoying the craic, but you see, Dan, there was never anything more to it than that." She paused for a moment. "You see, Mark O'Brien is my older brother."

Dan was taken aback, his mouth agape. He certainly hadn't seen that coming and felt a pang of relief. He asked about her father.

"My daddy is a bad man. A very bad man. And you've met him. That night you came round to my flat after you'd lost your money at Cheltenham, I told you I'd been out to dinner with Daddy. I was going to tell you then, but you were so drunk that I didn't want to explain everything to you that night. Then we had that fight, and you left, and then we split up," she said, her voice breaking again.

Dan moved back onto the bed and hugged her tightly. "Just keep going, babe. Kelvin O'Brien is your father, right?" he asked slowly.

"He is that. You met him with Mark at Cheltenham, and I met up with the two of them when they returned to London. He's a senior commander in the IRA. He was very strict with us as children. We attended Mass every Sunday. We were taught to hate the British. Our uncle was killed by British troops on Bloody Sunday in 1972. Anyway, it was expected of Mark and me to follow in Daddy's footsteps. We both came over to London in 1982 to join a newly formed IRA cell. We staged a robbery to raise money on a couple of East End bookies, the same bookies that invited you to the Grosvenor House Hotel tonight." Dan let go of her hand.

"Mm, hence the Mrs Thatcher masks. Go on," he said coldly.

"Oh my God, I just got so immersed in it all. I was in way over my head, but Mark and Daddy wouldn't let me out of my 'duty', as they called it."

"Ciara," Dan interjected, "did you and Mark have anything to do with the Tower Hill bombing?"

Ciara put her head in her hands. "That we did. We didn't want to kill anyone, though; just to cause disruption. Mark called the police station in Bishopsgate with a coded warning. He called them from a payphone in The Crispin while you were playing pool. And to think it was you who nearly died. Neither Mark nor I have ever killed anyone, I swear. We watched the chaos from afar and mingled with the rest of the office when the evacuation started. We knew precisely when the bomb would explode, and neither of us had seen you come out. We knew you were there because we'd seen you arrive in a taxi. I was terrified that you were going to die, and I got Mark to look for you. Thank God you survived."

"I've seen the guns in his desk, Ciara. They look like the same guns I found next to your bed last night. And I've seen those Thatcher masks in yours. Is there an attack planned for tonight? Why else would Mark have his dinner jacket in his drawer?" This time, he gripped her arms firmly.

She took her time to respond, her eyes glistening. "I couldn't go through with it," she stammered. "It's going to be worse than before, so much worse. There are going to be casualties."

"Is everything alright in here?" asked the ward sister in a curious tone. Dan got to his feet and gently placed his hand on the nurse's shoulder as he led her outside the room.

"You'd better call the police, Sister. There's going to be an IRA attack in London tonight, and our patient in there knows plenty about what's being planned." The sister went pale and hurried off to find a telephone.

Back in the room, Dan asked, "Okay, so it's due to go ahead, and it's looking very grave. But that still doesn't explain why you tried to kill yourself. And what are you saying? I'm assuming you intend for there to be mass casualties?"

"Dan, I know I've done some terrible things, but I couldn't be involved in this. I couldn't bring myself to be part of hurting you. You won't want me now, of course, but the truth is I love you. I've loved you since I thought we might have lost you in the Tower Bridge attack. Last night, just before I took the pills, I called the police. I don't have the coded password that we use; besides, there won't be one used tonight anyway. Mark and Daddy have taken a table for six of them; they think I'm coming with you. Mark briefed me this morning when he gave me my revolvers. They want me to be armed but not to take part in the attack myself. I'm supposed to tell them if I see anyone looking at them suspiciously. All six of them will be armed and will start shooting randomly at some point in the evening. They want me to leave just before the attack and drive a white van, which Mark has left outside my flat, to pick them up afterwards. I've told the police, but they don't know if I'm a crank or not. They probably won't believe me anyway. If they do manage to prevent it or even cancel the event altogether, the cell will eventually find out who exposed the plot, and my life won't be worth living anyway."

She was interrupted by two uniformed police officers and a WPC entering the room.

"We'd like you to wait outside, please, sir," one of them said to Dan. "Our inspector, DCI Logan of the Flying Squad, wishes to ask you some questions."

An armed constable stood by the door of the room, and an older man in a raincoat entered. He approached Dan.

"DCI Derek Logan, Flying Squad," said Logan, shaking Dan's hand. "I think we'd better have a little chat."

The DCI and Dan took the lift down to the hospital exit. Logan offered Dan a cigarette, which he gratefully accepted. The DCI explained that his office had received a call from a woman the previous night but had decided it was probably a hoax, as the caller was both drunk and had no coded password. They had informed the general manager of the Grosvenor House Hotel about the call and suggested they increase security for the dinner, just in case. Two plainclothes policemen had been ordered to remain discreetly near the entrance of the hotel. However, the call from the hospital had put them on red alert. The DCI asked Dan to remain in the foyer of the hospital and wait for him to interview Miss Ciara Rogers. After that, they were to pay a visit, not to the police station, but to what the DCI described as "a location near Waterloo."

The "location in Waterloo" turned out to be an Italian café. Dan was surprised to find that at 11:00 am, the sign on the door read "CLOSED". Inside, there were three men, two seated, drinking coffee, and an elderly Italian man behind the counter. The Italian man unlocked the door.

"Eh, Senor Logan, what do I get you and your friend? The others are here."

"What do you fancy, sir?" asked the DCI, slipping the Italian man an envelope.

Dan ordered a coffee. He noticed that the DCI hadn't paid for the coffees, nor for the sandwich that Logan had ordered for himself. A police car with two constables was parked directly outside the café. This is an arrangement, thought Dan, as Logan guided him to the table with the two other men.

"Mr Perry," said Logan, "these are gentlemen from MI5. I'm going to let them take over from here."

The MI5 officers spent nearly two hours grilling Dan. He explained everything from his relationship with Ciara and Mark (omitting the insider dealing incident) to meeting Kelvin O'Brien in the pub at Cheltenham. He detailed finding the masks in the box and the revolvers. It seemed they were already well aware of Kelvin's activities and had Mark on their radar, but were less certain about Ciara. Dan relayed everything Ciara had told him from her hospital bed just hours earlier. He described his relationship with the Archer brothers and how it had led to his invitation to the Grosvenor House Hotel that night. Throughout the two hours, one of the three men frequently excused himself, walking over to a back room in the café with his handwritten notes and phone to relay details back to headquarters.

"The dinner is going ahead," said the more senior of the MI5 officers. Dan was incredulous.

"How is the dinner going ahead when we know there could be mass casualties tonight? I don't understand."

DCI Logan answered for the MI5 officers. "Let me explain. You don't have to be there, Danny boy, and it won't be any fun if you are, I can assure you, but you won't be in any danger. The SAS will be all over these murderous bastards. They'll be arrested before you can say Jack Robinson. We wouldn't mind if you were there, however. We know Kelvin's appearance but aren't so sure of Mark's. You'll have a tiny microphone attached to your jacket; anything you say will be picked up by all of the gentlemen of the SAS at surrounding tables. And guess what? I'll be your date tonight, not Miss Rogers."

Dan didn't need any encouragement. He'd come this far; now it was time to see the end of this episode in his life. He agreed to meet Logan outside Sinclair Bank at 6:00 pm. He caught a cab back to the Fulham Road, picked up his dinner jacket, shirt, and bow tie while the cab waited, then returned to the City.

Logan was waiting for him as planned. He was driving a blue Ford Sierra and was immaculately dressed, hardly recognisable from his usual attire of jeans and a leather jacket. A traffic warden approached the Ford Sierra and peered inside the car, indicating for Logan to wind down the window.

"You can't park here, sir; you're on a double yellow," said the young warden. Logan reached inside his jacket pocket and showed the warden his ID.

"Police business, son," replied Logan. The traffic warden nodded and continued on his way. Dan, having spotted Logan and the car, climbed into the passenger seat.

"Grosvenor House Hotel, please, driver," joked Dan, trying to lighten the mood given the situation that lay ahead.

"The Grosvenor House it is, sir," replied Logan.

CHAPTER 15

— 4.00pm, The Same Day

The white van pulled up outside the budget hotel, its engine giving a soft, rattling hum before falling into a low idle. The building itself was as dull and uninviting as its faded signage suggested, with chipped bricks, tired curtains, and a lingering scent of damp and old cigars in the air. Mark O'Brien killed the engine and looked up at the building with a grim set to his mouth. He parked directly on a yellow line, uncaring of the parking violation, as if the law was nothing more than a faint suggestion in the face of what they were about to do.

One by one, the men disembarked from the van, each of them carrying suitcases that were heavier than they appeared. They looked like tourists, perhaps businessmen, but the atmosphere around them was too tense, too taut. Adrenaline coursed through their veins as the hour of reckoning drew near. Beneath the surface calm, their nerves twitched and thoughts raced. They were painfully aware of the scale of the operation ahead, the carnage it could cause, the message it was designed to send. The weight of responsibility settled like iron in their stomachs. But this wasn't fear. No, it was focus. This was revenge, righteous and necessary, at least in their eyes. It was vengeance dressed up in ideology, and in their minds, it was justified. They didn't see themselves as monsters. They were soldiers, freedom fighters in a dirty war.

Even if, by morning, the British tabloids would plaster their faces under the bold word TERRORISTS.

Inside the lobby, a young man with slicked-back hair and a crooked tie approached them with a rehearsed smile. "If you gentlemen would like to leave your luggage here, I'll have your suitcases and bags taken to your rooms," said Eddie, the nervous-looking manager of the shabby hotel in Earls Court. He was clearly trying to appear helpful, though his eyes flickered uneasily between the six men.

The group had booked three double rooms for a single night under the alias Mr Regan, a name chosen precisely because it sounded forgettable.

"We won't be needing you to do that, young man, thank you," replied Kelvin O'Brien curtly, taking a step forward and placing himself as the group's spokesperson. He gestured firmly towards the bags and continued, "Alright, lads, let's get our gear to the rooms and reconvene in the dining room over there in thirty minutes."

He extended his hand towards Eddie, and the manager responded politely, though somewhat stiffly. As their hands clasped, Kelvin discreetly passed him a neatly folded ten-pound note.

"You won't mind us having a private meeting in your dining room for a couple of hours, will you, son?" he asked with a tone of friendly authority that left no room for refusal.

Eddie glanced quickly at the note, felt its crisp texture, and forced a smile. "Pleased to help, Mr Regan," he said, though a ripple of unease slid down his spine.

O'Brien's mention of an "important board meeting" was accompanied by an air of secrecy. The young manager nodded, deciding that it was best not to ask questions. The dining room hadn't seen many visitors since breakfast, and it wasn't as if anyone else was likely to use it before evening. The foreign tourists who made up the bulk of their clientele usually went off gallivanting into central London, seeking more lavish experiences than the hotel could provide.

Eddie couldn't help but glance over the group again. These weren't the kind of men who laughed freely or made idle conversation. Their presence made the room feel colder. There was something in their eyes, not fear, but control. Silence, calculation, composure. Men used to command, or perhaps chaos.

Still, business was business, and Eddie reminded himself that a full house was a rarity these days. Besides, the ten pounds in his hand was worth more than its value. He knew full well he would have given them the dining room for free. But now, at least, he had an excuse to keep the other staff away.

The room bookings had been made two nights earlier. Mr Regan, or whoever he truly was, had phoned in advance and confirmed he'd be paying in cash. Not an unusual request in this part of London, but something about it now seemed calculated.

Apart from this peculiar Irish group, the only other guests had gone out earlier, leaving the hotel eerily quiet. The place felt like it was holding its breath. It was now four-thirty in the afternoon, a strange limbo hour between the bustle of daytime activity and the stillness of night. The six new guests wasted no time. After lugging their suitcases upstairs and locking the doors behind them, they returned quickly and assembled in the dining room, now their temporary war room.

Eddie's attention was suddenly drawn away from his thoughts by the shrill ring of the phone behind the reception desk. He picked up the receiver and answered with a bland, "Good afternoon, West Court Hotel, Eddie speaking."

On the line was a council representative, inquiring politely whether the hotel could accommodate a visit from the fire department—just a routine check for any fire hazards. Slightly puzzled by the timing, Eddie listened as the caller asked how many guests were present in the building and how many were currently inside. The questioning struck him as oddly specific. Still, with no reason to decline, he agreed.

To his surprise, barely five minutes had passed when two firemen appeared at the entrance, dressed in full uniform. There was something too precise about their arrival, like they had been waiting nearby. They approached the desk and asked to see the master key so they could inspect the rooms.

Eddie hesitated. Something about it didn't sit right. "Mr Regan" and his colleagues didn't seem like the sort who would tolerate strangers poking around their rooms. Still, safety checks were part of the job. Maybe the other guests wouldn't mind as much.

He checked their IDs, which appeared legitimate, and was just beginning to relax when one of the firemen asked to see the hotel's booking log. Eddie frowned. "May I ask why?"

"Just routine, sir," came the firm but polite reply. "We need to know the demographics of your current guests—dialects, nationalities, that sort of thing."

"Definitely Irish," Eddie replied cautiously, still unsure if he was doing the right thing.

At that, the firemen exchanged a subtle glance and asked to be left alone to complete their work.

Half an hour later, they were gone—driving off not in a fire truck, but a discreet red Volkswagen Golf. Eddie stood by the door, watching them leave, a chill creeping up his neck.

Meanwhile, in the dining room at the back of the hotel, Kelvin O'Brien sat at the head of the table surrounded by his five-man team. Their jackets were buttoned, faces serious, and their attention sharp. Spread before them were detailed, photocopied floor plans of The Grosvenor House hotel. The blueprints covered the expansive reception, the grand staircases, and, most importantly, the Great Room, the site of tonight's Racing dinner.

These weren't ordinary diagrams. They had been prepared with exceptional detail by Mark O'Brien, Kelvin's son, who had posed as a wide-eyed tourist two weeks earlier. Armed with a Polaroid camera, Mark had wandered the halls of the luxury hotel unbothered, taking dozens of photos under the guise of fascination with British architecture. No one had stopped him. The Grosvenor House staff, used to eccentric tourists, had likely thought nothing of it.But every picture had a purpose.

The men now studied the layouts with surgical precision. There were images of the entrance on Park Lane, the busy lobby, the reception desk, staircases, lift locations, bars, and more. Mark had even managed to attend a holiday event in the Great Room, using the opportunity to memorise the layout, count security cameras, and identify all visible exits.

He had chosen their future seating, pinpointed escape routes, and noted which tables would be occupied by which guests. Now, under the flickering light of the cheap hotel dining room, his plan was being reviewed one final time before execution.

Kelvin O'Brien presided over the meeting, outlining two plans. The first involved executing the attack in the Great Room itself. "My daughter, Ciara, will be at table 23 with a colleague and our old friends, the Archer brothers. After tonight, they'll wish they had settled for a beating and the hundred grand we relieved from them that night in Walthamstow a few years back. She will be armed but won't participate in the attack. The other guests at table 23 will know she works with Mark. If she notices anything suspicious, any odd looks, she'll come over to our table and inform Mark, who will be sitting next to me. In that case, we may need to act sooner than planned. An award is set to be presented around 9.00 pm to the leading trainer and jockey of the year. The lights will dim before the presentation, at least that's how it went last year. That's when we start shooting. She'll make herself scarce before we open fire. We'll shoot non-stop for ten seconds, targeting randomly while making our way to the separate exits." He pointed to the floor plan, indicating which exits each gunman would use.

"Plan B is the backup. We're unlikely to encounter any trouble on our way to or entering the hotel. The security was poor last year. God knows, they still haven't learned from Brighton," O'Brien remarked, referencing the IRA attack on The Grand Hotel in Brighton during the Conservative Party Conference three years prior. He continued,

"The only time we might encounter resistance is at reception. If we're in the lobby, which will be packed with guests, and anything goes awry, we'll open fire on my command. We'd much prefer Plan A, as the guests will be seated, focused on the awards ceremony on stage. In either case, whether it's Plan A or Plan B, after the attack, we'll make our way as quickly as lightning to the van parked in Hill Street just up the road. My daughter, Ciara, was fully briefed yesterday morning and will be driving, isn't that right, Mark?" He looked expectantly at his son.

"Yes, Dad. I briefed her with all the instructions yesterday when I gave her the weapons, and she knows where I've hidden the keys to the van," Mark replied.

"You're a good lad, Marky, that you are," his father said, before pointing to a location on a map, indicating exactly where the white van would be parked. "From there, we'll be driven to a different location on the other side of the park, where another vehicle will be waiting for us. Hopefully, we can cause as much damage as possible in the hotel without being captured. Under no circumstances are we to return here. Return to your rooms, arm yourselves, and leave the suitcases behind. We'll leave here at six o'clock and park the van in Hill Street. Fifteen minutes, and we're on our way, boys. Any questions?"

Meanwhile, on the other side of London, another meeting was taking place, this one in a car approaching Blackfriars Bridge. Dan Perry was sweating despite the cold December evening as he spoke to Logan.

"Mark O'Brien was in the office earlier but, unsurprisingly, left before I arrived. Apparently, he departed shortly before noon. One of my traders mentioned he looked very distracted and didn't trade at all, spent all morning on the phone."

Dan turned to Detective Chief Inspector Logan. "I'm shitting myself, Derek."

"You must stay calm, son," replied DCI Logan. "Since you went back to the office earlier, I've been working my arse off. We've had a stroke of luck too. Everything is under control. We're on table 23; they're on table 29. Each table for six surrounding table 29 will be exclusively filled with the highest-trained soldiers in the land. The SAS, MI5, and my department are all over it. We even know where the cell is. And I mean right now. We had a tip-off: a white van in Earls Court received a parking ticket directly outside a hotel at around 4:00 PM. Within half an hour, it came up on our system as the same vehicle used by the IRA in an armed robbery at a bookies a few years back. MI5 were crawling all over the hotel within minutes, posing as firemen conducting a routine safety check. It was the first one they checked. We believe the terror cell was there at the same time, having a meeting. My lads picked up on it straight away. MI5 are following that white van as we speak."

At 7:00 PM, Joss and Wayne Archer, along with an assortment of their guests, stood in the main bar located directly next door to the Great Room. Joss had already had a few drinks, not just back at his local in Walthamstow but also a few 'free' glasses of champagne generously offered by the waiters and waitresses at the Grosvenor House Hotel.

"Fancy a lager, Sir Marcus?" he called out, then turning to Diana, Marcus's wife, "Ere, love, Martini and Black?" He grinned as he handed over twenty pounds to the barman. "Bottle of Magnum bubbly, please, old mate." Joss wasn't sure who looked more embarrassed, the Holdernesses or the barman.

"Now come on, Archer, you old bugger," boomed Captain Neville Taylor, jovially slapping Wayne on the back as he approached the group. "We line your pockets all year, and this is a chance to pay us back a little. It's not called Magnum; it's called Moët, but we want a Magnum of that!" Diana shrieked with laughter. Joss reached for another twenty pounds and handed it over the bar.

"Fucking toffs, eh? It's free in reception," he winked at the barman with a broad grin. A rendition of *White Christmas* by Bing Crosby hummed in the background.

The white van had parked in Hill Street. Mark was annoyed not to see Ciara there; she had said she'd be waiting for them. Still, she knew where he'd hidden the keys, on the top of the back left wheel, as they had discussed yesterday. No doubt she'd decided to go straight to the hotel with that tosser Dan and his party. She would follow instructions and make her excuses to leave prematurely. He felt uneasy about how reticent she had been regarding the attack, but she had accepted the guns he brought to her and seemed to absorb all of his instructions.

Regardless, there was no point in waiting for her. She would be there, waiting for them, when the deed was done.

Following Kelvin O'Brien's instructions, each of the terrorists concealed their weapons in the inside pockets of their dinner jackets. They had no choice, as none wore overcoats to shield themselves from the biting December chill. Coats were a liability; there was no point in risking being spotted by one of those British coat rack attendants at the hotel, a Mauser potentially noticed as the attendant handed over a receipt. Coats would not be collected tonight. Tonight was solely about execution and escape. Triumph for the cause, and disaster for those who were enemies of Ireland. Mark recalled Dan Perry's musings on triumph and disaster at Cheltenham. How shallow was that? A poor little rich kid with a gambling problem, soon to become a poor, dead little rich kid. There would be no warnings or acts of rescue tonight.

The Irishmen entered the lobby of the Grosvenor House Hotel and quickly dispersed to different areas of the reception. Well over two hundred people were milling about. "Daddy, I'm going to peek into the Great Room, be back in a jiffy," Mark said, ignoring the waitress who tried to offer him a glass of champagne. The noise level was rising as it approached 7:45 PM. Everyone was still in reception, nearly time for dinner. Mark walked through the revolving door that led into the Great Room. It was empty. Silent in the vast space, but noisy behind him. He surveyed the beautifully decorated tables adorned with white tablecloths. The room was relatively dim, with light primarily emanating from candles in candlestick holders on each table. The atmosphere shimmered and sparkled. This felt surreal, a spectacular Christmas event in a London hotel, soon to turn into horror. As Mark scanned the room, he searched for table 29. It appeared to be in the ideal position to conduct the massacre.

Suddenly, he caught a strong whiff of cigar smoke behind him. He turned to find the trainer, Captain Neville Taylor, standing right behind him.

"Surveilling the scenery, old man?" Captain Taylor asked. "We've just been given the all-clear to go through. By the way, I don't suppose you have a light? This damn thing is cutting out," he said, gesturing to the dying embers of his cigar.

Mark was thrown off balance. He was in the midst of his reconnaissance mission, preparing for an attack that would dominate the headlines of the world's newspapers the following day, and here was this oaf asking him for a light. He felt flustered but knew he had to remain as calm as possible.

"No problem, Captain Taylor. Nice winner you had last Saturday," Mark replied, awkwardly searching for his lighter. His hand dipped automatically into his trouser pockets, fingers brushing past familiar objects—loose change, folded notes, his crumpled packet of cigarettes—but not what he was looking for. Where was the damned thing? He could feel the Captain's eyes on him, expectant, and time stretched thin as he delayed. A small bead of sweat formed on his temple, though the room was far from warm.

He knew he had the lighter on him somewhere; he had smoked on his walk from the van in Hill Street. It was then that he made his mistake.

The memory of that cigarette, the flick of the flame, the taste of tobacco, came back to him with unnecessary clarity. He just needed to get this idiot off his back as quickly as possible. The pressure of Captain Taylor's presence—the unblinking military composure, the way his shoulders squared—suddenly felt overwhelming. In haste, he opened the inside pocket of his dinner suit.

Captain Neville Taylor spotted it in an instant. His eyes, sharpened by years of service, caught the unmistakable glint of cold metal. He had handled a Mauser many times during his Army days, and his instincts as a soldier made him alert to danger. His body stiffened. His pupils dilated a fraction. Time slowed.

"What the fuck are you doing with that?" the Captain exclaimed, stiffening as he spotted the look of terror on Mark's face. The transformation in Mark was immediate—panic flushed his cheeks, his body tensed, and his gaze darted about like a cornered animal.

Mark instinctively reached for the revolver in his inside pocket, but he was far too slow. His hand trembled as it moved, thoughts scrambling for a way out, an escape route. But the Captain lunged forward, gripping Mark's wrist before his fingers could even touch the weapon. There was a sharp grunt, and then the two men grappled, twisting and turning.

Chairs clattered, glasses toppled. The Captain's grip began to loosen as Mark resisted with surprising strength, driven by desperation more than technique.

Seizing the opportunity, Mark used his free hand to pull the Colt from his other jacket pocket. His movements were jerky but determined, his face contorted with fury and fear.

"You bastard, you die now, you bloody British Army bastard!" Mark shouted, swinging the weapon to point at the Captain's head. His voice cracked mid-sentence, emotion spilling into violence.

Out of nowhere, a man behind the two wrestling figures smashed a candlestick holder into Mark O'Brien's head. It came down with a sickening crack, the polished brass striking his temple with brutal efficiency. The Colt slipped from his grasp, his fingers losing all strength in an instant. Mark let out a long groan and collapsed to the floor, unconscious.

The Captain quickly turned him over and sat on him, still unaware of who had just saved his life. His breath came fast, not from fear but from adrenaline, and he barked out an order in his old commanding tone.

"Get help, man, right now!"

Joss Archer replied, brushing his sleeves casually as though he hadn't just intervened in a life-or-death situation. "You hoorays never say thank you."

A waitress from within the Great Room had witnessed the scene unfold. Her eyes wide with shock, she had stood frozen for the first few seconds, her tray of drinks wobbling dangerously before she abandoned it entirely. Before Joss had left the room, she had dashed into the reception area.

Screams erupted as people on the periphery of the room noticed the commotion and began to panic. The social atmosphere of polite conversation and clinking glasses vanished, replaced with shrieks, toppling chairs, and flurries of movement. An Irish cry of "Now, lads!" was drowned out by the chaos.

No sooner had Kelvin O'Brien screamed the order than he was instantly overpowered by two other guests who had barely left his side since he entered the hotel. In a flash of well-rehearsed motion, their civilian disguises dropped. Underneath their dinner jackets were the tight formations and fluidity of professionals. He never stood a chance.

The same fate befell the four remaining gunmen in a split second. Each had a split moment of realisation before being brought to the ground by coordinated precision. The screaming, shouting, and panic raged on as terrified guests tried to flee the hotel by any means possible, while six men lay alive yet overpowered, now unarmed and handcuffed, with the weapons of the SAS trained on each of them.

Dan had hardly had a chance to say a word to his 'date', DI Logan. He was too nervous to speak. The entire evening had unfolded like a film reel he had no control over, and Logan, calm and unreadable, had simply watched it happen with the composure of a man who'd lived it a hundred times.

Logan had explained to him in the car from the City that the SAS soldiers were monitoring the terrorists' every move, having done so ever since the cell had stepped out of the hotel in Earls Court. The white van, linked by the Met's security systems to the Provisional IRA, had been followed all the way to Hill Street, and the cell had been tracked to the entrance of the Grosvenor House Hotel.

Logan had spent most of the journey from the City to Park Lane on his walkie-talkie. His voice had been clipped, firm, efficient, delivering instructions, receiving updates, each word loaded with silent urgency. He barely looked at Dan, except to reassure him once with a curt nod. Now that the SAS had done their job, it was time for him to finish the task.

"I think it's time for you to go home now, son," Logan said to Dan. "Now that the military have done the dirty work, and pretty efficiently, I think you'll agree, it's time for my lads to take over. I'll be in touch shortly. I'd go and have a stiff drink if I were you. Thanks for your help, Danny boy. You helped prevent a catastrophe, and we now have six Irish Republican Army commandos in our custody, shortly to be under lock and key. We'll extract a load of intelligence from these bastards; you mark my words."

Dan didn't doubt it. Not for a second. Every cell in his body felt the weight of the experience. His hands were trembling slightly, a nervous shake he couldn't quite stop. A voice crackled over Logan's walkie-talkie, distorted but urgent, and the policeman extended his hand to Dan.

Dan shook Logan's steady palm, his own still trembling. It was a strange sensation—part relief, part gratitude, part numbness. He knew it was time for him to leave. There was nothing left to witness here. The worst had happened—and had been prevented. Taking one last look at the chaos around him—overturned chairs, pale faces, the buzz of radios and murmurs of shock—he hurried from the Great Room, through the lobby, and out of the swing doors of the hotel into the cold winter night.

The air bit at his cheeks, a bracing wind sweeping down Park Lane, but he welcomed it. It grounded him. He resisted the urge to hail a taxi and walked alone from the hotel, the mile and a half back to his flat on Fulham Road. Each step seemed to echo louder than it should. The city felt bigger than usual, darker, deeper. But he kept walking.

THE END

ABOUT THE AUTHOR

James Douglas-Mann is a qualified freelance journalist and ex-City trader whose roots in British life and history shape the gritty, human world of his fiction. With an eye for character and a taste for realism, James draws inspiration from lived experiences and the people he once knew, those colourful characters that now breathe again in the pages of his work. From the East End of London to the City, down to the Cheltenham Festival, he perfectly captures the tone of the 1980s in this thrilling novel..

You can learn more about James and the events that inspired

TOXIC OPTIONS *by going to the website:*

www.toxicoptions.com

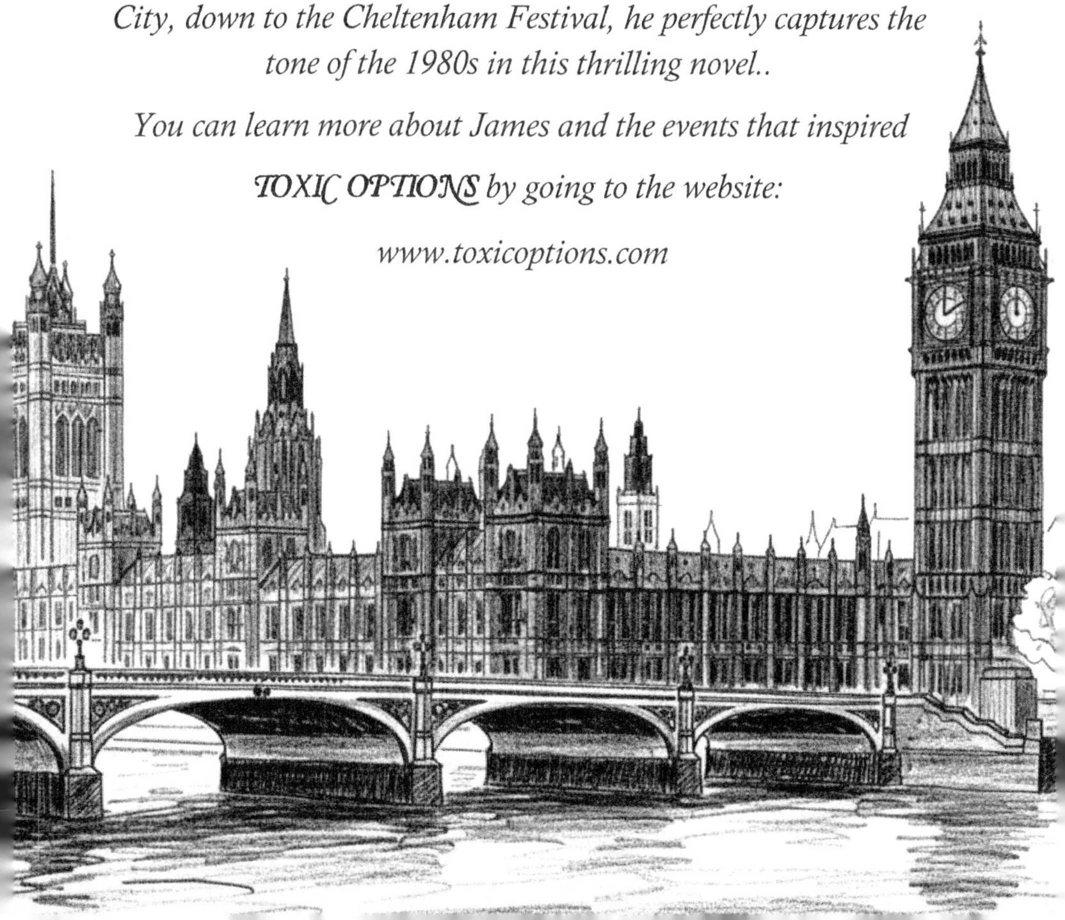

Printed in Dunstable, United Kingdom

77386308R00171